MW01438832

──────────── FULLY ARMED

Also by Bob Levin

The Best Ride to New York

FULLY ARMED
THE STORY OF JIMMY DON POLK

by Bob Levin

BASKERVILLE
PUBLISHERS, INC.

Copyright © 1995 by Bob Levin

Baskerville Publishers, Inc.
7616 LBJ Freeway, Suite 220
Dallas, TX 75251-1008

All rights reserved, including the right to reproduce this book or portions thereof in any form whatsoever without permission in writing from the publisher.

Library of Congress Cataloging-in-Publication Data

Levin, Bob.
    Fully armed : the story of Jimmy Don Polk / by Bob Levin.
      p. cm.
    ISBN 1-880909-38-3
    1. Polk, Jimmy Don, 1953---Fiction. 2. Afro-American men--California--Fiction. 3. Physically handicapped--California--Fiction. I. Title
PS3562.E8895F85   1995
813'.54--dc20   95-38286
                                              CIP

All rights reserved
Manufactured in the United States of America
First Printing, 1995

*To my mother and father,
who taught me books were valuable
and all men equal.*

*And to Adele,
Whose contributions to this text far
surpass those few words attributed to
the character with her name. She read;
she cut; she analyzed. She walked the
ground with me every step of the way;
she pointed out directions.*

INTRODUCTION

By the spring of 1989, a black man in a wheelchair had been panhandling near my law office for several months. He was in his mid-thirties, stocky, with a broad face, a wispy goatee, and hair braided into short pigtails. Usually he wore jogging sneakers, heavy wool pants, a blue, hooded sweatshirt, a gray pullover, and a blue baseball cap. The first time he truly caught my eye, he had the left drawstring of his sweatshirt in his right hand, the right drawstring in his left hand, and he was calling out, "Spare change! Or I'll hang myself."

On a downtown Berkeley street, with more than its share of riveting urban acts—nightmarish, comic or unclassifiably bizarre—the man carved a niche for himself through personality alone. To women, his standard greeting was, "You sure are looking jazzy today, my lady." To me, it was, "How's your day going?" If I said, "Bad" or "Crappy," he would answer, "Don't worry, my friend. Things will pick up." And he always smiled. At all of us, lawyers and derelicts, secretaries and punks, bank tellers and Dead Heads, he smiled.

In a world of AIDS and crack and rain forests burning, this man in his wheelchair smiled more than anyone I knew.

I had promised the daughter of a former client a summer job. She could not start until July. One morning, in late May, about two weeks after this promise, the panhandler, not without laughing, was telling me about hitting a new bottom: falling asleep in Provo Park and waking up covered by three dogs. By now, I had regularly been giving him quarters, occasionally a dollar, for one holiday ten dollars, and I had learned his name was Jimmy, he was from Texas, and he had been in Vietnam. ("My war souvenir," he had said, pointing at his legs.) He was homeless because the V.A. had overpaid him his disability pension for a year-and-a-half and, then, cut him off until it recouped its overage. His goal, each day, was thirty dollars, so he could rent a motel room.

"You want a job," I said, half-certain he would tell me he did better on his corner.

"Yes," he said.

"It's not much. Answering phones. Maybe some filing. I can't pay a lot, and it's only part-time and only until this girl gets out of school."

"When do I start?"

"How's Monday, ten o'clock?"

"Monday. Ten o'clock. Thank you for the chance, my friend. I will do a good job. I'll get myself looking sharp."

On the one block to my office, a toothless old woman, a man pushing three shopping carts, a skinny girl in a burnoose on roller skates, and a fellow tearing scraps of paper off a PG&E pole asked me for change.

When I give people directions to my office, I tell them, "Go past the massage parlor. I am over Pizza-by-the-Slice." My practice is mainly workers' compensation, some personal injury, a little this-and-that when I am hard-pressed. It is a low-budget operation. My Xerox machine belonged to an estate a friend administered. My I.B.M.-compatible came from a dope lawyer who was disbarred for defrauding the I.R.S. Amelia, my secretary, works Mondays, Tuesdays, Thursdays and cross-trains for triathlons the rest of the week. I have had it suggested, sometimes by myself, usually in the middle of the night, when I have woken, chilled, my malpractice premium unpaid, my Mustang in the shop facing major restorations, and too many assholes I can think of regularly cashing six-figure checks, that some significant character flaw has pinned me here: impacted immaturity; calcified non-aggressiveness; terminal fear of major league competition. Other times, when I have waltzed in late from a morning with my wife or scooted out early for extra laps in our club pool or simply bifurcated my afternoon with a double espresso at Cafe Frenzy, I believe my office fulfills the urge to untie knots and liberate one's self in all moments of being that is central to a rewarding life. "What I like about practicing law in Berkeley," I would tell ex-classmates in the east, "Is you don't have to wear a tie to the office. Or shoes."

"You don't know anything about the guy," Max said.
Max is bald. Max is fat. Max has a full, grey, twin-pronged beard that hangs down across his belly like sooty icicles. He wore a rainbow-striped, wool knit cap, a BE HERE NOW t-shirt, and camouflage pants. Max dropped out of graduate school in astrophysics to play electric bass. It was 1966 and people were doing that. He has lived in a straw hut in the Yucatan and toured Europe with a Portuguese circus. He has hallucinated on a slice of the same mushroom as Timothy Leary and meditated across a prayer rug from Allen Ginsberg. I have received calls at two a.m. from Max from hospitals protesting his medication and from jails requesting bail. He has come out of lunch beside me, bent over the gutter, and vomited up barbecued pork, four brandies, and blood. He has knocked on my door, asked to use the shower, and spent forty-five minutes under the tap reciting William Blake. We have been friends since the third grade.
When we were children, it was Max, of all my friends, my parents would threaten to forbid me to see; he was the only

one with whom I was in contact still. Max had always been the first among our group to the entertainments that were one step over the line: the comic books the P.T.A would burn; the rock 'n' roll the censors would cut; the stimulants the legislators would ban. He had led me as far as I would get into life's outlaw side. With him, at record hops and keg parties and acid tests, I had run into those West Philadelphians of my generation who would blossom into pornographer and biker, gun runner and drug smuggler, drag queen and trunk murderer. Then, when some inner chain of fear or conscience had yanked me tight, Max continued to race on.

Though we had both ended up in California, we were no longer so tight. Max's "Ommm" did not satisfy my discontents about the present level of permanent partial disability benefits. My yawns did not encourage his speculations about which punk rocker was the reincarnation of which apostle. Still we met regularly. I suppose I was an anchor of responsibility for Max; as long as I was there to tie up to, he could not drift too far asea. And his blessing my hum-drumness with his consciousness-expanded presence meant I had not turned irrevocably to Mr. Jones. Max had pushed the boundaries as far as anyone I knew. While, on the one hand, where it had gotten him was a room in a North Beach hotel, furnished more sparsely than a monk's cell, and gigging in a Columbus Avenue bar, where half the patrons looked like Charles Manson and the last benefit performance was to buy his tenor man teeth, it also provided him, in my eyes, with a stamp of incorruptibility. Max was the purest artist I knew. He lived and worked without concession to achieving commercial gain or accommodating public taste. His every word or gesture was consistent with the rendering of his inner vision. It was not usually Max who called for responsibility of action.

"I know his name's Jimmy," I said.

"Jimmy. Great. Consider the possibility. Tuesday, what's not nailed down will be gone."

"Look, he gets along with people better than Bill Cosby.

He's not schizzy, and he doesn't do alcohol or drugs. Or if he does, not so's they interfere with his work, which, in case you haven't noticed, is more competitive in this neighborhood than achieving due process. Besides, what the hell's he gonna steal?"

"Your Xerox machine, your typewriter, your desk..."

"Max, the fucking guy can't walk."

"Bob, liberalism's an historically discredited doctrine. Ronnie Reagan, Georgie Bush... remember? It's an era of avarice, deceit and plunder." He closed his eyes and bowed his head. "And what will other lawyers say when they see your receptionist panhandling in his off hours?"

"My old secretary, Jeanne, was a poet. Sydney made videos. Think of it as Jimmy's medium of self-expression."

On the wall of my office is a poster that says A CLOSED CONVENTION IN A CLOSED CITY. In the poster, Mayor Daley sits on top of a pyramid supported by soldiers with fixed bayonets and black men in chains. It was handed to me by a young man running through the tear gas in front of the Chicago Hilton in 1968.

I had graduated from Penn Law School one year before. I had not gone enthusiastically. I had viewed the law as a dim, dull, narrowing tunnel, at whose end awaited a wife and kids, a house in the suburbs, two cars, and waking up one morning, at age forty, wondering where my life had gone. In college, I had wanted to write, but my idea of a writer was Ernest Hemingway, and, by that standard, I had nothing to offer that anyone would read. It was 1964. I was twenty-two and needed a draft deferment. I had scored well on the Law Boards and was willing to gamble that the Princeton Testing Service knew more about me than I did.

What attraction I did feel for the law came from having been raised in a family that believed in working for social justice. (My father, a New Deal-minded attorney, and my mother, a school teacher, had met at a fundraiser for the Loyalists in the Spanish Civil War.) But "social justice" was not a term that was plentifully applied at law school. The emphasis was on practicality and advancement. The main value of the in-house culture was class rank. The higher you finished, the bigger the firm that hired you. The bigger the firm that hired you, the more money you made. The law school offered several courses in Trusts and Securities but none on trial practice or civil rights.

When I graduated, I joined VISTA. It sent me to Chicago, where I worked for a legal aid organization that provided assistance to community action groups. The major community action group to which I provided assistance was a 5000-member street gang. The main assistance I provided was to document cases of police brutality against the gang members for a massive law suit against the police department, which was drafted but never filed, because the legal aid organization feared offending Mayor Daley. At the end of my year in Chicago, the police, whose brutality I had been documenting, rioted at the Democratic Convention, clubbing college kids and militants, ministers and freaks, and eighty percent of the American people, according to George Gallup, approved.

I quit VISTA and came to California. I married and bought a house and cars. I started a law practice, which came to have less and less to do with social justice or community action. Some mornings, it seemed it had nothing to do with anything but trying to squeeze a few extra dollars out of insurance companies for a stream of clients with unending complaints. I had fallen into an eerie business, where one's sensitivities were steadily bludgeoned by the realization that one's livelihood depended on how badly others were maimed and one's philosophy progressively numbed, witnessing the passing parade of men and women struck down at random by failed brakes or slipped ladders or spilled oil, without regard to age or creed or extent of charitable contributions.

Each year was worse. Cases became more complex, more costly and took longer to conclude. The injureds' benefits did not increase, and since attorneys' fees were tied to these, I worked without a raise. Meanwhile clients, frustrated by the low benefits and long delays, became more hostile and abusive. It had gotten so that, when a social worker I had known for years and was representing for a cervical strain followed up her instruction to litigate her chiropractor's prescription for membership in a health club with a hot tub *and* sauna, rather than accept the sauna-*only* facility her insurance carrier was offering, with the comment, "I don't hear you being 100% supportive on this, Bob," it was all I could do not to scream, "What you hear, Carol, is me thinking, 'Jesus, here's more chickenshit work I'm being asked to do for nothing.'"

I no longer shared my clients' sense of passion or outrage. I no longer saw Truth or Rightness in their causes. "Well, you're not being unreasonable," was the most indignation I could muster. I had reached the point where every principle was as negotiable as a flea market rug. Every argument had an opposite to be flipped out of my briefcase like a card. Facts were things attorneys flicked at one another like second-graders' spitballs. When a prospective new client called, all I asked myself was "How big a pain in the ass will this one be?" and "What can I make off it?"

Even when I won a case, I didn't feel I'd accomplished anything. Usually the awards were too small to have impact on my clients' lives. Other times... Well, the last case I'd won was Richard Cullen's. Richard had been beaten with a lead pipe at his employer's gas station. He had a concussion, three lost teeth, two cracked ribs, and a fractured hip. The gas station denied liability, claiming Richard started the fight by spitting on his assailant. Its star witness was a close friend of the man who'd pleaded guilty to assaulting Richard.

It took a year and a half for the case to be tried. Meanwhile Richard could not work; his state disability ran out; he could not afford medical treatment; his phone was shut off; his landlord gave him a three-day notice, and his wife left. One morning, Richard told a collection agency that, if they did not stop sending him bills, he would blow up their building and was arrested for extortion, malicious mischief, and carrying a concealed weapon. At trial, I had Richard and two witnesses. The gas station had none. When I asked the owner in the hall what happened, he said, "Oh, Tony'd been out late and didn't feel like coming." The judge decided in Richard's favor, but I could only think of words like "cruelty" and "callousness" and "cocksucker," not "triumph."

Still I had my writing. I did it every day. It was central to my self-esteem. I was not just some sold-out, burnt-out lawyer, I told myself. I was this special artist guy. I wrote articles and stories for journals that no one seemed to read. I wrote one novel that was published and three that weren't. The most recent, a black comedy about an attorney, my agent termed "Repellant, morbid and grim." My publisher said: "The most depressing and most difficult to market novel I have ever read." ("I'm not asking you to change anything," he'd said. "I just want you to offer some affirmative alternatives." "Offering affirmative alternatives is changing everything," I'd answered.) I could derive pride from being rejected for the bleakness of my vision, for being too disturbing rather than too banal or trivial or weak, but it was disconcerting. My self-image was not based upon becoming the guy who sat black-suited, stubble-chinned, cackling bitterly in the corner of the bar, dribbling cigarette ashes on his lapel.

The leader of the street gang in Chicago was convicted of forty felonies involving a conspiracy with Libyan terrorists to blow up federal buildings. The police Sergeant, who'd led most of the raids I'd protested, was convicted of assassinating two drug dealers who worked for the rival drug ring to the one for which he moonlighted. When I looked at the poster, I thought of things like that.

I wondered what I was doing hiring Jimmy. I wondered if I could trust him with the front-door key. I wondered if his wheelchair would fit into the elevator and if he would sue me for discriminating against the disabled if it did not. I wondered why, if he wanted work and not someone to sue, he had not found a job himself. I wondered if I was planning to write some sappy t.v. movie: "Depressed, cynical, yuppie lawyer is redeemed by encounter with crippled, black, homeless person." Maybe I will get a case or two out of it, I thought, as if only turning a profit could make a decision reasonable.

"Your sister died when you were six, four, five?" Adele said. We were walking in Tilden Park, which runs along Berkeley's eastern border, north into Contra Costa County and south into Oakland. The Park has a lake and hiking trails. It has a merry-go-round and pony ride. Every night, raccoons creep up from its creek beds to steal garbage. Every few years, fire whips out of its brown grasses and devours homes.

"Five," I said. "She was five. I was eight."

"That's why you get involved with people like Jimmy. To fix things." Adele looked at me to see if it was okay. The sun dropping behind the ridge reflected on the lenses of her glasses, tiny as dimes, black as tar. The wind riffled her black hair. She pulled the zipper on her flight jacket tight. "To get back your happy mother."

Adele and I had dated in college, broken up, did not speak or write. After I left VISTA, I traveled 2000 miles and found her living in a converted garage at the end of a rose-choked lane. She had already dropped out of master's programs in french literature and urban planning and was about to conclude that, since she feared heights, cold weather and bugs, her engagement to a Cessna-piloting, ski-lift-jumping, wilderness-trekking Italian Count might not be the thing the doctor ordered—unless his name was Caligari. She and a friend, over one or three Southern Comforts too many, would trade men in their lives who had not quite worked out. Adele had a firm offer of a Missouri J-School graduate who had been a Second Team All Big Eight safety for me, but when I crashed through the brambles like the Prince after Sleeping Beauty, she decided to exercise her option.

Once, in the early seventies, at the espresso bar where Adele was working, a customer said to me, "You guys're always so happy to see each other. Every time you come in, it's like you've been apart for months." Twenty years later, she is still the best moments of my day. With loss, I suppose, as well as gain, we have elected against choices that would distract us from the pleasure we take in each other. We do not go to dinner parties or join causes. We have not had children. Sometimes, we joke we reconnected because of our compatible neuroses. Other times, it encourages belief in the Divine. Adele has become a psychotherapist. I can dislike her seeing things in an analyst's terms, or I can be fascinated.

"Go on," I said. My sister's death from leukemia had been something my family locked away. My mother said talking about it would upset my father. My father said it would upset my mother. I grew up knowing some boulder had crashed into us but unsure which bones had burst. We had all dusted ourselves off and limped away, not mentioning it again. With Adele, gradually, on visits east, we began to examine the pieces. "How long was Susie sick?" "What did you tell Bob exactly?"

Overhead, a grey-black turkey buzzard hung, dropping its cruel-beaked, sharp-clawed shadow on us like a curse. "Every child has fantasies of omnipotence," Adele said. "You may've been jealous of your sister; any older brother would be, but you'd've fixed her for your mother. When you couldn't, it meant you hadn't been big or good or strong enough to make her happy. I don't mean, now, you aren't a helpful person. You are. But this is connected to wanting things for yourself. If you 'fix' some person and they feel good, you feel good too. Your clients, me, your mother, Jimmy."

An owl, hidden in the eucalyptus, hooted. Somewhere, field mice shivered. I took Adele's hand. I stroked her wrist with my thumb. There are moments I wonder why all moments are not like these: startling, sweet, rich with intimacy and emotion. At the same time I catch myself unconsciously flinging sandbags to ward off their flood: this case that must be prepared, these pages that must be typed. I seem forever to be giving priority to the making of these payments on some debt I can not recall having incurred but whose demands I dare not ignore.

Jimmy worked Monday, Wednesday, and Friday, nine-thirty to three. He arrived promptly and regularly. He did his job eagerly and cheerfully. He said, "Good morning. Law offices." "He's on the phone. May I help you?" If I asked him to clean out a file drawer or water the plants, he did. When I asked him if he could pick up stationery at the printer's, he said, "No problem, boss. I'm on wheels."

Some callers complained. "A guy's answering your phone who can't speak English," one lawyer told me. "He can speak English," I said. Others raved. "Your new receptionist's a doll," said a woman in Sacramento, recovering from a second laminectomy. "So helpful. So sweet." I would return late from court, and my next appointment, instead of glowering, would have pulled a chair beside him and be chirping away. Amelia thought it was fantastic not having to answer phones. Even Max viewed Jimmy as "an all-right dude." When my ex-client's daughter started, I gave her two days and left Jimmy his three.

I thought of writing about Jimmy, but I did not want him to think he had to answer my questions. I watched and listened and made notes.

In June, Adele and I went to Philadelphia for my parents' fiftieth wedding anniversary. When I return to one of these assemblages—aunts, uncles, cousins, friends of the family I have not seen in twenty years—the only one living farther away than Long Island—I wonder how I have come to be so greatly displaced. My father, now a retired judge, is of-counsel to a firm at which, when—not if, *when*—you come to work on Saturday, you must wear a suit and tie but *when* you come on Sunday, a sport jacket and slacks is sufficient. Here it is my behavior which feels mad.

The party was in the backyard of my younger brother

Ralphie's in Bala Cynwyd, a suburb on the lower Main Line. A few miles from the rowhouse where our parents raised us, a few miles further from the immigrant neighborhood where their parents raised them, his house is three-stories tall, masonry and stone, set behind eight-foot high privet hedges, with a front lawn the width of Veterans' Stadium, and anchored at each end by a copper beech old enough to have known Betsy Ross. The house is filled with Santa Fe furniture and Eskimo art. Two bronze Mercedes SL's sit in the garage. Ralphie has become The Non-Fat Frozen Yogurt King of The Greater Delaware Valley. His wife Tessa paints oil portraits of race horses and hunting dogs for families in the Social Register at $5000 a pop. Their son Rory is the fourth-ranked fourteen-and-under singles player in the Middle Atlantic States. His twin sister Roxie models for Wanamakers, does commercials for Carl's, Jr., and has been hospitalized once, briefly, for an eating disorder.

After graduating Swarthmore, Ralphie had spent two years driving a cab in Boston, bussing tables in Boulder, and working on a freighter in the Caribbean. In a way, that behavior always amazed me less than his return to Philadelphia to settle in so successfully. I keep expecting a frantic phone call from my mother that he and Tessa have packed the kids into a wildly painted van to follow the Grateful Dead.

As we entered, a pink-haired woman I did not recognize told Adele, "We're so proud of Robert, giving work to that poor man he found sleeping in his doorway."

"He wasn't sleeping in Bob's doorway."

"Really? His father made it sound like he had to practically step over him each morning."

My brother's backyard has a hot tub, flower beds, and organic vegetable garden. Among the tomato plants, zucchini, and corn, I spotted three marijuana stalks. Ralphie saw me staring and winked. Given my feelings about the painted van, I found the sensimilla reassuring.

Children I could not identify ran about, tossing rubber

balls, peddling plastic cars, banging into each other, falling, and getting up. Adults fanned themselves at linen-draped folding tables and talked stock tips, tour groups, and what's-wrong-with-the-Phillies. Ghosts were present too. I counted two uncles, two aunts, a suicided cousin, a former law partner of my father's who went out a window, a golfing crony who had his ashes surreptitiously sprinkled on his favorite 18th green flitting under the suburban sun, gliding amidst the dahlias, before I was distracted by a white-suited waiter offering turkey sausages on whole-wheat buns.

My father, eighty-one, blind in one eye, deaf in one ear, veteran of a quadruple bypass, an arthritic back, and major abdominal surgery but still serving on civic committees, pointing out in letters to various editors the errors of their ways, and who, just the week before, had told off some body-builder who was letting his Doberman crap on the sidewalk, and my mother, seventy-seven, survivor of a childhood where her own mother died when she was five and so poor her only toys were pictures she cut from magazines, but still cooking, cleaning, shopping, sewing, and, now, administering drops and pills, ointments and medications to my father, as she had previously to my brother and me, had made clear their preference to avoid solemnity. They would not yield one inch to any heaviness that might press them too directly to recall the ever-increasing number of the gone. It was a request I welcomed. The challenge of putting into words my feelings at that moment would have been overwhelming. There were not sufficient words. There was not adequate time. The most important people in my life were leaving me with each tick of the clock. The idea that these partings were to be complete, unending, irreparable could not be sanely borne.

Ralphie gave a funny toast. Uncle Jules told a half-dozen Abe-and-Sadie jokes. Adele and I sang, our lyrics to Richard Rodgers' tunes: "There is Nothing Like a Herb," "That's Why Rebecca is a Champ." We were a hit. The clever son. The talented wife. People laughed until they cried. They clapped until they ached.

When I returned to Berkeley, I learned that Jimmy had been telling war stories to Amelia.
"That is incredible!" she'd said. "Absolutely unbelievable!"
"Oh, I have had the most fascinating life," Jimmy said. "What I been through, somebody ought to write a book."
"You ought to talk to Bob," Amelia said.

TEXAS

M y name is Jimmy Don Polk. I was born first—twenty-third—fifty-three.

My parents' names were Jasper and Geri Polk. My father was about six-two, shoulders like a barn, with a thin, inky mustache. He looked more like Creole. He worked construction. He also had his own little shop, making cabinets, chairs, tables, all kinds of carpenter work like that. He would work eighteen hours to provide for us. My daddy would work outside cutting boards, sanding, planing, two o'clock in the morning with me holding this flashlight in this icy cold to get us things. He tried to teach me that skill, but it was a bit too splintery for my taste.

My mother was a beautiful, high-yellow woman with green, pretty eyes. Stone-green, pretty eyes. She very tender, very strong, very independent. My mother was a secretary. She worked at the Police and Courts Building in Dallas, Texas, the famous Police and Courts Building. When Jack Ruby shot Lee Harvey Oswald, he shot him there.

The town I grew up in was called Waxahachie, a little country town thirty miles south of Dallas. Waxahachie had about 10,000 people. It was a farming town. Cotton was the main thing we grew. We used to pick it. We used to chop it.

And we grew lots of greens, okra, tomatoes.

I grew up with my sisters, Joanna, Sylvia, Beth, Vicki, Annette. I lost another sister before I was born. We was all in the house. The oldest, Joanna, was three years older than me and the youngest, Annette, about seven years younger. I was in the middle. I was the onliest boy, so you know I was spoiled.

My mother came from a poor family. Her maiden name was Faire. Most of her family was farmers. They mostly pick cotton. I didn't know my grandfather, but my grandmother died beside me. I was in the seventh grade. I had spent the night with her. She came in from work, sat on the couch, kissed me, said something about, "I love all my grandchildren. I'm gonna get me some sleep," and laid back her head. I tried to wake her and she wouldn't. I ran straight through the screen door home. Soon as I got there, my cousin called and said, "Grandma died."

My father's father was a farmer. He raised hogs and did gardening. He was also a minister of the Church of Christ. His father before him was a minister. My grandfather is from the Old School. He is a religious man. "Thou shall not do this." "Thou shall not do that." He has a church in Texas today. We used to call him Big Daddy. Didn't call him Granddaddy. Call him Big Daddy and Big Momma. In the South, that's the kind of name we use.

My father worked for my grandfather picking cotton. He was the oldest, and my granddad and them had five kids. The family relied on him to work at an early age. He picked cotton like hell. He paid for their whole house picking cotton. My father was grown to be a minister but he rebelled. He rebelled so hard against that he left the family. It was years before my father even let me communicate with my grandfather so much hurt and pain and anger there.

When I got to know my grandfather, we had a great relationship. My grandfather saw in me what he shouldn't of did with my father. They lost lots of years together. Trying to make up to me what he did to my father, he treat me with a lot more—love ain't the right word—kindness.

They good people I come from. My grandfather very well known in Waxahachie. The Polks are very well known. My Uncle Byron he's Fire Chief. My Uncle Lawrence Matthew he's kind of a builder. My Uncle Elvin he's a safety inspector with Standard Oil. Right now, the Polk family in Waxahachie, Texas, pretty prosperous. We very well respected. I'm glad to have the Polk name for that.

About one-third of the people in Waxahachie was black. We had very few Hispanic. It was basically a white town. In fact, Waxahachie did not start integrating the schools until I was in the seventh grade.

The Ku Klux Klan was active from the time I can remember thinking. I remember cross burnings. I remember being chased by the Klan.

I was thirteen. I was in Frankabetta Park, where all the blacks drink Thunderbird, play baseball, have barbecues and fish parties at. Black people had a curfew. Ten o'clock, we had to be inside. Me and some guys hanging out, having fun. All of a sudden, they start going home. I lived about twenty minutes from the park and I left about fifteen-to-ten. The closest route for me was along these railroad tracks. I met about thirteen guys with white hoods. They ran me down the tracks, the fastest I ran in my life. I remember falling down, getting up, falling down, getting up. They was saying, "We gonna get you, nigger. We gonna kill you." When I made it to my house, my whole pants was wet. From that time on, I started going home at nine o'clock.

It was a scary time. Playgrounds, swimming pools, all of that was segregated. We could go to the same theatre whites used but only Tuesday. They called that "Nigger Night."

My father raised me the old-fashioned way. Don't cuss. Don't talk back to your parents. Respect your elders. Say "Yes, sir," and "No, sir," and "Thank you." If you wake up Sunday morning and you late for church, you miss breakfast because you gonna be on time for church. You mess up, you get whipped.

My father was the type where I was a man before I knew what a man was. He put inside of me the value of work for what I wanted. No way you asked anybody for anything. Not him. Not my mother. Not my grandfather or grandmother. That was a butt whipping. If you couldn't get it yourself, do without.

I worked from the time I could push a lawn mower. I used to go into white peoples' area and cut their grass for $1.25, $1.50, $1.75. I would push that sucker from early in the morning to late that evening. I did everything from mowing yards to picking pecans to bagging groceries. I would bring that money home and give it to my father and let him give me what he think I should get. I always had jobs. I always did like to put some change in my pocket. If you was broke, it was bad. If you had money, you was glad.

I was well blessed coming up. Lots of my friends didn't have shoes. I didn't know the meaning of being real-real poor. I stayed clean. I had nice clothes. We lived in a one-story, four-room, wood-frame house. Had a big backyard. When my father started doing better, he had a couple rooms added on. Basically, we had everything in life I wanted.

Then something happened dramatically. My mother and my father split. She left us. I don't know if he was abusive to her or what. But she left us, and she took the girls. They stayed gone two years.

I chose to stay with my father. I always feel like I hurt my mother because I didn't go with her. I'll probably feel like that till I die. But then, I wonder how, if I would of went, I would have hurt my father. I felt torn in half. I didn't know which way to think, which way to do. I remember my father drinking and telling me, "Always be good to ladies. Don't do bad." He realizing he was wrong the way he treated her. I used to hug him and help him sleep. Sometimes he be so hurt and angry, I couldn't even talk to him. Of course, I'm hurting, but this was something I held inside. I wanted to show him I was a big boy. I wanted to show him that he could be proud of me, that I could take care of this and I could take care of that because he was in so much pain.

After my mother came back, things improved a hell of a lot.

I been hunting ever since I could hold up a fourteen-inch shotgun. I'm talking about the age of six, seven, eight. The guns be bigger than me.

Waxahachie had a wooded area on the east side of town. It was jungle-like, bushy, with lots of pecan trees, lots of acorns, lots of those kind of trees, lots of what-we-call cocoa bushes that sting you as you walk through. It had ponds and streams. It was very hilly. I liked hunting, but I hated to go hunting because I got hurt a lot. I always was falling down on some sticker bush. I fell into a river once and almost drowned. But it grew me up.

One time, about four months after I started shooting, my father was showing me how to load a .410. I told him, "Daddy, this gun is heavy." He told me, "Boy, you be a man." A big rabbit came by, and he said, "Shoot." I shot, and it kicked me backwards, and I shot him in the toe. It scared me bad. I thought I was gonna get a whipping. I started hollering. He grabbed me. "Boy, don't shoot me. Shoot them rabbits."

We took my father to the hospital, but the next day he put the gun in my hands and said, "Okay, you do this again. I don't want you to go off to no kind of place where you be afraid to shoot because you shot your father." I remember crying like a baby. I was holding my momma, and he was dragging me with one arm, "You going. You going." "No, daddy, I'll kill you." But he made me get back out there.

When I shot my first rabbit, I felt sad. My father said, "Don't feel sad. God put animals for humans to live." Hunting was a matter of survival. If you wanted to eat good, you had to shoot. The meat we ate was rabbit, possum, squirrel. We had to hunt for our meat, and we grew our vegetables, and the money we saved was for us to have clothes. My father was tight with that dollar bill. He figured you had to earn your keep. He trained me, in life, the less you do for yourself, the less you receive. That was the reward he was showing me. The more you try, the more you get.

We would leave about five o'clock in the morning. The mist still be out. We come back about six that evening. My mother pack us lunches. It was pretty fun. It was miserable too. Have these big boots on. Big thick clothes. It was hot. It was real hot, toting this gun that almost outweighed me. Bullets in this pocket. Bullets in that pocket. Imagine yourself in the jungle. Little kid with a big gun and stuff to bang you. Stuff sticking you and itching you and you looking for rabbits or squirrel or possum and looking out for rattlesnake, 'cause very-very lots of rattlesnakes in the jungle where we was.

When I was ten years old, I really developed shooting. It came natural. Somebody give me 100 bullets, I would hit ninety-nine and only miss if I wasn't trying. The average person aim and concentrate on the target. I aim and I'm firing. I was very accurate. I never had a bad day with a gun. Like when you get in your car and turn on the key and start driving, you have control from the first moment. That's the way it is with me and the gun. Soon as you put it in my hand, I have control.

I won all kind of shooting awards. Every summer, a fair would come into the town. They put the fair around the courthouse with a field for the shooting events. They had games like shooting barn arrows, throwing knives, shooting guns. You pay your $5—back then, that was lots of money. But you had a chance to win $100—that's a whole lot of money. I won about three years straight, competing against grown men.

My father said, "Boy, you got a gift. I hope it don't hurt you."

FULLY ARMED

I went to Turner High School, an all-black school, which the first to the twelfth grade went to.

When desegregation came our way, I went to Waxahachie High School. We almost had a big clash when we had to leave our school and go to the white school. They wouldn't bus white students to our area. They bussed the black students and closed down Turner. All the black teachers lost their jobs. The principal lost his job. They weren't transferred with the students. People started rallying because they wanted justice did. After the first year of desegregation, they started having black teachers.

Waxahachie High School was big. We ranked in what-they-called 4A. The senior class had 500, 600 seniors. The first time we walked through we could tell the advantage. They had better restrooms, better facilities, better everything. Turner's football field was a pasture. We played in parking lots with glass and stuff. You be afraid of getting tackled and getting cut. They had a stadium.

I started playing football my freshman year. I was so good I played with the twelfth graders. I had a good career. I was five-eight and weighed about 180. I was fast on my feet and solid. I played first-string, offense and defense. Fullback and middle linebacker. I loved the linebacker part. I didn't like getting hit, but I loved hitting.

I thought I would get a college scholarship. I had a dream I would play professional. I was getting lots of recognition, lots of special treatment, lots of free things. I got special jobs when school was out. I worked in a place called Kroger's. I stocked shelves. I worked at a fast-food restaurant, Super Sonny's. I was the first black in Waxahachie that, at that age, had a car. A '64 Mustang. Souped up and everything. The school gave my father money to get it for me. Basically, I had it pretty easy. I was blessed.

I didn't even have to do schoolwork. Teacher would tell me, "Don't worry. Just play football." But my father seen things I didn't. One time, I got big-headed because my name was in the paper and everything, and he noticed I wasn't bringing home no homework. I said, "They said I didn't have to." Dad said, "Boy, I be damned, you better do homework. Y'all gonna have to have something to fall back on. Don't let them make you dumb."

The saddest thing I remember in high school, my best friend—he played tailback—his name was Carl Square, and Carl Square was killed because he was going with this white girl. He was a year older than me, a great athlete, a good person, a fun-loving guy. They ran off together. They stayed gone six months. When they got back, they found him dead, his head smashed in, all his bones broken, on the same railroad tracks I escaped from the Klan on.

That happened midway through my tenth grade. We dedicated a ballgame to him against Ennis. Ennis was an all-black school, but it was a *big* black school. They played major white schools. When we was at Turner, we never could play Ennis. Waxahachie and Ennis hated each other. The worst riots would be because of Waxahachie-Ennis football games. That's about the only times the black and white would fight together, during football games.

I ran for 178 yards, scored three touchdowns. We still lost 42-21.

Vietnam was pretty hot then. I had knowledge of it, but I thought I was protected because, on a farm, the oldest son don't go. Plus, I figured football would get me to college. That was a deferment for sure.

Other guys were scared. The majority of black seniors got drafted the week they were out of school. Most of them was automatic going to Vietnam. It didn't seep into my head. I wasn't arrogant, but I knew I wasn't gonna go.

When I was sixteen, my sister Joanna was raped by this

guy, Erwin Barksdale. He was a big guy, big for his age, with a big ego. He was a football star for Ennis. His name was in the paper all football season every year. He was a well-known guy.

I been to the drag races. When I came back, lots of people in the yard. They told me my sister had got beat up and raped. My father was sitting on the couch with tears in his eyes. First time I seen my father cry.

I got really angry. Seemed like something jumped inside my body and transformed me to another person. I loved my sister. Joanna was the one cooked the chicken when Daddy and Momma was working. She made sure we had clean clothes. I always regard her more as a mother-sister than just a sister-sister because she took care of us. I felt I was the man and had to do something. I had so much hate in me my veins in my arms and neck started sticking out and beating.

My grandmother was telling me, "Don't do nothing bad." But I pushed her off of me. I went into my daddy's truck, a blue Chevy pick-up with a big-old long tool box in the back. I got the crowbar, and I went after him.

A friend drove me. He had come from the races with me. He was going to help, but I didn't give him a chance. I went straight to the park where I knew Erwin Barksdale going to be. I put the crowbar behind my back and walked up like I didn't know what happened. It seemed it took a long time to get to him. I didn't hear no voices. I didn't hear nothing.

I had my crowbar back, and I come up and started beating the hell out of him. I said, "This is for my sister." I wanted him to know what it was for. I wasn't trying to kill him. I was trying to mess him up bad like he did her. When I was hitting him, I seen my friend's tires spinning around and around and around. He was leaving me.

I turned back and hit Erwin Barksdale again. The police report says I hit him twelve times. They say I mashed in his skull.

The next thing I remember is somebody hitting me in the

head. Next time I came to, I was in a cell with my father saying, "You killed him, son."

I said, "How's my sister doing?"

So I got charged with first degree murder. First degree murder. They charged me as an adult. They didn't give me bail. They had me in a cell by myself. I was isolated.

I was a big story in the paper. *The Waxahachie Daily Light.* Big old picture on the front page. Big old black print:

FOOTBALL STAR ARRESTED FOR MURDER.

I had lots of people, black and white, supporting me. They knew what happened, plus, me being a football star had a lot to do with it. But in Texas, at that time, if you do something wrong, you going to Huntsville Penitentiary. That's a rodeo prison, very-very hard core.

I was in a state of shock that whole period. I was like a walking zombie. I remember going to court. I remember going back to my cell. I felt like my life was over. I didn't care what was going to happen, except I didn't want to die. The only thing going through my mind was, "Boy, you got first degree murder. They going to electrocute you." I started preparing to meet my Maker. I was reading the Bible every day. I became a Bible-frantic reader. I found comfort in it too. I can recite verses from the Bible now. I started trying to find that inner peace. I started trying to find that person named God. I wanted somebody to come to me in the middle of the night and say, "Okay, you going to be redeemed."

The County appointed me this lawyer, name of Groves. One night, he come to my cell and say, "We going to the judge. Whatever he asks, you look at me."

The Court House was a big round building like a church. The courtroom was hot and stuffy and small. The only people was the judge, the district attorney, my lawyer, and me. Two flags was on the wall. This fan was beating the air.

The judge said, "Your name is Jimmy Polk?"

I looked at my lawyer. He nodded. "Yes."

"You know the charges against you?"

I looked at my lawyer. "Yes."

"You know you entitled to a jury of peers?"

I looked at my lawyer. "Yes."

"And you want to plead guilty?"

I looked at my lawyer real-real hard. My hands was handcuffed. I had this brown jumpsuit on. I had my head up and tears rolling down my eyes. "Yes."

Bam! That hammer hit. "This is your sentence. You can either do twenty-five years in Huntsville or four years in the United States Military."

Damn, that freaks me out today. Things don't pop off like that. Sixteen years old, you don't go in the Army. You don't step out of jail into a uniform. I looked at my lawyer. He reading some file. I said, "Thank you, your Honor. I choose the military."

My father and mother saw me one more time in jail. My father said, "You know how to protect yourself, son. Please come home."

I said, "Daddy, I will not die there."

Two days later, two M.P.'s picked me up. They wore helmets and boots. They had big guns on their sides. They said, "Mr. Polk, we hear that you good with a gun. And evidently, you likes to kill."

TRAINING

The M.P.s took me by car to Dallas Airport. From there, we got on a plane. It didn't have no fancy seats. It wasn't a passenger plane as far as passengers would ride. There was a pilot and a guy sitting beside the pilot and the M.P.s. I sat by the door. The M.P.s sat beside me.

I had never been in any plane before. In fact, that was my first time riding out of Texas. I was scared as hell. It was like my whole life was picking up at a fast pace. I knew I was going into danger. I didn't know what was going to happen. I wanted to just lay in the corner and sleep and forget this whole ordeal. I had butterflies in my stomach. I had weakness. My knees started shaking so bad I couldn't stop them.

I tried to talk to the M.P.s about football or something. "You know, I used to play football?"

"Yeah. We know all about you."

They was so tightened up they wasn't about to give me an inch as far as being relaxed. They had to maintain that strong stability.

I remember one M.P. saying, "You have been chosed for a special assignment."

And I said, "What special assignment is this?"

Fully Armed

He said, "That's all you need to know." Like "Boy, don't ask no questions."

The plane landed at this, like, private field. I didn't see no other planes. I thought, "Oh my God, the Army gonna kill me. They gonna shoot me and report I was killed in the service." I said, "What's going on? This don't look like no Army. I supposed to be around lots of people in green uniforms."

The M.P.s started laughing. They said, "We taking precautions."

"Where are we going?"

"That is not for you to know. You in the United States Army now."

"Y'all fixing to kill me? My father know where I'm at. What's your name?"

Then I seen six jeeps lined up and six other guys in the jeeps with two M.P.s for each. When I seen these guys, I thought, "Well, I won't die alone."

We drove through some mossy, swampy places. We rode twenty-five, maybe thirty minutes to this base-like camp. It was night. Weren't too many people. I don't remember seeing Army trucks or Army tanks. I remember seeing jeeps and barracks and a flag pole.

Soon as we get out, two things happen. One, I see a mess of orange feet-prints painted on the ground. Two, these attack teams come running at us. Some had all-black uniforms. Some had all-red uniforms. Some had green-and-red uniforms. And they all cursing, yelling, screaming, "Asshole! Motherfucker!" and beating us, hitting, punching, kick us in the balls. Lots of guys, some no bigger than my belly-button, and they screaming "Cocksucker! Pussy! Get your feet in the marks!" I'm terrified. I'm serious scared. These guys are crazy. I thought, "They gonna kill me now."

Then this Major step out of the dark. Tall, straight, John Wayne-looking guy, starched and ironed and spit-polished.

He stand on a porch under the light. Attack teams stop their beating. I thought, "I'm saved. These guys gonna catch it." The officer saw me looking at him. He says, "Don't you eyeball me, maggot. Get your slimy eyeballs off me." Then he snatch a lizard off the wall. And he bites off its head. I was frozen. My stomach was like out of my mind. The officer say, "Straighten them up or kill 'em." And my last hope was gone.

They marched us down the feet-prints into a building looked like a ghost town saloon. It had lots of student deskses and a blackboard and podium. A man in a green uniform told us to raise our hands and swore us in. He called me "Asshole" because I had my wrong hand up.

We left that building and went around the corner. They gave us uniforms. Camouflage color jogging pants and black t-shirts and a hat, like a baseball hat but with pockets on the side, and black, lace-up, high-top Army boots.

From there, they gave us something to eat. We wasn't allowed to talk to other people or each other. We just sat at the table, while the other people were moving around. They gave us some weird-ass soup and rice. I said, "Okay, the Army ain't gonna kill me, but it ain't gonna take care of us too good."

Then we went to sleep.

Four o'clock next morning, Drill Sergeant woke us up. A short, stocky, no-nonsense man, with a shaved head like a bullet. Military all the way. This man go to bed dreaming about the military. He gave us fifteen minutes to have our bed made and our gear on. He ordered us to march outside and stand in formation. Hell, I didn't know what formation was. "What you talking about, formation?"

He told me to shut up and gave me 500 push-ups.

The Drill Sergeant said, "You going on special military assignment. You are a special, elite group. Your mission is to do missions that the regular R.A. army do not do. The chances of your survival are one in 1000. Don't expect to go home. If you're lucky, you might make it through, so you listen to me."

That was his speechin' words.

By then I was on about my 387th push-up, but I was steady listening. And he steady looking at me. I said, "Why were we picked?"

He said, "Boy, shut up. You should be proud of being in the Special Forces. You don't have to be in the jungle every day. Regular Army, R.A., has to fight every day. Sometime they be in the jungle for months, for years."

Drill Sergeant, he was glamorizing it.

We was a special unit. This the first time in the whole U.S. military history one group brought together and train together and fight together from Day One. The World War II German Nazi Army that way. Your Israel Army like that now. But the U.S.—no. U.S. military start you with basic training, everybody the same. Then it move you into separate units when you done. We was a pilot program. We was Make-it Break-it for the guys who thought us up. So everybody extra-tough on us. You mess up, you get beat up. That just how it was. They hook your elbows over the top of the bunk and beat you.

Our code name was Bumblebees. We didn't have like a 51st Division or a Bravo Company or things like that. We had a insignia we had to sew on our shirts and on our jackets and a special scarf that had a bumblebee stinging with a little rifle. We had to wear that scarf all the time. We had to tie it a certain way. The Drill Sergeant said, "That scarf more important than that gun. Whenever you guys get leave, people gonna respect you, because they gonna know y'all an elite team."

They called us Bumblebees because we buzz in, we sting, and we buzz out. They stressed this point: go in; do your mission, and get the hell out.

Our training wasn't the kind of training that other veterans had as far as being around lots of people marching and singing and stuff. It wasn't about that with us. It was all about business. It was serious tension all the way up in the air, because you never did know what was going to come next.

We'd get up, do calisthenics, an hour sometimes, maybe two, depending on how the Drill Sergeant felt. If we was sluggish or dragging or if one person had a bad attitude on his face, he would extend it to two hours. Push-ups, sit-ups, jumping jacks. Then we'd march in this swamp, where every time you march mud and water be coming over your whole feet damn near.

Sometimes, we be carrying stretchers when we marched, running over ridges and gullies, carrying this heavy damn load. We run two, three, four hours, on account of we not allowed to leave no bodies behind. If you got hurt or tired, you allowed to lie in the stretcher. But this laid this guilt trip on you, because you a burden to your buddies. So you hop off the stretcher and start humping. Plus, while you lying on the stretcher, your buddies cursing and beating you for making them carry your ass.

Then we'd have lunch. Piles of rice and vegetables, with a little fish or chicken, just like the gooks. They made us eat, and they made us trim down. There was no fat guys on this team. Everybody was well-muscley built.

After lunch, things'd get heavy. Weapons firing. Parachute jumping. Hand-to-hand combat. Hand-to-hand fighting with knives. If you cut somebody, they consider that a point and everybody clap. But you could not literally hurt the person. You supposed to cut and nick them here and there. That make them fight harder, make them more cautious. I been cut two or three hundred times before I got good. I started listening to the instruction more.

We had grenade-throwing patches. They had this whole village just like in-country. Our mission was to crawl under this barbed wire, with your face all sunk in the mud, and hit whatever target the Drill Sergeant designate. They always had a way where you could crawl out in case something go wrong. One fool I was behind didn't get a good hold on his grenade. He threw it, and it went straight up. Me and him set a record for crawling up from under this barbed wire. We had a good fight after that. I never went behind him again.

Then we had special classes, sometimes together—escape, survival, village surveillance, house clearing—sometimes apart. My main class was Shoot-a-Gun-All-Day. All I had to do was lie out in this hot-ass sun and listen to these guys telling me to shoot this bolt-action Winchester 70, which I already know how to shoot. They would lay down with me. "I can't shoot with you laying beside me like that."

"Shoot the rifle."

I would shoot.

"You didn't even aim. Let me see what you hit. I be damned! This boy can shoot."

Every time I hit a bulls-eye, they moved the target back. They kept moving it till it got out of bullet range. After that, it got easy for me. I'd shoot about 200 rounds and then drink beer with them.

The other guys were going through their routines. I never was allowed to watch. They wasn't allowed to watch me. Some guys was on the team just for fighting. They just mean guys. Mean, bully, ugly-looking guys, where you sleep with your eyes open.

But some guys had a special skill: bomb making; knife fighting; grenade throwing. We had a brother, whenever we wanted something to blow up, we call him because he always hit the target. Reggie was a minor league baseball player, fixing to be called up to the majors—the Red Sox or White Sox, one of those Sox, but he had to go into the service. He was a pitcher, but he was loony too.

Another guy, Jorge, had a strange religion: no shooting but you could stab all you want. His religion said, "Never believe in any gun, but believe in knives because Jesus Christ was pierced with nails." Jorge killed his father. He got tired of his father beating his mother. You know how sons are about their mothers.

He had little knives, big knives, fat knives. Knives covered his whole body. The Army made him special belts to put around his self. Jorge wouldn't shoot nobody, but before you shoot him with a gun, he'd kill you with a knife. He was fantastic. One guy made him mad one time. He said, "I'm gonna ask you one more time, my friend. One more time, ear go off." The dude kept harassing him. Like you slap at a fly, the knife cut a piece off the dude's ear. The dude never did mess with Jorge no more. Jorge was the youngest one in the bunch after me. All the rest was grown men. We was children compared to them.

Michael Flint—Flint Michael—was a thin fellow of a man with innocent blue eyes. He seemed like the loneliest man in the world. Seemed like he was schizo-schizo-schizo. The guy never smiled. He loved fire. I think he was an arsonist. He would look at a match and let it burn on him. He set his bed on fire three times. It got to where everybody scoot their bed down and he was by himself.

He was also a bomb expert. He had a special black box that he go into the jungle with that had little vials of stuff in it. He could make a homemade bomb like that. Or he could rig a Claymore out of hunks of old metal and plastique. We had to burn this village one time. He was so smart and so great that he knew exactly what point to set the fire to cover the whole area in thirty seconds.

Wee Willie was our main muscle. The dude was a biker from Compton, near L.A. He had tattoos with skulls and eagles all up and down his body. The man couldn't say one sentence without the word "Fuck" coming into it. "Fucking hello." "Merry motherfucking Christmas." But if you need a neck broke—or you need to hump an M-60 through rice paddies and over mountains, which we did—he was your man.

The Professor was a guy who, no matter where you be at, always knew how to get back to the point from where we was. He was great as far as choreographing. In the jungle it was easy to go in circles. The Professor knew how to keep us from doing that. We called him the Professor because we never did realize how you can jump out in the jungle, in the middle of the night, and it's pitch dark and know the exact place to bring us back to the next day. We never did know how he had that talent.

We were all Loony Tunes. We all had messed up personalities. I don't think everybody was convicted of something, but one day the conversation came to me—here I am, everybody else got a mustache and stuff, I didn't have one string hanging down my chin—"Boy, ain't you too young to be in this?" And I told them what happened. After that other guys started exchanging stories. This guy convicted of rape. That guy convicted of murder. All of a sudden, Hot Rod, a big-old hellova guy from Chicago South Side said. "Yeah, we all convicts. We all disposable."

We never did force each other to talk. That's a bad habit in a game of war. The same person that you might force to talk gonna be the same person that gonna watch your back. You don't want to cross him no kind of way, you know, upset him or make him feel bad. So you think about consideration like that. The Drill Sergeant said, "You guys got to kiss each others' ass if you want to make it through this. Which y'all probably won't no way." I caught on and said, "Hey, I better start liking this guy because this guy might be the one to save my life." We didn't like each other, but we had respect for each other. And that's how we got along. Only thing we'd say to each other sometime would be, "Hey, hope you make it out of here. Good luck, buddy."

The training facility was like out of a Hollywood motion picture. You know how they put up these fast buildings. Like that. Like it was built in a hurry. It was all wood. Everything was the same color. Greenish-brown. There was no red or yellow or orange. There was no lots of greenery as far as grass and trees and stuff. It was always hot. I'm talking about 107,

113. I'm talking about four o'clock in the morning it's hot.

I was there two months. When I started, there was maybe eight other guys in the barracks, and it end up being thirty-two. The team had its own barracks. It was something like a barn but flat and long. Each one of our beds was lined up beside each other, and we had lockers with our name on it. As far as socializing with other units, we couldn't do it. The damn Drill Sergeant slept in there to make sure we couldn't communicate with nobody.

Thirty, forty miles off was a little-bitty town. I never found out the name. We were not allowed in without an escort. There were military guys there, but you wasn't allowed to talk to them. One time, a military guy come up and asked me, "What branch are you in?" My companion, whoever was appointed to go with me, snatch me and say, "Hey, none of your business." This place I was at, you don't supposed to ask questions.

I never even found out what state I was in. All this was hush-hush. Things happen so fast you never did wonder what state you was in. You just wanted to get through it. They kept applying pressure to your mind. They kept trying to school you, and you knew that you had to listen to these people if you wanted to make it through. They had your full attention. I knew that I was in something that was bigger than big. I didn't even try to understand it. I just wanted to be strong to survive.

At night's when you got to asking yourself, "Where am I?" but you'd be too tired to focus; you had to get ready for the next day. It was a well-designed plan, because everything was rush. By the time you get through doing what you be doing during the day, you be so exhausted that you might think "Where am I?" or "What the hell am I doing here?" for a minute; then you fall straight to sleep, because you know, come four o'clock next morning, sometime three-thirty, you got to be up.

The only persons we could socialize with was our selves.

And the guys in the unit were so damn crazy that they really didn't want to socialize that much. Once a week, we might get together and go off to a garage-like place, built out of cinder block, and do a little drinking. That was a reward.

When we'd go have a beer and stuff, somebody was always assigned to us, somebody other than who was in the group, like a guardian or something. I mean, strangers you don't even know. They always would wear a red hat too, a beanie. They would sit with you and talk to you. But as far as me and my guardian and somebody else and their guardian going and communicating two-on-two, no-no. That was very rare. You talk to somebody outside your unit, that was 1000 push-ups in the sun. You don't do that. You drink your beer and listen to your guardian. Guardian would tell you, "Okay, you know you got to kill babies," and you just drink your beer. We didn't have to pay for it either. We could sit and drink until our guardian say, "Okay, that's enough."

I could write to my family, but the Drill Sergeant took care of the mailing part. He said, "Give it to me." We didn't have a Post Office. We didn't know where things went. We handed the letter to him. He sent them out. Anything come in, he read it first. I couldn't make a phone call for a month. Then when I made that phone call, there was somebody sitting beside me, looking at my mouth.

And we wasn't allowed no endearments. No kinda comforts-from-home. One time, this guy, Pettis, his girlfriend sent a box of chocolates. Drill Sergeant was all over him. He put him on his knees in front of the group. Punched him in the chest. Called him "Maggot." "Maggot got cookies from his dog-fucking whore." He filled two canteens with salt tablets and hot water. Each time Pettis ate a chocolate, he made him drink. First, Pettis tried to play it cool, like "Hmmm. Good." But uh-uh. Drill Sergeant knew his business. Pretty soon he puking. Drill Sergeant really brutalize him then. He beat him and made him clean his own vomit off the floor.

35

We got no newspapers. We couldn't read a book. They let us read some magazines, but they was six or seven months old. We never had nothing up to date. Only up to date things we got was papers, wasn't no title on it, and they would say, "Read this. This is what happened to your brothers." And it was saying, "United States lost this many soldiers." "This many soldiers being held in this place right here." That's the only news they would give us. As far as sports and stuff, you read about something happened six months ago that you already seen before you went into the company. Only material up to date they would give us was how Charlie was doing this, what Charlie was doing to get information out of you. "They sexual molested this soldier because he didn't give information." "They cut this guy's dick off, stuck it in his mouth." "They skinned this one alive." They would have pictures of them doing this.

It would make you mad. It gave us this attitude where we was going to kick ass. We hated Charlie that bad. We hated Charlie. We hated his momma. We hated his children. We hated everything about Charlie, and our objective was to kill Charlie and take his women and kill them. Because this is what they did to soldiers. This is the anger that we all was feeling. I don't know about everybody else fighting, but our team, this is what we felt. We didn't respect Charlie at all. We wanted to hurt him best as we can, mentally and physically. That was our objective, and we got a thrill off it.

Mostly, now, we drilled at night. We made tremendous marches at night, all night, up, down, over, under.

We'd be out for days, for weeks. You got, maybe, three hours sleep. Your name was "Maggot" or "Asshole." Nobody talked to you any other way. You had one set of clothes. How many shirts can you wear? That was the whole idea. You didn't carry another shirt, that was more bullets you could carry. It was all about killing anyway.

All our work was done at night. You couldn't make no

noise. Days, you just sit and sweat. You could sleep a little, but it was 110 in the shade, and there wasn't much shade. You couldn't drink water on your own, just when Drill Sergeant said. You live like that, you start going crazy. One time, I thought the Nazis won the war. I thought the Drill Sergeant had swatzikas on his sleeve. No way Americans would be treating other Americans this way. I thought I was in one big outdoor concentration camp, and this one more torture they thought up.

One drill was: set ambushes in groups of three. Two guys be awake and one asleep. But you only get to sleep one hour. Then it be the next guy's turn. After a while, Drill Sergeant let us swap our hours. It seemed like a generous thing to do.

One night we had a real mock mission. We had to take this peak. Mortars and artillery firing live ammo on both sides, and we had to go down this corridor between. They were steady exploding, exploding, exploding, and we're running down the middle, carrying ladders we got to throw against this cliff. I'm not talking about no rope ladders like Batman. I'm talking heavy metal ladders weigh a ton. It's night. We run down the middle, and we're climbing the ladders, and we're carrying mortars, rockets, the kitchen sink. I was freaking out so much my hair was shaking. One shell goes wrong and we're wiped out.

On top of the cliff is a road. Soon as we hit it, this RUMBLE RUMBLE CRUNCH CRUNCH coming at us through the dark. Godzilla! No, tanks! We flop down. We got to hide or be crushed. We got to decide whether to attack the tanks or keep on with our mission. We got to decide in a minute. Drill Sergeant told us it be totally clear when we get up top. He told us he had reports. That taught us not to trust nobody.

No matter what anybody told you. No matter how much you want to trust him. Don't. It always turn out different.

One night a man walked in the barracks with drills and

stuff. He said, "My name is..." And gave his name. "I'm a full bird Colonel. I'm here to do a little work on you guys, so you might as well get your nuts up. Come on, get in line."

The rest of the guys was bigger than me. By the time I realized it, I had been pushed up front.

He made me smell some kind of smelling salt. I got real dizzy. I remember hitting on my knees and him picking me up and dragging me to the chair, and I remember the drill. ZZZZZZZZ. He was drilling a hole in the back of my tooth, and one of the guys was holding me.

He come out with white pills. "This is cyanide. You ever get captured, bite down to the left of your tooth. And fools, remember, while you're in the jungle, when you eat, take this pill out of your mouth. But when you get through eating, place it back in that hole. Always bite down and slide your teeth over to this side. The capsule will break. You will be dead in three seconds. This is to keep the enemy from torturing you. Do you know what these guys do when they torture you? They pull out your fingernails. They cut your balls off. They cut each toe off. This is what happens. You guys are United States Military. You should be proud to die for your country. Don't suffer. If you're gonna die, die quick."

The guy had a Southern accent and he talk with confidence. You knew this guy was telling the truth. After I got mine did—and it hurt like hell—we all had it did. That was like a safety valve for us. We knew that, if we got hit bad and couldn't take the pain, all we had to do was slide our jaw over to the left and—BAM—in three seconds it over.

After that Colonel told us what that pill was for was the first night I seen everybody on their knees. Everybody got upside their bunk-bed and prayed. The atmosphere was quiet, and it seemed like death was walking the halls. We knew it was time to put in session things that they was teaching us. We was scared. I was probably the scaredest one. I was the baby.

That last week, there was lots of prayer sessions. We got

lots of visits from the Chaplain. Lots of us came together closer. Like one dude had called me "Nigger." He said, "I'm sorry I called you that." And I shook his hand. We knew it was time for battle, and we had to fight together. And all those bad things that we said to each other or hurt each other some way, we made up for. That last week was a special moment. We became closer and we got very religious. We found God real quick. Real quick. I mean guys who would cuss all night and all day was reading their Bible out loud. When you're scared, things change.

NAM

When I landed at Cam Ranh Bay, I didn't know where the hell I landed at, but I knew I flew twenty hours to get there. We got dressed that morning at three-thirty. They said the plane will be ready in thirty minutes. We said, "Hey, can we change our minds? Can we postpone this?" They said, "No. The mission is on."

We was the onliest ones on the plane. When we wanted cocktails, stewardesses brung 'em. We flew for a long time. I went to sleep for eight hours and woke up, and we was still in the air. Then I look down, and I'm seeing green and brown. I'm not seeing smoke or fire. It don't look so bad. But when we landed, it was hotter than Hell, and it smelled...

I can't tell you how bad it smelled.

The first night we jumped, I don't think none of us knew what a real jungle was. All we knew was the play jungle at camp. We almost had a rebellion against the Drill Sergeant. He was telling us, "C'mon, let's take care of this mission." And we was sitting up there, "Hey, no, man, we ain't going off in no jungle. Jungle got lions and tigers and shit." Then he pulled his gun on us. "Yes, you are."

He told us to hook up our latch lines. Normally, when

you jump, the next guy wait three seconds and go. When we jumped, it was instant. Doom doom doom doom doom doom doom.

When we parachute out, it was pitch dark. All you could hear was "Cricket! Cricket! Cricket!" That wasn't lions or tigers, but it was scary enough.

Our mission was to kill this Charlie. He run a P.O.W. camp, and he was torturing the men bad. Our mission wasn't to rescue but to attack the prison. Don't bring back no captives. No United States. None of our boys we couldn't bring back. Just kill dinks.

I was to be the first one in and the first one out. My mission was to go through, see if I see any sniper. If I do, eliminate them, get on the radio, say, "Bumblebee clear," and they come behind me. They don't have a call from me in twenty-four hours, the mission is off because I'm dead.

I go alone, because I have more chance succeeding by myself than when you have two people. Things work out better when one mind is working on a certain thing. When you got two minds working, as far as in the jungle, looking for a sniper's point, there tend to be disagreement. Those disagreements can cause confusion. Confusion can get your whole unit killed. I dig to be the first one out, but the first one in I didn't like.

I had a M-16 with twenty or thirty clips. I had two Smith and Wesson .38s. I had two silencers, a short one and a long one. I had eight hand grenades and a machete, a K-bar knife, and C-4. My nickname was "Fully Armed" because here I am, the little-bitty person on the team, and I'm the one they depend on to make sure their life was safe when they come through.

Sniper is a guard that protects certain perimeter areas to make sure that it is not being invaded. He's moving around, but he's never leaving his perimeter. When I look for those snipers, I crawl in and look for him—or her. There was a lot of hers. The hers was the best shooters anyway.

Charlie normally had three snipers on any trail. And you know, once you in a perimeter, you only had one to knock off. You ain't got to worry about three or four other guys. That was like a protection to me. I knew, once I got this person, I could go on to the next perimeter and get the next person. They had three points where they said snipers would be.

Certain areas of Vietnam we had fully mapped. When we land, we had maps telling me in this area might be a sniper, so be careful. Go 300 yards, look to your left. Might be a sniper there. We know where the prison camps are. All this stuff is pin-pointed down. All you got to do is not be hardheaded and listen.

When we left, everybody's pack was filled with drugs. We was told not to open up until we parachute. After we landed, the Drill Sergeant said, "You have Inspiration in that package." It was amphetamine and coke mixed together. More of amphetamine.

We had a doctor in our unit. He was a quiet person. He would not conversate with you. You could pass down the street, he wouldn't say nothing, but if you in the jungle and you get scratched or hurt, he's on it—BAM—you get the best care. He was damn good. We loved that guy. This guy took bullets out in the jungle. He stopped bleeding with a string. I saw him, one time, stop a chest wound from sucking with a wrapper off a Camel's pack. He had a way of talking to you, so smooth and comfortable, you would kick back and not be afraid, because you knew you in good hands. If he see you panicking, he would stick a needle in your ass. He was very observant about the people. This doctor shot us up.

It took me a while to get my nerves together. I was the baby, and I was scared, but once that Inspiration hit me, I was ready. I was so drug up I was out of this world. The drug made me feel like nothing gonna happen to me. I could've gone to sleep in that jungle and not worried about being shot. Only thing I wanted to do was go in, kill those three Charlie, come back, let the other men go do their thing.

The Drill Sergeant was talking to me and eased my mind even more. After a little bit he said, "You ready to take care of your business?"

I said. "Yes, sir."

The terrain was very green. Very soggy. It had lots of wait-a-minute bushes. Lots of elephant grass. Lots of trails where somebody had went stomping through, cutting down.

I got lost. Hell, I didn't know how to read this piece of paper they telling me to. I figured it out after I went around in circles. I came to this vacant ex-village which, on my map, was where that first sniper was gonna be. From there, it was easy to reach the other two locations.

I went through quiet, walking slow, an inch at a time, looking for booby-trap wire. I was so comfortable I wasn't afraid of anything. The fear of death didn't bother me. I could walk by a snake, pick it up, and sling it around. I thought Vietnam was gonna be a snap.

I knocked off those dinks quick. The first one I knock out of a tree. The second was kind of difficult because I had to sneak up behind him. That was my trouble one. I had to shoot him in the back. Number three was easy. He was beside this stream, with his M-1 on the ground, like I caught him taking a leak.

When I shot the first person, I felt like I won a trophy. It made it easy for me to kill the next person. And that made it easy for me to kill the next person. And that made where killing became—and, God, please forgive me—it became fun. Damn, I hate to say that. But it got to where it felt good. Where I mean... Hell, it felt good, that's what I mean. It sound bad, sound crazy, but that's the way it was.

I got on the radio. I said, "Bumblebee clear" and got the hell back to Safeland. They had told me once I came back I was safe, but I climbed in the tallest tree I could. I sat there, and they came back about seven hours later smiling, shouting, "We're Number One!"

I said, "What's the count?"

They said, "No count," meaning we had no casualties.

I felt damn good. I figured that we was the best elite team the government had. I said, "We bad, y'all."

A couple guys was crying. They said, "Damn, man, we could of brought at least two or three home."

We had to meet the Hueys three miles the other side of the river. Charlie was pissed off, but they wasn't gonna come on our safe side, because they was outnumbered twenty to one. We sent up a flare so it was easy for the pilots to get us.

Only my chopper drew Captain Chaos, this pilot-fool. The man had a suicide drive. Bullets and shit shooting at us—man, we be scared as hell—and he's like, "Beautiful day, isn't it? Let's see how traffic's moving in Beverly Hills." Shit like that. "Let's take a trip, check out East River Drive." "Man, you better get us back where we supposed to go." We had to make it clear we wasn't gonna go down with him.

After he had five guns put to his head, he stopped doing that.

He just started flying slower.

We had a safe haven in a village six or eight klicks from the Cambodia border, near where the N.V.A. was fiercest at. Sometime the best hiding place is in front of your enemy's nose. The times we did go there, we go on another mission in the next week. Normally we had a month, maybe five weeks lag time, so that was a reason why they sent us there.

We stayed in this...something like a cottage. It had lots of rooms. We wasn't allowed to go outside. We wasn't allowed to stand by the windows. We had a contact that would come in, bring us food, cigarettes, booze, *Playboy* magazine. We didn't see no females. We couldn't even peep our head out the door. When somebody knock, we had to rush to certain spots like we was hiding. Drill Sergeant was the only one could leave. All we was able to do was sleep and eat.

And old Doc had enough supply for our withdrawals. We wasn't allowed to do drugs after our mission. That was a complete no-no. You would get an Article 15 against you if you did, so he was shooting this vitamin-shit in us to bring us down. Most of that time, we was going through withdrawal. I remember throwing up for four days, just gagging one time. I thought, "This is it; my time has come." I was throwing up every two hours.

But what we was in was cool because we didn't have to fight every day. Fighting sometimes is better than fighting every day.

At this time, the war was heavy. Charlie was kicking our ass. Charlie was at his highest peak as far as killing. Like a football game, Charlie had us beat 42-10. Our mission was to track Charlie and eliminate him. We had to send a message through.

That second mission, we had to destroy a whole village.

"No mercy," the Drill Sergeant said, like a coach give you a pep talk before a game. "Line the women and children up, and kill them. Let the men see, and kill them next. The village is harmful to the United States. Daylight, it is cool. Night time, they will destroy anybody from the United States. They is treacherous. G.I.s dying like hell in their area. Get those who responsible."

We was pumped up. But when we got those kids, weren't nobody pump up no more.

That mission, I couldn't go in and come out. I had to follow the group. When I found out, I felt I had been lied to. I had to kill snipers first, and when I got back, they tell me I got to go. You know how pissed off I was? I argued with the Drill Sergeant. In fact, he pulled a gun on me. I was fixing to kill him, and he was fixing to kill me because I wasn't gonna go. Until the rest of the guys put their guns on me. Then I went.

It was a hard game played. If you didn't shoot who you supposed to shoot, then somebody in the squadron was gonna shoot you. You never knew who. The Drill Sergeant would pick somebody out secretly. He told me one time, "If Billy Junior don't do this, blow his fucking head off." Billy Junior and I was friends. And one time Billy Junior wouldn't pull the trigger, and I came out with my .38 and stuck it to his head. He looked at me, and he pulled it with one tear rolling down his eyes.

So we did that village.

That was to send a message to Charlie that Bumblebee was on the job. When we first went in, people run up with food and stuff. Old men, women, children. Before they got ten yards, we killed 'em.

We killed everybody. When they started rushing to us, we started killing. They started running back. We started putting Zippos on each hooch, knocking people off as they run out. It was bad. It was pitiful. They offered us sex. They offered us everything to let them live. One mama-san I had to damn near hit to get her off my knees, begging me, begging me. We got to a certain section, everybody was in a crowd. We killed 'em like you slaughtering cattle. We killed 100, 150 people.

Then the Drill Sergeant made us hammer cards with a Bumblebee picture into their foreheads with our pistol butts.

The next village we destroyed was more modernized. We was ordered to destroy the people in the village but not the food, not the transportation, not anything our people could use.

This time we didn't have to kill the womens and children. Before we went on that one, everybody said, "You might as well kill us now, fuckers, because we not gonna kill no more babies." We all meant it, because we all had bad flashbacks about killing those kids. It took a hell of an effect on the group. Maybe they took that into consideration, because we was told to round up the women and children, take them in the jungle, and tell them, "Ditty mau!" "Get-the-hell-out!" "Ditty mau!" But the men, we had to kill.

We accidently did shoot some womens in a crowd. Once that M-16 starts shooting, it don't have no target, and some of 'em got in the way. The ones we didn't kill, we was able to round up, take into the jungle, and tell them haul their ass. They was very happy.

But we shooting men as we saw 'em. We killed about seventy people, maybe seventy-five. My buddy got ready to shoot this one man. Before he could pull the trigger, the guy had shot hisself. He said, "No, you Yankee son of a bitch" and blew his own head off. When they had firearms, they was shooting back at us. Then we did their foreheads like before.

I think that town was a drop point Charlie use to get supplies. There was hooches with fifty pair of chopsticks, big iron pots of food, corn for 2000, like you feed an army. There was a fucking barn full of ammunition. They had guns, guns, guns. They had American guns there. We couldn't understand that, and the Drill Sergeant said wasn't our business to understand. I believe that was why we was told to destroy that village. Maybe they did know what they was doing.

Saigon was a pleasure. We stayed together in a nice hotel. We had our own rooms. We was in a friendly part of town full of G.I.s. It was like a G.I. city: G.I. bars; G.I. restaurants. We could move around but we could not talk about our missions.

They took care of us. They fed us damn good: steak; lobster; stuff we didn't even eat. They gave us cartons of cigarettes every other day. They brought us boom-boom girls to take out our fantasies on. We weren't able to do drugs, but we was able to smoke weed. We had the best marijuana you could smoke. We had marijuana that wasn't green or brown; it was black. You hit it one time and you hallucinate. They was giving us boxes of the stuff. It was like a party. We got rewarded very well. We knew that, when we be successful on a mission and we go into the safe side, we had everything we wanted. It got to the point every one was saying, "When we go on the next one?"

When there was a mission, we had memos slid under our doors. First thing we do when we walk into the room is look on the floor, see if there is any white piece of paper. Memo would say something like "Poop Meeting: 1500 hours." If it was important, it would have "URGENT." We would meet together like a conference. We was told what we was gonna do and devise our strategy.

This meeting had two URGENTs on the memo.
The Drill Sergeant said, "We have a sourball in the group." We started looking around. We knew the word "sourball" meant "defector," "traitor," or whatever.
He said, "No, not in this team. In a P.O.W. camp. Our order is to eliminate him."
Then he look at me. "Jimmy, this is your biggest assignment."
I say, "Sir, Private Polk requesting permission to speak." He say, "Speak."
I say, "Is I going by myself?"
Everybody started laughing.
He say, "Hell no, boy, you get a squad with you."
I say, "Thank you, sir."

Fully Armed

The choppers dropped us in the jungle above the D.M.Z. It wasn't bad. We wasn't gonna run across no whole lots of Charlie, because it was very underground. It was gonna be easy to get in there. I didn't have to knock no snipers out.

Only trouble was when we had to cross this long, wooden bridge, where, you look down, you can't see nothing but rocks. I mean, it was a big, swinging bridge. Every time you walked, you was afraid the boards was gonna break. You didn't know how safe it was, if it was gonna fall. That scared the hell out of me.

It was about a four-hour hike, but this was no serious hike. We was all crazy loaded. Before I was on the ground, I was loaded. Doc did it. And we had an emergency kit he taught us to do, in case the drug he administrated wear out. We was all taking our time. It wasn't a push-type thing. It was a more relaxing go-as-your-own-pace but do-it-within-this-period thing. It took us four hours to get to the job because we was lagging, but it only took us forty-five minutes to get back.

The camp had six mid-size buildings, halfway big as barns. They had maybe thirty-five G.I.s in there and forty ARVN and forty Charlies. They had barbed wire all around. At the foot of the wire it was very well laced with mines in case a P.O.W. tried to escape.

The bomb man checked and said, "No way you should go in there. You got to make the hit from the outside."

That was a relief off of me because, if I had to go in, I had to go by my damn self. As long as my teammates was around, I was safe. Me, being the sniper, I had to be the one performing these so called hit tasks, while the company, their job was to cover my back. They was off in a certain area waiting for me, but they wasn't far. It was up to me to set up my range, my rifle, and what I was going to do. I had control of that.

I made the hit in a tree. I had to pick him off at 200 yards in the midst of a crowd. He had been a high-ranking officer, a high-classified person. To keep his self from getting killed, he was giving away pieces and pieces of top military information. Evidently he was throwing out little crumbs here, little crumbs there in order to have a meal, a bed, not to be sleeping on the ground, not to be thrown in the hole, not to be kicked, not to be bullied. He had enough information to survive in that P.O.W. camp for three years. That's a long time.

He always stuck around this high-ranking Charlie. He didn't have hard duties like the other prisoners do. He was gonna be with him the entire time. He was his flunkey, his personal slave. Where Charlie go, he right behind like a dog. I had a photograph of the guy. I had a photograph of the Charlie he worked for.

I had binoculars, and I'm steady looking, trying to find this guy. It took me forty minutes. I kept looking the whole damn time, looking around, looking around. I got frustrated after twenty minutes, 'cause this tree I was sitting on was hurting my butt. Also I had to watch out for snakes crawling up everywhere. So I'm steady looking everywhere. I'm looking for this guy. I'm looking down for snakes. I'm looking around.

I threw up in that tree too. They was torturing people in the yard. They took this brother, and they had something like a hanging gallow. They slap him upside the head and tied his feet and pulled him upside down, and he was hanging upside down from this gallow. They had this white bag and this guy with this rat big as a dog, and he dropped it in the bag, and then another guy dropped another rat in, and they pulled the bag over his head and tied it. The whole thing started shaking and then made one final jerk, and when they took the bag off, the rat was in his mouth. And I threw up.

Then they slap him to the ground and start stabbing him. And Charlie was clapping and speaking their little language and giving each other cigarettes and walking with their arms around each other and having a fucking ball killing him, man. That was the most horrible thing I ever seen.

Finally, I spot the Charlie coming off this porch. And no bullshit, soon as he out the door, here came this defector. I hit him right then. I hit him dead in the head with the first shot. I didn't have no problem knocking off this guy. It was an enjoyment.

I was mad. I was really mad. We all got feelings. We ain't so super macho we going to destroy those feelings, but I was able to keep hold of myself and do what I had to do. I regret to this day I didn't hit that Charlie, but my first objective was to hit that defector. If I would've hit that Charlie, I might've got caught, but that always have bothered me.

Then I jumped out of that tree. I did not climb down. I jumped and ran. I ran past the guys, and they started running behind me. We ran a long time.

I'm not gonna talk about three missions.
The team had missions in the jungle, and I had missions out of the jungle. I was a trained assassinator. I had to kill people on the peace side. Those missions I won't talk about.

When I got hooked up with drugs, I got unafraid of death. Only thing I cared about was taking care of my mission and getting out. They took that fear out of me.

It got to where I liked going into the jungle. I felt like nothing was going to happen to me. I felt like I was invincible. Nothing could touch me. Hell, I couldn't wait. When I came back to Safeland, as we called it, hey, I'm bored. I'm ready for another mission. It got to that point.

One time I almost got my leg blown away because I wasn't as cautious as I should. We was on a mission to snatch'n'snuff this V.C. tax collector in the Bo Lo woods. That's all I know about him. They never give us much information about the person. The less we know the more protected we are. If Charlie catch you and you know a lots, Charlie gonna get it out of you. Charlie highly skilled at torture. He can torture you hard, and he can torture you soft. He can drug you; he can cut off your private parts. I have seen horrible stuff in that damn jungle. But if you don't know nothing, he ain't gonna get nothing out of you.

I was walking point. I stepped on a mine and didn't know it. It pitch dark, and the mine say, "Click." I froze, because I knew, if it say "Click" again, I was gone.

I reached and felt for it. My feet was on it. I got a piece of tape and sustained the pressure on that mine and kept from blowing myself up. I got halfway back, and "Ba-BOOM!" It had slipped and went off.

That put the whole team in jeopardy. It alert Charlie where we was, and we have to come out of there. Once Charlie know where you at, Charlie come down on you quick. And let me tell you, they were little-bitty people, but those little cats will fight the hell out of you.

I was trying to get to the company but I couldn't fast enough. They was gone. Charlie caught me. Charlie wanted to know who I was. I wouldn't talk. They took me to their camp, which was cut out under the trees, so you couldn't spot it flying up above.

They threw me in a cage. The cage was in a hole dug in the ground like a grave. It was past six-feet deep. It had wooden sticks across the top. I could look up, but all around was walls of dirt. They threw me in and got the head Charlie. He started spitting in the cage and laughing and calling me "Black monkey." "Black monkey, why you fight the white man's war?"

I wouldn't answer, so he pissed on me.

Then he said something in Vietnamese, and they put a ladder in and got me and took me inside a barracks and sit me in a chair.

"Who are you? What's your mission?"

"No speak. No speak." I'm playing dumb.

He's got a knife he's tapping on my ears, my eyes, my balls. Then he stick his knife in my shoulder and pulled like a lever. I'm steady hollering. I'm crying, and he's steady hitting this knife. I'm flipping my tongue up over my pill, but I'm still thinking, "I don't want to die. God, help me. Please help me. God, forgive me for my sins." Things like that are running through my mind. I'm shaking bad. I'm flipping back this pill, flipping back this pill and—BAM!—he's steady hitting this knife.

I'm in the most torment pain. A bright light came, and I went out. I came to, and this Charlie do the same shit again. I was there twelve, maybe fourteen hours, and they tortured me for six. After I passed out the second time, I was laying in this hooch. I'm stripped naked; my wrists are tied to my ankles; I had this gash, and blood was everywhere. I hear POW! POW! POW! POP! POP! POP! Bullets was coming. Lots of bullet fire coming. I look up, and here's the Drill Sergeant. Here's Doc. I think I'm dreaming now.

Doc start pushing the shoulder. I holler. They gag me to keep me from hollering so loud. Doc start pouring alcohol. I'm semi-conscious. I'm thinking I'm dreaming. I'm not realizing it's real. It hurt so bad I was in a sweat. Doc shot me with something, and the pain went away, and he start pulling a needle in me.

The Drill Sergeant say, "Hurry! Hurry! Is he gonna be okay?"

Doc say, "Sure."

Next time I came to, I was in the chopper. The team had not abandoned the mission. They postponed it till they could find out what was going on. The Drill Sergeant told me, "After we surveyed the area where you was and didn't find no body parts, we knew they had you." When they had taken care of business, they came back for me.

After we got to Safeland, the guys joke with me. "How do it feel to be catch by Charlie?" "It felt pretty good, man."

That's when I seen the emotion we had for each other. It did seem that they did care. Remember, when we go off on a mission, we don't free nobody else. Evidently, it didn't hold with our own. I felt proud of that team. We was damn good. We became a family. Even though we kept our own ways and never did talk to each other much, we got the assurance that we looking over each other.

The next mission was our first casualty lost. We lost Flint Michael, our buddy who liked to play with matches. We lost Johnny K., this light-complected brother who loved killing. This guy kept a Hav-a-Tampa cigar in his mouth all the time. They got him, and his Hav-a-Tampa was still lit.

This was the most delicate mission. What we was going off to was an extra-suicide movement. You don't go off in a lion's den and you the prey. You don't jump into a pit fire. We jumped into a pit fire. We had a fight soon as we landed.

We were gonna free this Colonel in a high security Charlie camp. This guy was another Oliver North. This guy was top brass. The United States Army was willing to lose a special attack team for this guy. He only been captured fourteen hours when we got the orders. "Get him. Don't give no gook time to examinate his mind."

Most of the time, when we landed, we was able to relax, do our drug, get our composure, go. This one, the Drill Sergeant told us, "Okay, you big boys now. Y'all been on several missions. Y'all haven't failed. Y'all haven't lost nobody. This one here's your roughest. Have your triggers pulled; have your clips ready. When you hit the ground, Charlie's gonna be on your ass." The Drill Sergeant wasn't lying.

Soon as we down, bullets start coming. From that point on was action. Steady action. Steady movement. Luckily, we was in the range but out of the range. We took cover. We managed to fight 'em off. They was only about twenty Charlies. We killed them, but we lost two men. We lost two buddies.

Johnny K. caught it in the throat. A B-40 took off half Michael's head. We was able to chill out for thirty minutes. Then we marched off in a zig-like pattern, so everybody had their back watched. Thirty minutes from the camp, we climbed in trees and rested till night.

We had lost our main man as far as checking out the booby trap situation. It was scary. Who we gonna send to check this out? Drill Sergeant made a decision. "We all go."

"Good decision, Drill Sergeant!" I'd rather stick together as a team anyway.

It wasn't booby trapped. So we cut the wires.

This compound had a main barracks and hooches for the guards. They had five guards guarding the main building and guards around the perimeter.

Me and Jorge and this guy Lassen from D.C., went this way. Some of the guys went thisaway. Some guys went thataway. What they did on their side of the job, I don't know. Me and Jorge were the main one to get this guy out. Number one, Jorge had a talent for killing silently. I had a talent for being able to shoot. Lassen had the blow torch and bolt cutter if we needed that. We all supposed to meet at a certain point once we got back.

It worked good. Jorge killed three guys. Two of 'em was taking a smoke. Jorge cut both their throats. He hit one guard behind his back from twenty yards, and I wanted to kiss him. I thought, "How in the hell could that man throw that good?" That was a pressure throw.

After we knocked off the guards, it was simple. We creeped through the barracks and located the guy we wanted.

"Sir, is your name..."

"Yes."

"Let's go."

Everybody else was begging us to take 'em. There was four of 'em. "Please take me. Please take me." They was dragging us by our knees. They started screaming. "Oh, God, please don't leave me here! Oh, help!"

We had to shut 'em out. We wanted to bring 'em, but we couldn't. It was dangerous to our welfare. We didn't have time to focus on feeling. Tears was coming out of our three eyes. We wasn't crying like really-really crying-crying-crying but like, "Damn, could we bring 'em?" But we couldn't.

This guy said, "I know how you feel. Y'all gonna get medals for this."

We said, "Man, stick your medals in your ass. Let's get out of here."

Damn, they made us do some rotten stuff over there.

When we passed the barbed wire, shooting started. One of our teams on the other side started shooting back. Lights came on. Then we started shooting like hell. I gave the guy one of my .38s and said, "Here, asshole, you fire too."

We was able to hold 'em off. We started throwing grenades. We started blowing up the place. I had about eight grenades and I threw all of them like eggs. I remember hitting a barracks that was holding United States soldiers probably. In time of war, you start throwing and you start shooting. Things don't have an aim. I'm not looking where I'm throwing, but I'm throwing in the direction of the fire to create a screen.

We got out with no further casualties. We was good running. We was, also, heavy armed. Everybody had extra stuff, and when things break out, it was like Fireworks City. We might of been thirty men, but we made noise like 300. That may have played a big role in what was happening. Charlie heard so much artillery fire, blowing-up, and stuff, they think there's a whole damn 1500 soldiers out there.

Once we got back to our point, this top-brass bastard smiling, want to shake everybody's hand. We all looking like he got dirt on him. We didn't shake his hand because we lost two damn men.

He come to me. "You're a hero."

I said, "Kiss my ass. I lost two good friends for you. Military might think you are worth it, but I don't."

"I still think you should be honored."

"The hell with you, man. None of us should be honored. We lost two men. We're fixing to go get the bodies."

"No! Leave 'em there."

"Man, fuck you."

Our men's bodies were located, maybe, 100 yards away. The chopper was coming down. The hell with it. We got our mens.

Before we got on the chopper, we put our buddies' bodies in bags. We took the dog tags out, and each of us kissed their foreheads. Jorge started the kissing shit. Then everybody did it.

Captain Chaos said, "This sonofabitch run on the chopper, wanted me to leave you all. I told him, 'I'll kill you right now. I'm not going nowhere without those guys.'"

The guy almost got threw off the chopper. But the Drill Sergeant said, "Remember your mission." When we made it back to Safeland, the guy had champagne sent to us. We got two cartons of cigarettes. We got a bag of weed. We got R& R. We got prostitutes. He laid out the red carpet for us.

When we lost a guy, we didn't get a new one. We had lost our explosives man, and they wouldn't give us a new one, and we had to blow this bridge on the Red River. This was a well-made, steel bridge. We basically didn't know how to blow it. We never could set the explosives right. We tried three different times. We kept failing; we kept failing; we kept failing.

To set those explosives, we had to go into water. Every time you go in, there was leeches and snakes. It was awful. It was more dangerous in that water than fighting Charlie. That water was a cesspool of death. It had all kinds of dangerous things in it. You never know if you gonna be bit by a snake, but you knew you was coming out with leeches. I came out with so many leeches it was a shame. And once leeches get on you, they automatic start sucking your blood. They start getting bigger. You can't pull 'em off. You got to burn 'em off. That was painful, very painful. It don't matter how much clothes you wear. It don't matter what you have on. You couldn't stop the leeches getting on you.

And they had these black-and-white snakes. One bite, you dead. Those things we was watching like hell too. Lucky we didn't get bit. We seen lots, but we managed to get out of that water fast or climb one of the poles that hold up the bridge. One dude climbed up one pole, and that snake swum around for forty-five minutes. We couldn't shoot the snake because we would of alert Charlie. He had to stay on that pole, shaking like hell, leeches on him, growing bigger and bigger. When we did get his ass out, the leeches was like ten-dollar cigars. Had sucked that much blood off him.

We got under attack from Charlie twice. First time we failed blowing the bridge, five or six Charlies came out. We eliminated them. Then we took refuge in the jungle. We stayed four days. When we seen Charlie wasn't protecting that bridge, we tried again. We failed again. This time we knocked off six or eight Charlies. We figured the third time Charlie was gonna have a whole squadron up there 'cause they knew we was trying to blow this bridge by now. Common sense would tell them that.

We stayed in the jungle two weeks. Basically, we lived in trees. Everything we did was from the trees. Urinate from trees. Sleep in trees. Eat in trees. If it rained, you soaped up and took a shower like that. Charlie had this habit, when he came through the jungle, he didn't look up. That was our ace in the hole. That was a safety net for us.

We would have four or five guys in each tree. You tie yourself to the tree in case you slip. You sleep for four hours while your buddy watch out for you. Our rucksacks was full of C-rations. Beanies-and-weenies was good; ham and beans was bad. We had instant coffee and pound cake and applesauce. One day, one dude killed a monkey, and we boiled up some of that.

Drugs was a way of surviving too. We had to administrate ourselves. One of your buddies would hold your arm to make a vein, and you would pump the needle, and, when the blood draw in the syringe, you know that you in. These are not regular syringes. The tip and the plastic part was like a syringe, but the top was a balloon instead of the up-and-down. You had to be easy with that balloon when you shoot that stuff once the blood come through. If one of the guys had trouble hitting hisself, one of us hit him.

They gave us speed for that mission. We was able to shoot thirty or forty units and stay up days, no problem. We wouldn't be afraid of nothing. There was no heroin given on that mission. Heroin make you brave too, but speed have you feeling the same, and it have you rushing. Speed make you see things before it happen. You think faster. You act faster. Everything be way ahead of time. You very calm until you come down. We shot speed every eight hours. We got real pushed up. When we made it out, I slept for three days, and it seemed like I slept overnight. They had us in a hospital place.

If we would have had our explosives man, that bridge would have been blown first time. When you blow up bridges, you have to hit a certain perimeter to make the whole thing come down. You can't set a hunk of C-4 and just blow. That's what we didn't know. We knew how to hook up the explosives, that's all. Nobody knew what the hell they was doing.

We got really frustrated the second time it didn't blow. We was telling the Drill Sergeant one night in the tree, "Hey, man, looka here, if we go back, Charlie gonna have a whole damn army with tanks."

But he didn't see it. "Y'all gonna bring your asses back

over there. We gonna blow this bridge."

"How we gonna blow the bridge if we don't know how?" So we tried something different. We tried a sure way of blowing it. We set C-4 all over the bridge. We musta had 400 spots we set it at. That sucker had to come down like pick-up-sticks. And when it did, we cheered.

Drill Sergeant said, "Shut your damn mouths. Y'all making more noise than the bridge."

As we was flying, our door-gunner got caught by fire from ground. He got killed off in a fluke. Captain Chaos went sightseeing again. Any time you come out of the jungle on a chopper, you under fire. But this cat loved the route where you get fired at the most. Again, the door-gunner might of fell out. We don't know. Somebody hollered, and we seen a body flying around and around and around, hitting the ground.

The gunner was damn good. He was one of the guys you love was on your side. Lots of times he pulled somebody's ass up on that chopper. When we come out, we had what you call flanks. The head man of the flank have to hold off until the next party come by. One time the party was coming by and coming by, and I slipped, and he grabbed me by my belt and managed to pull me on. We getting higher and higher. He's shooting with one hand and pulling me with the other. I never did know his name.

We had a good rest. We was treated like royalty. Every time we got treated like royalty, we knew we were fixing to do something funky. When we got orders to destroy another village, we didn't want to go.

We didn't mind killing Charlie. Charlie was a sport now. The whole war became a sport thing. We even counted how many guys we killed. We had a pot. Everybody put in twenty-five bucks. Whoever had the most killings before it was over pick up the whole pot. But when it came down to the kids and women, we didn't like that game.

The village had about 400 people. It wasn't in the middle of the war. You see a lot of G.I.s there. They had a hospital not far away. They had P.X.s down the street. This was a peaceful place until we got there. Then all hell broke loose. That was one of the dirtiest missions they had us doing.

We didn't destroy the whole town. Only certain things. Bars. Brothels. Opium dens. A couple so-called churches the government felt was disrupting us. We had to do it undercover. We would blow something in the middle of the night when nobody around. We got orders, any time we seen by anybody, including people on our side, eliminate 'em. Kill anybody that get in our way. Make it look like the V.C. did it. One night I set explosives to this bar with a timer for an hour on it. I set out by my jeep, looking at my watch. Thirty minutes passed, and three G.I.s hadn't come out. I ran in and faked like Charlie was coming to get them out to protect their ass.

We stayed eight, nine days. We was able to party every night. We didn't have to spend nothing. Everywhere we go, everything was spent for us. All we had to say was "Bumblebee." In fact, some guys from other outfits seen what was going on and started saying, "Bumblebees. Bumblebees. Bumblebees." This guy in this one bar gave each one of us a case of beer, and we had to kill this same guy. We had to blow his bar up, and he was sleeping inside.

The next day the village retaliated. They had their network too. This group of United States soldiers walk up to play with this baby. Heads go off their bodies. That baby was hooked with grenades.

We stayed in the village, but we wasn't sleeping. Things got so intense after the third blowing, we got orders from some head-honcho to stay in a group because we was suspicious. Everybody was speculating, "Who are these jerks? They appear; they don't wear no army hats; they dressing cool. We know they Special Forces. What the hell they doing in town?"

Our own people started treating us funky. We got stares. We got beer cans thrown at us. We was very unwelcome, and it wasn't a good feeling.

In this bar one night, an E-4 from a different company said, "Shit didn't start till y'all came. Who are you? I know we fight on the same side. What's going on?"

The Drill Sergeant slapped him. Then his company came, and we had to fight his company. I got my jaw disconnected in that.

I think these places they had us bomb was like a drop-in for Charlie. I think they got information there. The black market was wide open. There got to be lots of spy shit going on. But at that point, I wasn't really thinking. At that point, our feeling was mixed. We cared, but we didn't have time to care. We had to stay in a negative mood to be successful. When I was taking away lives, it would have an effect on me no longer than five seconds. After that, it would be erased from my entire mind. I wouldn't allow myself to feel for over five seconds. Course my heart will always be sick with some kind of something, but after five seconds—BAM—it's gone.

The Drill Sergeant told us this: "Don't allow yourself to feel. Not even for the person beside you."

It confused us. "Don't care for him? And this guy might have to save me?"

"Fuck him. You got to worry about you, not him. Just 'cause he got the same uniform you got on doesn't mean you got to watch over him like he's your brother's keeper. He's on his own."

That's gonna tear you up inside. You gonna wonder, "What the hell are we? Who are we fighting for? What are we doing anyway?"

They kept us in a state of confusion mentality-wise. Any time we came back, we had to turn in our drugs. We turned in a little and kept some for ourselves. When we had this kind of speech, we would shoot dope to forget it. By then, we was a bunch of junkies. We was a messed-up unit brainwise. But I got so good with that syringe I could hit myself in the dark. And that's good.

When we ran out of drugs, we was able to go to a buddy and say, "I'm sick." That's all you had to say.

"C'mon. Let's take a walk."

One time a dude said, "I'm sick" in the group. In five seconds, everybody's hand came out with balloons. Everybody started laughing, but everybody got quiet too. Somebody said, "We do care for each other." A moment of silence came over the whole bunch.

Then somebody said, "Fuck us. Let's party." We was getting sentimental, and we wasn't supposed to get like that.

While we was on this mission, the Drill Sergeant told Jorge to blow up this temple. This is how dirty the Drill Sergeant was. Jorge was very religious and didn't believe in destroying no church. The Drill Sergeant knew Jorge was religious. Everybody respected his religion. He was a very religious man, but he was a hell of a killer. Jorge say, "No."

Drill Sergeant stuck a .45 in Jorge's mouth, pull out the trigger, gonna blow him away.

When the Drill Sergeant did that, you hear clickclickclickclickclickclick. Everybody have their shit on him. Jorge had become very well liked. Jorge had saved every ass in that outfit in one way, form, or fashion.

"I am your Commander."

"You pull that trigger, you our ex-Commander."

Drill Sergeant dropped the gun.

Jorge spit in his face, say, "May God bless you anyway," and walked away. As he was walking away, everybody was walking with Jorge. Jorge didn't have to blow that temple.

Drill Sergeant didn't talk to us for four days. That's when we became a rebel group. That's when the Drill Sergeant lost his power of command. The group had become uncontrollable to him. The temple was blown, but it wasn't blown by Jorge. Two other cats blew it to cover Jorge's ass, in case the Drill Sergeant tried to put some kind of Article on him.

We had longer off than usual. Two damn months of R&R. The only drill we had was basically exercise at our own pace. Normally, a formation be called every morning. I'm talking four-thirty, five o'clock a.m. There was no formation call. It was very suspicious.

Second, they transferred us to a city away from the war. We stayed at this luxurious hotel, like a resort. It had that French look. It had beaches with white sand and palm trees. It had a discotheque. It had people serve you food with white cloths over their hand and shit.

It was old, but it was respectable. You felt like anybody couldn't stay at that place. It was big. It was real big. We had our own rooms with balconies. When we eat breakfast on the balconies, you see mountains and green valleys. I'm talking about elegant.

Civilians stayed there. Men in business suits. Blonde women with round eyes. We was told to act in a civilian-like manner. We was ordered not to wear khakis. We kept our scarf—that was like waking up and putting your underwear on, damn near—but we told people we were a construction crew. Or that we was U.S.O. We was there two weeks. I was so relaxed. Two best weeks I caught in Vietnam.

The Drill Sergeant didn't stay with us. He was at a place not as pretty and comfortable. We figured that, because we had rebelled, he didn't want to be part of us. It was strange that the Drill Sergeant was across the street, but that wasn't in our minds until the Chaplain came.

We having breakfast on somebody's balcony. The Chaplain pop in out of no damn where. We hadn't seen him since before Mission One.

FULLY ARMED

"Father, what are you doing here?"

"I came to give you your blessing," he said, like he knew something we didn't know.

The Chaplain stayed two days. He visited each person. He asked us if we wanted to ask the Lord to forgive us for different sins. He came to my room one night and said, "Private Polk, you have lots to ask the Lord to forgive you about."

I said, "Chaplain, you talk like we fixing to die."

"Every mission, you about to die."

"Why are you here now? This is our twelfth one."

"They asked me to bless you guys."

So I asked the Lord to forgive me for killing and stuff like that. I repent for my sins.

We started paying attention when the Professor said, "Something is wrong. This shit ain't right. Look where we at. What's happening? War is happening, man. Bodies being killed every day. Look at us. We like a bunch of multimillionaires on vacation. What the fuck going on? The Drill Sergeant is across the street. What's this, man? The Chaplain's here. What the hell's going down? Y'all better wake up and see what time it is."

He was one of the most serious guys in the company. When the Professor talked, we listened.

We was playing volleyball when the Drill Sergeant came over and said, "You guys moving out in a couple days."

"What we gonna do?"

"We not gonna talk here," he said, like spy cameras around.

He marched us to this church. He set us down on benches.

"We have this person in this camp. Bring him out. If he don't want to come, kidnap him. If you can't kidnap him, kill him."

Talking killing in the House of God was freaky. And how many people in a P.O.W. camp ain't gonna want to come out? That blew all our minds. I don't think nobody slept that night.

In this team, you taught to be suspicious. We started holding secret meetings. We started putting pieces together. "Hey, man, the Chaplain been here." "We talking killing in the House of God." "We could've talked where we playing volleyball. Nobody watching. People in that church."

We made a pact. We put all our hands together like a football huddle, all kinds of black and white and Mexican hands stuck upon each other.

Seven jeeps came to pick us up. That was weird. Jeeps never picked us up before.

When we getting in, the Drill Sergeant came across the street. Somebody said, "Sarge ain't going."

Everybody started looking at each other.

The Drill Sergeant said, "You guys been on eleven missions. You know the routine. You don't need me. Your orders are in packages. Tie them around your neck. Do not open your package until you on the ground. Do not look at anyone else's package. Kick ass! Do your mission!"

They drove us to this field. Three new, black choppers waiting for us, instead of our old ones. Our regular pilots wasn't there either.

Normally, our pilots would have our weapons with our names on it for us. It was very important to have the same weapons. To shoot somebody else's rifle was uncomfortable. That rifle was more important to you than anything. It was more important to you than a human life. That rifle was your woman. That rifle was your best friend. It was your wife; it was your mother; it was your daddy. It was everything to you. You love that weapon. You know every spot on it. You know every grain. You know everything about it. I could take my weapon apart and clean it in thirty seconds. It is like your shoes or something. It is something you love. I loved my rifle. I loved the fuck out of my rifle.

The choppers had weapons in them, bazookas, all kinds

of fucking stuff. They loaded like hell. When I seen this arsenal, I'm looking through it for my gun. Then I caught myself. We all caught ourselves. "Our weapons ain't here."

"Might be on the next chopper."

"Or the one behind it."

Some punk fool driving the chopper say, "You got issued new material."

"Man, who in hell are you? You don't even know us."

"Yeah, I know of you guys."

"Who gave you permission to speak to us?" We had attitudes then. Plus we couldn't find our guns, okay. We pissed, okay.

His co-pilot say, "Hey, man, they nuts. Leave 'em alone. They gonna die anyway."

"Hey, fuck you! Fuck with us, and we'll blow you both away."

Things out of proportion now. Sarge ain't there. Jeeps never picked us up before. We in a different chopper. We ain't gonna carry our own guns. But nobody was thinking none of this. When things happen over there, it happen fast. They don't give you time to think. You got to do shit fast. That's the way the war is: it's fast; it's unpredictable.

We started going through the firearms, picking out what we wanted.

When we on the ground, we asked Doc, "What the drug?"

Doc said, "Tar. We gonna do thirty cc."

"Tar" is a word for heroin. Every time Doc said "Tar," we knew it was time to pull our drawers up. It be dangerous. Tar was a death-like high. You not afraid of nothing. You don't give a fuck about dying. You don't care about shit. You was fearless. You so mellow you could skip through the jungle holding hands with Charlie. But you ain't gonna do that. You gonna kill Charlie if you see him.

Normally, the kind of heroin we was getting, twelve cc is enough. Thirty, you be loaded twenty-two to twenty-six hours.

But by now, I've opened my package and find out I didn't have no back-up. It had me going into the damn place by myself. It had an "X" and a map going straight in. Usually, you got an escort; you got a couple more X's behind you. Wasn't no X's behind me. I said, "Doc, give me sixty cc."

While we was holding our arms, doing the drugs, we was looking at each others' packages. We wasn't supposed to, but we had a bond. We had made a commitment to each other. We didn't trust nobody, the Drill Sergeant, nobody; so we looking at what's going on. You can call us rebels, but I call it looking out for each others' back. By now, we were a brotherhood.

When we started comparing packages, everybody had back-up but me. It seemed like we was all on a suicide mission, but it seemed like I was supposed to go real fast, real quick, real first, real alone.

Jorge said, "I'm going with you." He was disobeying orders. He could be court-martialed. He was doing mutiny out of his love for me.

Everybody said, "Hell, the Drill Sergeant ain't here. We don't know nothing."

We knew the whole damn thing didn't make sense. We was crazy, but we wasn't fools. We knew it was a trade-off. In Vietnam lots of Special Forces was traded for certain key individuals. The government and the generals was playing with toy soldiers on fucking deskses. Life was being exchanged for lives. Our group was well-known in the jungle. We had eleven successful missions, no failures. The Viet Cong wanted Bumblebees bad. This was brought up while we was talking, trying to figure out how come they going to sacrifice our lives.

We knew we was dead. The guys started hugging and kissing each other and saying, "Bro, if by God you do make it out, here's my wife's address and name or my mother's phone number." We started exchanging pieces of paper. In that jungle, nobody even dreamed of coming back.

I did. I figured I was too young to die. Goddamn, I'm still

a baby. I haven't even started growing whiskers yet. I haven't started shaving. It's too early for me to die. Those other guys grown men. They older. They got wives and stuff. I'm a little kid. I ain't even finished school. I want to know what's happening. That was my attitude.

I'm thinking fast. I said, "Hey, guys, we ain't got to go nowhere."

The whole group got silent. One guy said, "What you talking about, Jimmy?"

"The Drill Sergeant ain't here. We can say we had to abort the mission." I was doing my damnedest to talk these guys out of going, not because I was afraid... Hell, I can't say that. I was scared. It was a suicide mission. We all knew that. I was thinking of a way to protect my ass and also the company but my ass first because I had to go first. "We ain't got to go in. If we do, we ain't coming back. Fuck it. We all loaded. We can sit here until the time's up and go where they supposed to pick us up and say it was too heavy a fire."

I almost had the guys. We took a vote, and the vote was sixteen-fourteen that we would not go.

And, then, here comes this motherfucker. This asshole Wee Willie turn into this red-white-and-blue patriot dude. "We ought to be fucking proud to be United States Special Fucking Forces. We ought to be fucking proud to serve our motherfucking country with dignity."

I'm here saying, Shut up, fool. Shut up. Man's already burned women and babies. Don't say no more.

He got off a long-long speech. "We could be fucking court-martialed if they fucking find out. Will you be happy going through life knowing you didn't do your motherfucking duty? Will you be happy knowing you has been a fucking coward?"

That's what got everybody: "Knowing that you has been a coward."

I said, "Hey, man, you calling me a coward?"

Something fixing to break out. The guys hold me back and hold him back and say, "He ain't calling you a coward.

He's got his right to speech."

We took another vote. The vote was to go in.

Realizing it was my last chance, I said, "Let's break the tie."

Then Doc said, "By the time we get through voting, y'all gonna have to shoot more drugs, and there's not enough for everybody."

So we went into the jungle.

Jorge went with me. That kinda relaxed the pressure.

There was three snipers. Jorge killed one with his knives. I got the other two.

It was peaceful going in. The only thing you could hear was birds and shit. Normally you would have heard a BOOM or a BAM or a shot or something. As we was ducking through, being careful, looking both ways, Jorge caught me on the ass. I said, "What's wrong?"

"Too quiet."

"Way too quiet."

When we got in position, we had binoculars, and we was looking inside the camp. We noticed it was little movement there. That was the strangest thing I ever seen in a P.O.W. camp in my life. It was a big old ass camp, and there was hardly no guard protecting it.

We had a certain time to infiltrate the camp. We had a time limit that we had to be out. You had some people on the north. You had people on the west. You had people on the south. Different groups had taken different routes, but when the routes end, you had this camp covered from each side, like a circle. But they couldn't move without us. You can't move without your point man saying, "Move." I could of stayed there until next week, and they couldn't've moved.

There were times I thought of not going in. But what kept coming in my mind was this coward thing. You got to live with that the rest of your life. And you really don't want to think it's a set-up. This thing impacting in the back of your mind say, "Don't believe your government do this to you. You guys are too valuable." You forget that you expendable from Mission One. That was your purpose: to never come back. To ease the United States conscience, as far as if in this crazy game anything happen to us, "What the hell, they was gonna kill or rob or rape somebody anyway; so the world was saved from them." That's the way they categorized us.

Me and Jorge looked at this camp for two hours overdue, scoping the place out. We turned the radio off. We didn't want no contact. The position we at, it wasn't cool to leave your radio on. Somebody could of heard. We didn't want to risk that chance. It was dark. We high; we freaking out; we know we gonna die; that's guaranteed. No "if," "and," or "but"s about it. I know the guys thought me and Jorge ran out.

When we came back on the radio, I said, "Bumblebee clear." Everybody started saying, "He's not a coward." "He's not a coward."

"Where the fuck y'all been?" Somebody said that.

I said, "Shhh. Charlie might hear you."

"Man, don't you know you two hours over the limit?"

"Shut up, fool. Are you in position?"

"Yeah."

"How's it look on your side?"

"It's quiet."

"How's it look on your side?"

"It's quiet."

"How's it look on your side?"

"It's quiet."

"Something is fucking wrong, guys." That's the first thing I say. "This is a set-up. Watch your brother's back. Let's go in. Do not talk. Do not communicate."

We go in. We don't talk. We communicate by hand signals when we was in position.

There was no problem. There was no mine at the edge. The door was wide open. The damn place was so clean. It was like somebody said, "Okay, here the keys. C'mon in." We got in the damn front gate the jeeps and trucks use. I said to Jorge, "Once we pass this gate, if we don't do no shooting, kiss my black ass goodbye, because we're gonna die."

Our map had a building in which this person was at. The whole team gathered around the building. Me and Jorge and a couple more guys go in. We walk up to the dude. "We come to get you out."
He shake his head "No."
I said, "Look here. We risked our lives to get you."
"No." The guy was well groomed. He was dressed as somebody who should be in a state job. He wasn't military. No damn way he was military. I can't even imagine what the hell he was doing there. He probably was a negotiator. In Nam we had lots of negotiators, big-time politicians, trying to make behind-the-closed-door deals to end the damn war. Lots of 'em wandering around on Charlie's side with troops covering their tail.
Jorge started crossing his chest. "Look here, motherfucker, I'm gonna die for your motherfucking ass. You coming out of here."
There were six or seven more guys in there. I asked 'em, "You want to go?"
They shook they head.
I said, "Is this a set up?"
One guy nodded.
"Where Charlie?"
He pointed. He wasn't talking. Like Charlie was in there somewhere.
Jorge was really crossing his chest now. He come over, crossed mine, and grabbed this dude by his neck.
I looked at Jorge and the other two guys. I said, "Charlie's waiting. Hell gonna break out."

The dude didn't want to come. We were dragging his ass. I was kicking him. I'm mad. I'm drug-up. It's a set-up. We fixing to die for him, and he don't want to come. Our whole team was fixing to die, so, of course, you gonna die with us, man. That is all there is to it. I was kicking him like a dog.

I say, "Y'all ready to boogie?"

One guy say, "Hell, no, but we don't have no choice."

"Let's go."

We start creeping out. We pass where the jeeps come in. BOOM! BOOM! BOOM! BRRRRRBOOM!!! BOOM! BOOM!

Fire coming everywhere thick as stink on shit. It was litten up like a 4th of July. It was fuck-up. It was bad. Blood was shooting in the air.

I started shooting with the M-16 in my right hand and the .38 in my left. Then I switched to the left hand with the M-16. I put the .38 in my right hand because I got this dude on my right side. He's down now; he's down in the dirt. I got this gun dead on his temple, and, as I move, I'm making him move too, and I'm shooting. I'm steady shooting, trying to get out of this shit.

At the same time, I'm seeing blood. I'm seeing some of my best friends shot down. I'm seeing guys shot thirty, forty times. Pieces flying offa bodies: arms; legs; insides spilling out. I'm scared. I'm real scared. I'm shooting like crazy. All of a sudden, a splat of blood hit the side of my jaw. I thought I was dead. I wasn't dead, but I thought I was hit. I wasn't feeling no pain, so, automatic, my mind responded. Things are happening fast. Things are real-real fast. I look down as I'm shooting. There's Jorge with half his fucking neck damn near off. I say, "Oh my God..."

I ain't got time to dwell on that. I got to look out for this guy. That was the first priority. You protect who you go after. If you got to throw your body in front of flying bullets, you protect him. The whole time we was fighting, I had him crawling, holding a gun to him, and my body over him. In case I do get hit, at least, I did protect him. That was like a code of honor. It was crazy, whatever it was. I got to keep shooting and crawling and running at the same time, till we get out of this fire.

By the time we made it out, I was crying. I had blood all over my face, blood on my chest, blood on my pants, blood everywhere. Man, I was bloody up. Everybody was bloody up. There was only six of us. We all broke down. We cried together for a minute. I said, "Let's get the fuck out of here. Let's go."

We go. We get to marching through the jungle. We real-real scared. This one fool stand up and he's shaking.

"Get ahold of yourself, brother."

"Fuck this shit." He hug a frag-grenade to his chest and dive on it.

"No!"

POW! Brains and shit shooting in the air. You know how a lettuce bust? He did like: POW! Brains pop out of his head.

This guy I got the gun on is crying and shaking, making all kind of noise. I pull the trigger back. "Be still."

We go on down. We meet three more Charlies. We destroy these Charlies.

We crawl on to where my map said the Hueys supposed to be. The Hueys wasn't there. In fact, a chopper couldn't land there. A chopper can't land in trees.

Oh my God! What the hell going on? Maybe they made a mistake. Maybe they gonna pick us up where they dropped us off. That's what come to my mind, but everybody's map had that spot on it.

So we go back. This dude, the other guys, me. We covered with blood. Our minds are freaking. The drugs are on us but not as heavy, so we feeling more fear.

We had to backtrack through the place me and Jorge came through going in. I figured it wasn't gonna be no more fight-

Fully Armed

ing. I say, "Stay here. We killed the snipers going in, but let me check."

I went and checked if the bodies been moved. I didn't check if there were more snipers. I figured that, if there was more, the bodies would have been moved. My mistake. Costly mistake. We was taught to be cautious and suspicious. I didn't put that rule in effect. I let the emotion part of me take control. You can't let no emotion control you while you fighting in Nam. Once emotion take control, you miss a second or two, and a second or two can cost you your life. In my case, it cost me my legs. It also cost me some lives.

All the snipers' body was in the same position. So I figured it safe.

I go back. "Okay, guys, we damn near home."

One of the guys say, "What if the chopper don't be there?"

"We find another company in this damn jungle, and we fight till we get out."

I be damned. After we pass the last body, the motherfuckers open up on us. They popping out of holes. It was like an execution squad. They was standing up, from our blind side, shooting. I mean, fucking wild, man. One minute, wasn't in no trees. Wasn't in no grass. Wasn't nowhere. Then just like a hit-man walk up and start shooting, they cut us down like flies.

I got hit so many times. I got hit lots of times. One that hit me was a female. She was pointing right at me. She could've killed me. Everything slowed down damn slow. I was making all kind of movement. I was conscious, but I was hurting so bad, I said, "Help."

This same guy I had kicked on, same guy I had drug, same guy I had pulled through the fucking jungle with a .38 to his head, same guy been through all this hell—he's the only one living—all of a sudden, he got brave. I remember him taking my M-16 off me and firing. I remember him grabbing me, and I'm hurting. And I remember him dragging me.

"Stay woke." This guy was talking to me. The guy kept

75

me conscious. He saved my life. "Are you married? Do you have a family?"

I kept slipping.

"Wake up! Wake up! Which way we go? Left or right? We got to get to the pick-up. Where is it?"

I was saying "Left," "Right." I'm trying to get back to where we landed.

And when we got back, there it was. The chopper. Whhhh. Whhhh. Whhhh. Just one. Wasn't none of the ones that brought us. Was one of those motherfuckers you can put a jeep in. I don't even think they supposed to be there.

People come out in green R.A. uniforms. They said, "Who are you?"

One guy say, "Shit, this got to be Special Forces."

They started slapping me and sticking needles in me. A voice said, "Any more?"

The dude started crying. "They all dead. They all dead."

And I remember blacking out.

HOSPITALS

I didn't know if I was dead.
　I was crying in my brain. I was scared in my brain. I even found peace in my brain. For days, I was walking in my brain. I couldn't find no way out.
　Inside my mind, I was woke. I knew I was around people. I was saying to myself, "Well, Jimmy, are you dead?" "I can't be dead because I'm thinking." These are the questions I was asking. "Maybe you're dead." "But I can breathe." These things are running through my head. "God, where are you?" "God, please forgive me." "I hope I'm not in Hell." "Jorge, are you here?" All these questions going through.
　I remember reading books say, "If you look for a light, you come out of whatever you in." One day, in my brain, I was saying, "I'm gonna go to sleep and wake up outta here. I'm gonna go to sleep and wake up outta this. I'm gonna go to sleep and wake up. It's gonna be all right. I'm not dead." And in my brain, I was laying down in a dark place, and—BAM—a burst of light came through, bust open—BOOM—like when you in the dark and someone shine a flashlight on you real real quick, and a nurse is hollering, "Ahhhhhh!!! He's woke! He's woke!"
　People coming in, coming in, coming in, telling me I been

in a coma for six weeks. They got on a phone, and here come a Colonel. Here come a General. Here come a Lieutenant.

The first black sonofabitch came was the Sarge. I wanted to kill him. I wanted to get to him. I couldn't. I was in so much pain, and my eye was blinking, my eye was just blinking. And he was telling me, "Stay woke, stay woke, stay woke, stay woke."

I think I was in Germany when I came to. I kept hearing the words "Danke schoen." When the nurses leave, I heard "Auf weiderschoen." So I'm speculating I was in Germany, or I was around German nurses, one.

I was laying flat down. I couldn't move.

They didn't tell me I was paralyzed.

The Sarge was trying to deprogram me. After every mission, the Sarge would deprogram us. When they deprogram you, they ask you everything that happen. Then they throw the Holy Book at you to swear with the right arm that you not gonna say this to nobody. It's totally secret. This is like an oath. This is every time. You got to realize, when we was doing this stuff, God was pretty mighty with us. When we put our hand on the Bible and swore, it was like, "I would not dare say anything." We figured, if we did, the Good Man take us off on the next mission.

They had me hooked up on machines. The Sarge upset me so much the machines saying BEEP BEEP BEEP BEEP. I wanted to kill him. I wanted to know why that bastard didn't go on the last mission. When I opened my eyes and that the first face I seen... Shit!

The lights started zig-zagging, and the doctor say, "This man gonna die if you don't get outta here." The doctor grabbed the Sarge by the chest and dragged him out.

The nurse kept saying, "It's gonna be all right." She was wiping my forehead and rubbing my arm with a gentle stroke. It calmed me down.

They kept trying to deprogram me. Normally, when you get hurt like that, they fly your mother and father wherever you at. They wouldn't fly my mother and father. They threaten me. "We won't let you see your mommy and daddy because you won't let us deprogram you."

They were asking me: "What happened?" "How many men lost during the first round?" "Is anybody captured?" "Is everybody dead?" "Do you think it was a set up?"

That got me suspicious. That was a trick question. And that's the only one I answered. "You're damn right it was a set up."

They got frantic. They got scared. You could see 'em perspire off their cheeks and brains.

Next day, I had a General come. He told me, "It's your duty as a United States soldier... You should be proud to have served your country... You gonna be taken care of."

I said, "General, sir, I'd like permission to speak."

He said, "You don't have to call me 'Sir.' Speak freely."

I said, "Sarge was telling me you guys not gonna take care of me if I don't let him deprogram me. That's not right. Now you're telling me you're gonna take care of me. Fuck y'all."

I caught some sort of infection and slipped back into darkness. It wasn't as bad as the straight calm. I struggled like hell to survive.

After a week, a nurse told me I was paralyzed. She got in trouble for that.

I was paralyzed from my neck to my toes. I hadda have help with everything. I couldn't eat food. They fed me through a tube. I had no control over my bowel movement. I kept having accidents on my body. That was very embarrassing. I had tremendous pain. I had no control over nothing. I didn't have a life. It was awful. It was really bad.

When she told me I was paralyzed and that I never would be able to walk and use my hands again, I just said, "Oh, fuck, God, take me away." It put me in another state of shock. I went off in a daze. People on the staff would try to talk to me. Psychiatrists and psychologists. I wouldn't talk. I would just sit there. There was no t.v. I didn't have no radio. I would just sit in a four-corner room by myself.

There was lots of loneliness and lots of crying. I didn't think about life. I tried my best to die. I tried to die. I was praying to die. I was praying to die every moment. Every minute. Every second.

I wanted drugs like hell. The doctor would give me morphine. Morphine give you a happy-happy-happy feeling. It make you search for reasons to keep going. I got hooked on morphine.

One time, I overheard a conversation. You can hear lots of things when they think you asleep.

Someone military asked the doctor, "How is he?"

The doctor said, "Y'all fuck him up. This man is paralyzed. He's a quadriplegic. He's a junkie. He's a addict, and I don't think he's gonna live."

He was a good doctor. Fisher or Fletcher was his name. This guy became a friend to me. He never did ask what happened over there. He tried to deal with me as a patient-doctor relationship. I wasn't going to open up for nobody, but it got where he would make me smile. He would say, "At least, you gonna have a pretty woman bathe you every day."

But I could see he wanted to cry for me too.

They put the Medal of Valor on me when I was in Germany. They come all dressed-up in their dress-up attire. The General pinned the medal and shit on me. Whenever they honor you, they have top brass there. I cussed everyone of those bastards out.

"Take the sonofabitch off! Throw it away!" I started hollering. "Take it! Take it!"

They had to take it off. I knew, if I got upset, the doctors would make 'em leave. I was mad, but I put on an act to make them get out.

They took the medals. Somehow my father end up with 'em. He wrote me, "Son, you should be proud of that."

I said, "You keep it."

I was in Germany for three weeks, maybe a month.

They came to me and said, "You going to the States. You gonna see your mother and father."

They took me to the V.A. Hospital in Houston. I stayed there a year-and-a-half, maybe two years, in the Spinal Cord Unit. I was among veterans, but most of 'em didn't get hurt in Vietnam. Lots of 'em got hurt in the street. Old veteran, young veteran. Couple of 'em got hurt in Nam.

I was in an open ward. I wasn't in a room. Something like thirty-two beds in that ward. People lined up on both sides, and everybody messed-up. They can't control their bowels and stuff. I didn't want to be with those people. I felt I was a freak in a Freakland. I said, "Get me out of here. I don't want to be with y'all." That's how I felt.

And I was one of them.

Every morning, they would stick a suppository up your butt. The damn thing was like a bullet. It was awful. It was awful for me because sometime the nurses would be in a pissed off mood.

When they serve the food, sometime I had to wait till my food got real-real cold. They were trying to punish me. I think the Army told them to do that shit. For about two months, I didn't eat no hot food. I couldn't feed myself. I had to wait for somebody to be feeding me. So I would be watching everybody eat, and I would be hungry. I would be crying, and they would be feeding everybody else, and they wouldn't be feeding me. They wouldn't feed me at all. Then when they do feed me, my food be cold, and whoever feed me act like they got an attitude problem, sticking stuff in my mouth fast. It was bad.

But at that time, I was cruel too. I probably put lots of that on my own self. I was rude to people. I wouldn't talk. If I didn't want to be bothered, I told 'em, "Get the fuck out of my way." Bad things came out of my mouth. I was screwed-up.

I didn't want to live. I didn't want no friends. I didn't want nobody to see me. When people from Waxahachie found out what happened, lots of people was making a three-hour drive to Houston—football coaches, teachers—and I wouldn't let them see me. "I don't want to see those assholes." I was like that.

The first year was bad. When I got where I could move my arms, it was still bad. Even now, I got to deal with lots of things just to function through a day. When some equipment screw up on me, I'm still embarrassed. For the rest of my life, I never know what's gonna happen. But at that time, things was new: being hooked up to bags; the things you had to do just to go out. It's still bad, but it was worse then because everything was new. It felt like I was a grown man in a baby's body. I didn't have no say-so over nothing my body wanted to do or didn't do. My brain was working, but that was it.

I asked for death twenty-five hours a day. Every day, I begged for death. I offered to buy death. I cried for death. Then I got mad at myself 'cause I didn't die over there. Then I got mad at God. I started cussing God out. Then I got mad at the Devil. I started cussing him out. Then I got mad at everybody. I shut myself off from my mother, my father, from the government, from everybody. I got to a point where people would come to see me, I would just look. They would talk to me. I would say one or two words: "Hi" and "Bye." They thought I had lost my voice.

My father would cry beside me. I would just look at him.

No tears would come outta my eyes. The only thing I would say to him: "Kill me. Help me. Kill me." That's the only thing I would say. He would say, "No." Then I wouldn't talk to him. I would say, "Go away." I would tell my mother the same thing. "Y'all can't help me. Kill me. Go away. I don't want to see you. Get the fuck out of here!" I would start shaking and screaming until the nurse would shoot the drugs.

They gave me physical therapy. I hated that.
They had me in these long, white stockings and this dress. I felt like a punk.
They would move my arms and my fingers and put their elbow on my knees and move my legs. They said, "Try to move your toes, Jimmy. Concentrate. Close your eyes." They would do that for fifteen minutes on each leg and fifteen minutes on each arm. Then some pretty woman'd massage my neck. That's the only time I would smile. They would do that in the morning after lunch, and, after dinner, they'd do it again. They was trying their best to get me to walk. Lots of guys wasn't given P.T. three times a day. They would give it to them one time. But they was coming to my bed all the time. I guess they was trying to get me to change my attitude because my attitude was bad.
 The only people I did respond to was physical therapy people. I figured they could help me. But I gave up on them after six months.

I played asleep a whole lots. Every time, I come to find out information I could use.
I remember a doctor telling one of the nurses, "Whenever he asks for some drug, give it. I don't care if it's two hours apart and it's supposed to be every six hours. If he asks, give it. He doesn't have control over his body. It's not working right. He can go into convulsion and choke and we can lose him." So I knew that was the key for getting drugs.
When I hurt, I wanted drugs. When I didn't hurt, I wanted

drugs. When I was depressed and wanted something to feel good, I got drugs. They was sticking me six and eight, nine, ten, maybe twelve times a day.

I got to where morphine didn't get me off. "Doctor, I need something stronger."

I don't know what the hell they gave me, but it made me go to sleep. "Doctor, this stuff is making me sleep. I need something that will make me feel good."

I don't know what he gave me, but it made me feel good.

It was a year and four months till I got my arms back.

A lady slapped me. A big-big black woman, about 300 pounds. A big, mean, Aunt Jemima-type woman. She say something, you say, "Okay." I would hate when she come on shift.

She told me, "I'm gonna make you come out of this shit." But I resisted her.

One day she kept washing me because I kept urinating and having bowel movements on myself. I got tired of being washed. I said, "You black bitch..."

POP! She slapped me.

All of a sudden, I sit up.

She started hollering, "Doctor, come in here."

The doctor trip out. "Move your arm! Quick! Move your arm! Move your arm!"

I started moving. I was shaking. And I was burning from my chin down to my knees. It stopped right at my knees. It didn't go down to my toes. I was on fire. I was sweating so bad, sweat wasn't rolling, it was popping. You could see sweat sprinkling off my face. "I'm hot! I'm hot!"

Doctor said, "Pack him!"

They start putting ice around me.

I got happy as hell. I started saying, "Thank you, God. Thank you, God." I tried to move my leg; then I got depressed because I couldn't. But I started thinking I could move my arms. And I got happy again.

That night, I didn't go to sleep. I moved my arms all night.

When the doctor came in that morning, I was still moving my arms. He said, "Haven't you been to bed?" They gave me a sedative. I wouldn't go to sleep. I kept moving my arms because I was afraid it was a dream.

Later on, when I got depressed, this nurse had a way of making me smile. She got my respect, plus I was thankful to her. We would joke sometimes. I'd say, "How come you didn't slap me harder? Maybe my legs would've came back."

Once I got my arms back, it relaxed a little pressure off of me. I didn't have no more cold food. Sure didn't. I said, "Well, you got to live like this, Jimmy, accept it."

That made me happy for a month. Then suicide start coming in my mind again. Suicide play a big part in me. Since I got my hands back, the first thing went through my mind: "Good. Damn good. Thank you, God. I can kill my fucking ass now."

It was like a Russian roulette game. I would find something to make me happy. Then I would start thinking about the bad things, and it made me sad. I had anger in me. The same time I'm a junkie. And I'm still pissed off at the government because the government is still sending psychiatrists three times a day to talk to me about the Twelfth Mission.

Every time I think about the bad things, it depress me. I try to put everything in perspective. But you can't put these things in perspective. You ask yourself, "God, why this? Why that?" You can't ask yourself those questions because you ain't gonna find the answer. And then it confuse you more and more and frustrate you more and more. The next thing you know, you want to put something through your head and take yourself out.

Once I got my arms back, they worked fast. Next time I looked around, they was rolling me to classes. I started lifting five-pound weights. When I got strong enough, they put me in a wheelchair, and I had to push my own damn self.

They moved fast to keep me from being depressed. Lots of activity, you ain't got time to dwell about what you can't do. That was their motto. After I asked about fifty times why they was taking me through this real-real fast, a lady told me.

They taught me to walk with braces. They had me hopping around in circles. Guys who had been there six or seven months wasn't hopping more than I was. I was a natural. I had determination. I thought they was gonna get me to walk again.

They wasn't. It wasn't walking. It was hopping. It wasn't doing no damn good.

They kept telling me, "Jimmy, you should do this. You walking."

"That's not walking. That's hopping. Walking is when you lift your leg, you take a step, you take another step, you take another step. Y'all just got some fucking stuff on my leg for me to hop around like a fucking silly, illy formed rabbit." I thought they was trying to make me out a fool.

I got pissed. "Fuck it. If I can't stand up like I used to stand up, I'm not gonna stand up and hop around like a bunny rabbit." I threw those damn canes through a window, broke the window, took those braces off my leg, and went back to my room. They said, "Don't mess with him. Let him get through it." They told me not to come back for a week. I never did pick 'em up again.

They learned me to drive a car. I got my license in Houston. I don't drive hand-control, even though they taught me. I keep a big old stick, long enough for me to hit from the brake to the gas.

The reason why I drive with a stick is, when I went for my license, me and my instructor drove off in the car. Hand-control, you pull down and the car go forward; you push in, the brake hit. We on a highway, and I'm pulling down, and he take me by this school house, where these children crossing the street, and I had to brake, and the damn hand-control got stuck. I was hitting the brake, trying to slow down. The man was hitting his brake. His brake wasn't working. The man's eyes got real big. I got so desperate I tore the whole hand-control from the column, and the car disengaged. I got on the sidewalk and almost killed myself. Cat say, "You pass! You pass!" He was soaking wet in his uniform. "You pass, buddy!"

I made a vow. I never drive with hand-control again. And I never had a wreck with my stick. It's amazing what you can adjust to.

Every week, they took a group of guys on a field trip. They took us to a couple lakes. We would go to a Budweiser plant and drink all the beer we wanted.

We went to Gilley's. Man, that was all right. Gilley's a good guy. I was the only black in the whole place. He set right beside me, bought me beer. He said, "You from Texas?" I said, "Uh-huh." The guy talked to me without looking at this wheelchair. You know when this is coming before you. He ignored that. He talked to me like a human being. He became a good friend. He would come to Houston to visit me.

Every weekend, they used to give us two Schlitz Malt Liquor six-packs in twenty-four ounce cans to make us mellow.

We could smoke all the weed we wanted to. The doctors would pass by, and we wouldn't hide it. The police and security guard pass by, we wouldn't hide it. The doctors find weed in the drawers, they wouldn't move it.

They never gave us permission to smoke, but they never stopped us. They knew we was dealing with our paralysis. They wasn't gonna stop us because they afraid they mess up our rehabilitation. We knew that. We knew we could get away with it, so we did that a lot.

They never gave us weed, but weed was brung to us. Guys were getting good money every month.

I seen a couple of miracles.

This one guy was paralyzed for eleven years. The phone rang. I'm fixing to jump in my chair and go to it. The bastard got up out of his bed and walked to the damn phone. I said, "You're walking! You're walking! You're walking!" He looked down, dropped the phone, and ran out the door. Nobody never seen him again.

It gave me a carrot. I said, "It can happen to me." It gave me faith. But faith can only last a minute some times.

I was getting twelve shots a day, a shot every two hours. They flew me to Long Beach to detox me. I was in Long Beach six months, maybe longer.

J-Ward was an entire unit with people in wheelchairs. Some had drug problems; some had alcohol problems; some was just plain nuts. You had two psychiatrists, one hard core, one sweet core. One sting you with guilt, as far as being straight-down hard on you, like, "Fool, you knew what you was doing." The other talk to you nice. "I know it's easy for you to do things because you been through so much." They see if you pick the strong person or the lovey-dovey person to open up to.

That hospital was a lock-down place, but they had a movie show, bowling, bingo, swimming pool to get your mind off things. Didn't nothing cost nothing. It was a country club to me.

When I got there, I'm moving around in a wheelchair twice as fast as I can. My attitude day-to-day was, "Hey, take me tomorrow." I was cooperative, but I didn't care. There wasn't no goal for me. No objective. I was just going along with the system. I wasn't gonna try, so it wasn't no big deal if I failed.

You had freedom, but they had all kinds of screw-up rules. You couldn't drink or have no alcohol or nothing in you as long as you there. If you didn't follow the rules, they take your cigarettes for a week, or they cut your t.v. privileges for a week.

They had all kinds of crazy groups which had meetings run by Robert Rule Books of Order. After three months, you were allowed to go outside, but you had to get permission from these groups. They have a meeting; you state why you want to leave. To go have a MacDonald hamburger, you got to do this. I hated those groups.

They was giving us Methadone. That solved problems with cocaine and heroin. I'll make a lot of junkies mad by saying this, I'll have the whole methadone program cut off, I might be another Salmon Russkie, whatever his name is, but the Methadone was better than heroin. The high was exactly alike; it lasted longer, and it was free.

When I got weekend passes, I did drugs all the time. I got smart. In this condition, you have to wear these leg-bags because you can't stand up to take a leak. I started filling up a leg-bag with urine before I left and hiding it, instead of disposing it. Before I got back, I'd change that one for the one I go out with. When you get back, all the nurses tired. They want to book, so when they run a urine sample, they take it from your leg-bag instead of putting a syringe in your bladder, so I was covered.

One night, they punished everybody. They wasn't gonna give us Methadone. By then I'm hooked. I left the place without permission. I went over to this person's place and did drugs for a week. When I ran out of supplies, I went back. I claimed I had amnesia. Shit like that worked because they think you crazy anyway. I still had to go through a trial by the people who was in the program. They said, "Hell, everybody gonna mess up once." One dude said, "Hell, two or three times."

Finally, the hospital said, "We can't cure you."

I told them I didn't want to be cured.

They told me they was sending me to New York for psychotherapy.

New York was a psycho-emotional place. More a military type thing. Houston was civilian-military. Long Beach the same, except you got a drug program. New York was totally United States Military.

It seemed like a cold, dark place. The feeling was heavy. Heavy as hell. Every time you moved, you going through a dark tunnel. Physically dark. Mentally extra-dark. Nothing was fast. Everything was slow motion. Going to sleep was slow. The whole day would drag by. Twenty-four hours seemed like forty-eight.

I was in a wheelchair unit again. Vietnam veterans. Young guys. I was one of the youngest still. You couldn't leave. You didn't go nowhere, and when you did, you went as a group. Wasn't lots of people inter-reacting with you. Just you among the group. I was still on Methadone, but they was reducing the dosage.

I was lots of trouble. They couldn't control me. I was rebelling against everything. I kept me a gun the whole time. It was like a teddy bear. They knew I had a gun, but they didn't move it. They had me pegged. They knew what they was doing.

The rest of the guys had hospital rooms. I said, "I got to forget this." I fixed my room up like a little apartment. I had a t.v., flowers, plants, a Tina Turner poster on the wall, a nice stereo. I listened to everybody. James Brown was hotter than a firecracker then. Temptations was deadly at that period. Four Tops, my God. My room was tough. I freaked 'em out.

They had lots of therapists. They threatened you. They had fun and games they played. They take you in a room and show you circles and pyramids and shit, asking you to concentrate.

They had classes to tame you. Teach you to be cool. Teach you keep your anger in. One class, the whole objective was to get you mad as you could. I would never do it. I would block myself out. I didn't care.

See, it was totally strange. Vietnam was fast. Then things broke down. I ain't hearing bombs. I'm not going on missions. It was like stepping out of one world—the jungle, fighting, coming out with teeth-marks on you—into a totally nother world. And I was stepping fast. Here I am, fresh out of the military, paralyzed. I ain't adjusted to civilian life, let alone my own life. I ain't adjusted to none of that.

It was like I went off the deep-end somewhere, nobody telling me what's happening, and I just now stepping back. I can't get myself adjusted for the real world. I still don't know what the hell happened in the old world. I started convincing myself that Nam wasn't real. I damn near had myself believing it didn't exist. You convince yourself, it works. But I kept remembering that Twelfth Mission, Twelfth Mission, Twelfth Mission.

That's when I snapped back to reality. That wasn't no game. That was the real thing. I got this wheelchair to prove it.

New York scared me bad. I was turned off in Houston and Long Beach. New York clicked me back on. It made me function. I was jungle-like again. I said, "Boy, this shit is real. You got one thing you can do. Dwell on it and get schizophrenic, or deal with it." I decided to deal with it. Till I decided if I wanted to live or die. I knew nobody could take that from me. That was my decision. So I decided, "Let me run through here and see what happens."

I was going to classes, but I wouldn't let them help me. You don't care, you don't concentrate, and I didn't care about nothing but having a good time. I left so many times they gave me the nickname "Escape Artist." I'd stay away a night or two, then I'd come back. It got to where they said, "Hell, let him go."

One morning, I said, "I don't feel like going to no class." I got a cab to Kennedy Airport. I caught the plane to Dallas. When I got home, my father said, "I knew if you were gonna come it would be on Friday night."

TEXAS

I was screwed up when I got back. I had a hell of a drug craving, plus, the way my father put it, I was a cold-blooded, cold-hearted murderer. I would stare at people like I wanted to do something to them, even with my paralysis.

I was a mean person. Nobody liked to be around me. I was mean, and I was dangerous, not only to whoever pissed me off but to myself. Very dangerous. I didn't hurt nobody, but I didn't care. If I got mad, I did some crazy things. Pull out guns. Stick 'em on peoples' necks. I mean, playing with death. I couldn't sleep without a gun. I couldn't leave my house without a gun. I always kept me something.

I was still programmed. You couldn't walk up behind me. If I saw somebody who looked like a Vietnamese person, I would take 'em down. I seen one Chinaman in a supermarket, and I just dove off my chair and started choking him.

My family reacted, out of love, by over caring too much. My family be hovering over me like a hawk. They thought I was so fragile, it made me feel helpless. If I coughed around my mother, she'd dial 911. Everybody had to watch me jump out of the chair. Everybody had to watch me jump into the chair. Everybody was worried if I took a ride with a friend in a car.

If I be sleeping, my sisters come and check on me. Grandmother come and check on me. Grandfather come and check on me. Come praying for me. I had more people praying for me than Oral Roberts. The Good Lord have to know Jimmy Don Polk. I think that's how come he enabled me to live.

I was out of place, but I was trying to fit back into the world. I did normal things. I went to parties. Concerts. I went anytime they come around. And one thing about this wheelchair, anytime I go to a concert, they push me up front. I be on the stage. I had a good time. I said, "Fuck it, if somebody gonna like me, they gonna like me for the wheelchair or not. If they don't like it, they can kiss my ass."

One time, I took a lady out for dinner. My leg bag popped. I said to myself, "Oh shit, whachu gonna do?" I thought quick. Bottle of wine up there. Knock the wine on your leg. "Hey, sweetheart, we have a problem." It worked.

Basically, I did the things I did before. Still, you go through this state of depression because you never know what's going to go down when you go out in everyday life.

My friends played a major part for me. They came by every day with their cars, black friends, white friends, pick me up, try and get me back into society. There was a crowd everywhere I went. I went to a football game, people would gather all around me. I go to a movie, people around me. I went to a party, I had a crowd. Maybe people was just giving me love and support, but people come up left, right, back, forth; people sneak up from behind me, and I couldn't breath.

I got to feeling I was the black sheep among the whole bunch. I felt like a freak. People was too good to me. I felt they was doing this out of pity more than anything. Even though I accepted it, I felt these people doing this because they felt sorry for me.

I was treated very well before I went into the service. Especially for a black person from Waxahachie, Texas, I was treated damn good. I was treated like I didn't have a color. I was always appreciated and respected, but I felt like I didn't have that respect when I came back in that wheelchair. I felt like people felt, "It could've been me."

Some people felt bad out of their heart, and some people felt bad out of pity, and some people was happy. Those who envied me before it happened were happy, and that was the most hurtful thing. A couple guys who would challenge me for my position and challenge me for my girlfriends was thrilled. They come looking at me, have a smirkey-smile on their face like, "Good. Bastard." That messed with my mind a little bit.

The schoolhouse gave me a Return Home Party. I was the Guest of Honor. Everybody from the school and people from outside the city came. It was supposed to be a happy occasion, but it drug me down lots. Everybody who hugged me and kissed me dropped two or three tears. It made me feel badly-badly like, "You poor, crippled little man." I got sadder and sadder. So when it came time for me to make my speech, I had left. Here I was rolling down the highway, leaving thousands of people there. My father come up behind me in the car. He said, "Get in, son."

I jump in the car, and he put my wheelchair in. We got a case of those little-bitty, eight-ounce, pony-neck Miller's. We got thirty-two of them. And Waxahachie's not a wet town, so we had to go thirty miles to Dallas.

First time I ever got drunk with my father. First time I ever told my father exactly how I felt. I was raised up, being a man, to protect your deepest feelings and emotions because they could be used against you. I was able to unleash them.

We talked and we cried and we talked and we cried. We laughed, and he said, "The people waiting for you."

He drove me back. We was gone two hours, and the people was still there.

I rolled up, and people started clapping. I said, "I appreciate you all for coming. This town is my life. Lots of people here is my life. I had to leave because people hug and kiss me, but everybody was crying, and it made me feel sad." I'm drunk now. I'm rocking in my wheelchair. My father right beside me with his chest all out. "I appreciate the sympathy, but I will not accept pity."

I rolled out, and people started clapping again. Soon as I went outside, I had another accident with my body, and it depressed me again. It got me real down again. I was on an emotional roller coaster. Up and down. Up and down.

We call those things "accidents" or "equipment problems." I have to deal with that today; that's part of being like this. Now I have accepted it; it's not like I'm doing it on purpose. But during a one-day period of time, not too far after New York, I went through eight or nine different pairs of pants, and, the ninth time, I cried so hard, I got so frustrated, I said, "Fuck it. That's it. No more. No more." I didn't give a damn. That was it. I was tired.

I put my hands on a .38. I tried to commit suicide. I tried; I tried; I tried. I shot the gun and shot the gun and shot the gun, and the gun didn't fire. I turned around and shot at the ground. I be damned. BOOM! It went off. My daddy come in, grabbed me, threw me down, and took the gun.

A little while later, I went over a good friend's house. He lived up these big old steps. They tote me up there. I had a accident, but it wasn't bad. I could make it to the bathroom. Coming out, I heard his wife say, "I don't want that smelly, crippled person over my house no more." It hurt me so bad I rolled by and tried to throw myself off the stairs.

The first step, I fell off. Only thing destroyed was my wheelchair. I said, "The hell with it. I can't even kill myself. Ain't no use me trying no more."

FULLY ARMED

After that second suicide attempt, things changed. I think God took affirmative action with me. I married my high school sweetheart. Evelyn Corrinne Hodges. Corrinne very light-skinned. She was half-Indian and half-black with long, reddish-black hair. The most pretty woman in the whole town. She was Miss Teenage South Oak Cliff a couple years in a row.

We were at a movie, and she said, "Don't you think it's time for you to settle down?"

I said, "What do you mean? I'm already settled down."

She said, "You need some substance in your life."

"What you talking about, woman?" She was still in high school.

"Will you marry me?"

"You want me with my screwed-up body?"

"I love you, not your body."

It touched me so much, I said, "Yeah."

My grandfather married us. My grandmother gave us a three-bedroom house to live in.

Life began to be different. My wife opened up a new door for me. She started me on my journey back from the dead. I was still in the dead, but I was steady climbing up. I wasn't going backwards. I still felt cheated, but I wasn't as lonely as I was. I had somebody to hold.

We'd go out. We had friends come over. I joined a wheelchair basketball league. I ran wheelchair races. I got trophies. I tried to stay active. I tried to do everything I did before I lost my legs. But it wasn't the same. When I won a race or we won a game, it wasn't the same feeling I was trying to recapture, so I faded off.

I went through a change. I was planning Suicide Number Three.

This is how I was feeling: I got this beautiful woman; she loves me, but I'm holding her life down; I'm gonna pick me the best fucking freeway, the crowdedest one, and get out of the car...

I had planned this for a Friday night. I was gonna go on 35E, the highway that runs between Dallas and Waxahachie, wait till an eighteen-wheeler come up, and roll in front. I was pumped up. I was drinking gin. I'm stoned. My nerves are up. I'm gonna do it. I'm gonna do it.

When I was rolling out the door, my wife walked in. I'm drunk, wheelchair bumping into every wall in the room. She says, "What's wrong?" She never would stand up to talk to me. When she had something direct to tell me, she would get on her knees and put her hand on my chair. She looked me dead in the eye and say, "I got good news. I just come back from the doctor. I'm pregnant. We gonna have a baby."

WHEW! All of a sudden, I'm not high no more. It seemed like I didn't drink no gin. I was completely sober. I said, "Okay, Jimmy, let's don't do this. Let's go back thisaway."

My daughter, Marvetta, was born November 8th, 1974. That was a proud day. I didn't even smoke cigars, but I had five cigars that night. I almost choked. It was like, "Thank you, God. You gave me a gift. You gave me a reason to live."

That made me want to go off on life with a big BAM BING BOOM. I said, "I'm gonna straighten up. I'm gonna quit talking crazy. I'm not gonna let these accidents bother me. I'm gonna be a good daddy." My wife and I got closer. Our attitude got better toward each other. I learned to put up with her ways; she had already accepted my ways. Remember, I was growing up too; we was both kids when we married.

But I still had Vietnam in my picture. Vietnam was not completely over. We still had M.I.A.s. I was still sensitive toward certain issues about the war. I was split down the middle. I had peace of mind on one side; on the other I had Vietnam. It had me divided straight down the road.

Things was so bad when my wife was pregnant, when we go to bed, every time I woke up, I had a knife or gun on her.

Many knives and guns I stuck in her mouth, her ear, her eye. It was hurting me.

She was putting up with it. She stuck by me good. She kept saying, "You'll get over it."

One night, I had been drinking, and I was half asleep, and I felt someone get in bed. When I pulled the gun this time, my eye was still closed and the trigger was cocked back, the first time I cock it on her. Even though the gun was cocked and my eye closed, she slapped the shit out of me, and I woke. Only one person could hit me, and that was her. Good thinking woman! But it scared us both. She said, "Baby, I'm tired of this shit. We got to develop a code. When I wake you, I'm gonna kiss you. Or if I come from another room, I'll knock three times on the wall."

I stopped pulling a gun on her.

But my mind was still playing games with me. People be pushing me down the street, a car would backfire—BA-POW!— and I'd dive out of the fucking wheelchair. People be pushing the wheelchair by itself; I'm sitting down with my gun out. It got to where I was carrying my gun in Waxahachie. People keep calling the police: "There's a fool in a wheelchair with a gun." "Okay, we'll come talk to Jimmy." But they knew what I had been through, so they never did take me in. They just said, "Jimmy, unload the gun."

One time, though, I was having flashbacks and drew my gun in public. A rookie police, who didn't know me, came and drew his down on me. I'm holding mine on him, and he's holding his on mine, and I'm thinking he's Charlie. I heard other people say, "No! He's Jimmy Polk!" And this police officer, he's looking amazed, like, "Who in the fuck is Jimmy Polk?"

By this time, my father's coming, my grandfather coming, my wife coming. It took them an hour-and-a-half to get me to drop the gun. I had to go in the hospital to get some counseling.

I was living two different people. One was fixing to be a father. Another was an ex-Vietnam veteran. I always did search for an answer to certain things. But I couldn't find an answer for Vietnam. I couldn't find an answer for being crippled. I couldn't find an answer for "Why is God letting me be punished like this?" or "Is God punishing me, or is the Devil holding me down?"

I even tried to turn religious. I went to Faith Healers. I went to one guy had his own ministry in Dallas: "Give me $12.50. You'll never be cut on again."

Next week, I'm in the hospital having surgery. I got out and went straight to his ministry. This guy had about 4000 people there. I rolled in, rolled straight up there. "This fool lied to me!" I pulled my pistol and was fixing to shoot him. In a church house. I was mad. Things taken over me. Everybody hollering.

I was arrested. I told the judge, "Your Honor, he lied. He took my $12.50." I did ten days in jail, until the Army sent some people to explain my situation. The judge let me out. He told me not to carry no gun, but I always did.

One day I'm in the world of being peaceful, being a father. The next day I'm back in the jungle. It steady blew my mind. Lots of funny things happened while I was coming out, but lots of bad things happened too. There was times when the car broke down on the highway, two or three o'clock in the morning. I wasn't about to let my wife go out, and I wasn't about to leave her in the car either. You don't do that in Texas.

There was times we had to roll all night. I'd put her in my lap, and she'd be asleep, and I'd be rolling down the highway, and people pass by laughing. Those were hurtful things. One night, I rolled fifteen, sixteen miles with my wife on my lap, just rolling, and I'm tired, smelling bad, my car back there. Dallas Police wasn't shit then. They'd say, "We can't put you in the car. We'll call you a wrecker." Discriminating things like that. It was bad. I would say, "If I had my fucking legs I could've changed that flat." It made me feel less than a man.

Whenever we'd get gas, my wife had to get out and pump. Those things offending me. They offending me real-real bad. Really bad. Really bad. It's offending me today. If I have a young lady with me today, I ask her to get my chair out of the trunk before I let her pump the gas. Things like that were affecting my mind. I had to deal with situations like that every day. And how in the hell can you do that when you're still a kid? It's hard. You can't.

I was in a ball of confusion. Everything was confusion to me. Here, I can't walk, and I was blessed with the prettiest woman in town, fixing to have my baby. I got a nice home. I got two nice cars. I had an El Dorado and a Continental Mark IV. I had money in the bank. I was getting $3350 a month from the V.A. That was good money. I was like a rich man. My wife was great with money. "What was you gonna pay a dollar for a hamburger when I can cook it for less than thirty cents?" She was that kind of woman. She would not let you do it. "What we gonna see a movie for? We got a t.v." She was very good with that, because I like to spend.

At this time, I'm still shooting drugs like hell. I had a $600 drug habit back in seventy-something. That's about $3000 a month today, maybe $4000. Drugs I was buying for five dollars is going for sixty, seventy dollars today.

I wasn't shooting drugs to get high. I was shooting drugs to be normal. I couldn't be normal unless I was poking myself with needles. I would leave the house, two o'clock at night, jump in the car, take my stick, put my wheelchair in, and go way to Dallas into the most dangerous neighborhoods, get out, and look for my drugs.

I was mainlining four to six times a day. I knew if I ever got popped I'd only be in jail two or three hours because of the government. That was my edge; I knew how far I could go. We'd go to church, I'd go in the bathroom and shoot dope.

We'd ride down the street, I'd pull out the syringe and shoot my dope. Before I'd go to bed, I'd fix up my dope. In the morning, my syringe was like a cup of coffee to me. Before I ate my breakfast, my drug came first. Before I wash my face or jump in the shower or if I had an accident, my drug come first. Before I kissed my wife, it came first.

My wife would sit there and cry while I shot drugs into my veins. She would sit there, crying and crying. Then she'd come over and sit on the floor. She wanted me to feel normal. She'd say, "Get out of the wheelchair. Let's get on the floor." She'd hold me and rock me to sleep. The next day, she'd be there beside me. I hurt my wife a whole lot, but she stuck with me. I sent that woman through periods of hell, but she was trying to understand. They had counselors, and she would go to the meetings. I would say, "The hell with those people. I ain't going to no meetings." She would say, "Well, I'm gonna go." She was way ahead of me as far as thinking. As I look back at it now, her way of thinking was very educated, but then it was very silly to me, very crazy. I was still a kid in a body I didn't want, in a state of confusion, angry, mad.

Whenever I got frustrated, I would blast away into another world. I would shoot my dope, and—all of a sudden—I'm happy. The drugs won't let me think about the negative things. I think positive things. I didn't give a damn I was hurting my wife. Even though she's crying, I was feeling good.

When my daughter first said, "Daddy," I made up my mind. I seen that pretty little thing, and I couldn't deny her. I had incentive to be happy and start living. She made me become drug free.

I said, "I'm leaving this shit alone."

My wife was cooking chicken. She dropped a whole thing of grease, almost burnt herself. "You gonna do what?"

"I'm gonna quit shooting drugs. I'm gonna go to rehabilitation."

"How long you got to stay?" She got to worrying: they

Fully Armed

gonna make you stay; they gonna make you do this; they gonna make you do that. She say, "Sweetheart, you strong enough to stop on your own."

And I did.

It was a different life. I threw away my syringes. My weed consumption and my beer consumption rose considerably, but the drug part was gone.

I had fun with my daughter. She called my wheelchair a "Thing." I'd be in the bed. She'd say, "Momma, get Daddy's thing, so he can get up." Anytime I'd jump in it, she'd climb in my lap. "Let's ride, Daddy." That was everyday for us: jump in the wheelchair and take us a ride.

She was a bossy little girl too. We'd be rolling down the street. "Go this way, Daddy. "

"I want to go this way."

"Let's go *this* way, Daddy."

Got a way of looking at you make you say, "Okay, girl, let's go this way."

My daughter used to bring me orange juice every morning. If there was no orange juice, she'd fuss. "Now, Momma, you know Daddy like orange juice in the morning."

My wife would be, "Jimmy Don, you hear how she is talking?" And I'd be, "Yeah, honey,"

"You gonna say something to her?"

My family was great. They took my mind off lots of stuff, but more problems with my body was surfacing. Vietnam was still there, but Vietnam played second fiddle to my body then. It moved next door. My resistance was low. I had bladder infections, urinary tract infections, kidney stones, bladder stones, liver problems. I had operations for the bullets in me. I broke my leg one time and didn't realize it because I couldn't feel.

My little girl was the most precious thing in the world to me. She was a joy, and she changed my whole world, but I started having depression and negative feelings about what she was gonna go through, what she might be missing. "Damn, I wish I could put my daughter on the back of my neck and walk down the street." "Damn, I wish I could chase after and play with her." I remember how it used to feel to race barefooted in the sand. I remember how it used to feel to go to the lake and curl your toes up in that nice Bermuda grass. Little things like that I was missing. I was longing for those feelings. Every time I would end up crying.

My daughter never did understand how come I couldn't walk. She didn't care 'cause I was Daddy. I'd say, "Daddy's sorry he can't chase after you. Daddy's sorry he can't walk."

She said, "That's okay, Daddy. I love you." She hugged me so tight she was choking me.

My wife bust down crying. And I cried for three hours.

I stayed in a depression for a week. Things like that would happen, and it wasn't lasting me over night. I was off the drugs now, so I couldn't run away. The weed and the beer wasn't strong enough. I had to deal with this straight-on. Many times, I bought dope and come back with it. My wife'd come in the bedroom, and I'd be there looking at it. I would fight it. I'd throw it down, and I'd lay down, and I'd cry myself to sleep. My old lady would just rock me to sleep.

I went through a lot of emotional things. Emotionally, I should be destroyed. Emotionally, there should be no way I should be existing. My emotions have been through so much, I am lucky to still have some. It feel like getting on a fast car or a fast plane and never stopping. It haven't stopped today. Emotionally, I'm drained.

Pressure was coming on me so much and so fast. Every month it would build up. More and more frustrating things was happening. I got frustrated with things my body was going through. I got frustrated with people crying. Every day I was in Waxahachie, somebody would come up to me crying. Didn't miss a day. If I be at home with the door locked, somebody'd come to the window crying. And every time it happened, it'd bring me down.

I felt pity for myself. I was angry. I was having flashbacks. I would wake up in the middle of the night, hollering. I would relive that twelfth mission over and over again. Nothing else. Just the twelfth mission. Step-by-step. I would wake up hollering and screaming. Especially when I got hit. I would feel the burning of the bullet. And I dreamed about when they tortured me. Except I kept dreaming I didn't make it out. I almost convinced myself that I was dead. I would be so glad when morning came.

All these events were steady bringing me down, bringing me down, bringing me down. I got down over lots of things that weren't working out how I wanted. I started thinking about things that were being taken from my family because they was with me. I felt I was dragging them down. I got to thinking, "I don't want kids to meddle my daughter, saying her daddy can't walk." I tried to push my family away. I would start fights with my wife to make her leave.

I went into another depression. Depression is a hell of a thing. Depression is powerful. Depression won't make you stay clean. Depression will make you kill yourself. I kept going through lots of depression.

I didn't know who I was. I didn't know where I was going. I was in a cage, and I had to get out. I figured, for my daughter to be happy and not feel ashamed I can't walk, I should leave. Even though my wife and daughter meant the world to me, I couldn't be productive for them if I didn't make that move. I loved them too much to make them suffer. The pressure got on me so hard I had to escape or I would have killed myself.

I went to the bank. I withdrew $2000 and left everything else—between forty and $60,000—for my wife and child. That night my wife and I got to fighting. I roared out, "I'm going to the store," and jumped into a beat-up 1963 Chevrolet Impala I had.

I thought about getting some beer. So I left Waxahachie for Dallas. When I got to Dallas, I went to this gas station. I got a six-pack of Schlitz tall-neck bottles, and I bought a map. I was looking at the map, and I said, "I got people in California." My grandmother's sister lived there.

I drank a couple beers, looking at the map. I was thinking to myself, "If I was to drive to California, how would I go?" I had a pencil and started outlining sketches to get my mind off my wife and all I'm going through. "You take 35E, then you go to Highway 5, and it turn to 10, and then it hit 99."

Next thing I realize, I say, "Fuck it, I'm going."

CALIFORNIA

That trip was a hell of an adventure.

There was like two little monkeys on my back. One monkey say, "Go back to your family. It's your obligation to take care of your family. Your family's taken care of you." Another little voice was saying, "You gonna be alone like you want."

Then another little monkey... I guess I had monkeys all over my back. We had like a monkey conference. "You had somebody to love you and take care of you, and you leaving them."

Another monkey would say, "You should go, because it's better for their lives. You got a beautiful woman. You got a beautiful daughter. In the long run, it's gonna hurt them. What will you do if you see your wife with another man? Will kids tease your daughter because her daddy crippled? Save her from that disgrace." I was listening to that monkey hard. It was making sense. Maybe I used my daughter as an escape route out, but, still, that's the monkey I paid attention to.

The trip was rough.

By the time I made it out of Texas, my hand got so swole from pushing the gas pedal and hitting the brake with my stick that, when I got to a motel room, I had to stay there for two days and soak my hand in ice. I had to do that every state I went through.

Several motels asked me to leave. They told me I was throwing things. One time, in Arizona, I woke up in this motel, and I did notice the room was different. The t.v. flipped upside down with the tube busted out. Pictures crooked. I was saying to myself, "What the hell happened?" But I was in a daze. I didn't pay much attention.

When I came out the door, I had fifteen police rifles pointing at me. "Do not move! Put your hands in the air!"

"Okay! What I do?" A couple of them run up and handcuff me behind my wheelchair. "What have I did?"

They took me to the V.A. hospital. "I think we got one that went over the cuckoo's nest."

I stayed there seven crazy days. They gave me a drug called Lithium. It made me hallucinate. I got hyper-paranoid. I thought they was trying to make me crazy. I thought they trying to kill me.

They wouldn't let me leave. That was a scary moment. I stopped being violent. I started being nice and calm. I knew it was the onliest way to get out.

They had a committee meeting before some Board. I had to talk to eight different people. Each person was saying things I needed to work on. Other people was telling me other things. Anyway, they decided to let me go.

I got back on the highway. It had never entered my mind, "What you gonna do when you get a flat tire?" I was coming up on California, out of Arizona: BOOM! That's when I got my first taste of feeling there was something I couldn't do.

It was late at night, no phones nowhere, no cars. Nobody is riding up and down, except for these big trucks now and then. I jumped out of the car, got in my wheelchair, and started rolling.

It was two hours before I got help. Some guy with his

family. I was smelling bad. The way his wife and children looking at me, I'm feeling like I'm a Zippy or something.

We open up the damn trunk, and the spare is flat. The people helped me inside their car and took me on a forty-five minute ride to where they was going and brought me back the next morning with a tow truck.

L.A. was my destination.

I was going to surprise my grandmother's sister. Her name was Ethel Richards. I had stole her address from my father to keep him from being suspicious. But when I got to L.A. and found her address... Hell, she done moved.

I went into this depression, missing my wife and family. I wanted to jump in the car and go back. I went to this motel and cried myself to sleep. But I said, "The hell with it. I'm here. I'm in a new place. I might as well try and start my life over." I felt I was doing the right thing. Nobody knew me. I had a chance to live without my family around me, without being crowded, without hearing the words "I'm so sorry," and watching tears happen every day.

One of my aunt's neighbors said she moved to San Francisco. I got the number and looked on the map and seen it was another 400 miles. But I was brought up that I needed to be around family, so I came to San Francisco.

When I got to San Francisco, I found out she went to Dallas, Texas. So I said, "Ah shit! Ah shit!"

I got a motel room, about three blocks from where my aunt was living, to stay until she get back. After a week, things started coming in my head like, "This won't be wise, Jimmy, to have your aunt know where you're at. Jasper Polk will jump on a plane and come try to take you home."

I got in the car and left. I ended up in a place called Antioch. I don't know what drug me to that spot. Maybe a work of God. A-N-T-I-O-C-H. It seemed like a nice little town, seemed like a cool place to live. I didn't have no plan. I just stopped and started resuming my life.

Antioch was small, but it was friendly. People wasn't prejudiced there to me. It was the first time that, being a black, crippled man in a wheelchair, people would come up to me and smile and look at my eyes before they look from my feet down. Back home, they look at me from the feet down. Then they raise their head and look at my eyes. Antioch made me feel comfortable because people looked at my eyes. Even if they did look down at my feet, I didn't care because, first, they made contact with my eyes.

In Antioch, they didn't have hotels with elevators. All their hotels got steps. I got me a cheap room in a motel. Easy 8. Super 8.

I called Social Security to have my check transferred out there. I found out where the nearest V.A. hospital was.

I would go to the park every day. People would come over and say, "Hey, my name is This Person. You seem like you're nice. What's your name? Where you from? And this and that."

I never would say where I was from. I said, "I'm from Texas."

"Maybe I can show you around town."

I didn't do nothing.

All I did was meet people and try to get to know the town. I hung out. I drunk a little wine, a little beer and stuff. I went to the movies. I met a young lady. I met whole lots of young ladies. They invited me to some of their family. I was experiencing a different kind of life. I felt freer.

That depression I was experiencing left. It went away for a year or two because I found this new freedom. Then, when I got together with this lady, it came back on me. I started doing the same thing I was doing with my wife. This woman didn't take it. First time I came out with a knife or gun to her

Fully Armed

throat, the next day she was gone.

It broke me down again. I would cry. I would get mad at God. I would cuss the Devil. People would come up, "Lemme pray for you." I cussed them out. I transformed into a mean, ugly person. I was just rotten. I thought things would never get better. The word "suicide" came through my mind, but it wasn't so pressing as before.

I was battling every day with my mind and body. Something was telling me, "Get out. Do something. Prove something." It was like a soul-searching mission.

One day, another dude in a wheelchair talked to me in the park. "You know, just 'cause you in a wheelchair doesn't mean you can't get an education. I graduated from Los Medanos Junior College." This guy was in a wheelchair, and he was happy. He was talking like he was proud of what he did.

It made me feel bad. It made me feel, "Boy, you been to the war and youse a punk sissy." Here was this guy: his mind was straight; he looked like he could get out of his chair and walk. I looked paralyzed in my head and in my body. Curiosity, he killed the cat. I wanted to know, like, "Hey, what pills have you had, buddy?"

He said, "Brother, I haven't had no drugs. I'm trying to give you some advice. I look at you every day in this park, man. You seem like you got a mind. We lost our bodies; let that go. Quit feeling sorry for yourself. Get you some kind of skill. Go to school. We people in wheelchairs can work. We can do this. We can do that."

I mean, my chest started coming out. I got prouder and prouder. I don't know why that guy started talking to me. He just popped out of nowhere. I never seen him before. I don't know his name. Maybe it was an angel God sent down in a wheelchair. This man was coming from the heart. When someone come from the heart, you can't do nothing but listen. He gave me inspiration. He gave me energy. He changed my life into the Jimmy of now.

So I went to Los Medanos College.

I said, "I want to go into Small Engine Repair."

They said, "We don't think you can take that. With that course you got to be able to weld. Nobody in a wheelchair ever been through welding."

So, Jimmy Polk, I always had to do something people said I couldn't do. I said, "Are you going to discriminate against my right of what I want to do?"

"Can you weld?"

"Will you let me try?"

I had to get a G.E.D. degree first. I got that in six weeks. Then they let me start taking welding, computers, some math. The V.A. bought me a $300 welding outfit, shoes, big old, hot-ass, buckskin material to protect the little sparks and shit. I got really involved. School was something to keep my mind occupied; plus, I'm around lots of people; plus, it was an extra $300 a month. Next time I look around, they taking pictures of me.

And I did it. They had a party because I was the first guy in a wheelchair to complete welding. I learned how to weld damn good. I could fix lawn motors, rotor tillers. It was like a proving thing to me. Once I got over that bridge, goddammit, there was nothing I couldn't do. I got highly motivated. I started liking myself again.

I said, "I got to get involved with something else."

I read a sign said: WANTED: STUDENT GOVERNMENT REPRESENTATIVE.

Interesting! I liked helping people. I always liked standing up for people's rights, even though I never stood up for my own hardly.

So they interviewed me. We had about eight people representing the students in cases. We had cases where women felt like they was discriminated. We had one case where this teacher kicked this student out 'cause he was gay. I was still a rebel,

Fully Armed

but I was more of a rebel with my mind and not my mouth. Plus, I was getting the Thrill of the Kill. We had these meetings with these judges, and I had the thrill of saying, "Hey, you wrong," and proving it.

After that, I got into student government. I was the first black to head it. I ran because a young lady asked me. The guy I was running against had been in school three years, but I had all the ladies' votes. They got together secretly and made me head.

I did lots of traveling. They would give us money to travel to Santa Cruz, San Diego, L.A., to universities to educate our minds as far as what's happening with the students and what we can do for them. I liked it because there were lots of other people in wheelchairs out, moving around. In Waxahachie, Texas, I was the only person in a wheelchair I seen. I felt like, "I'm not out of place. This is okay."

I met lots of politicians. We went to Sacramento to try to get bills for students passed. We got AB 179 passed to have tuition lowered. I met a cat named Campbell. He represented Contra Costa County. I met Governor Deukmajian.

Two to three months into junior college, my V.A. checks changed.

First check came was $6000. I did not even think about calling 'em to say, "You guys sent me too much money." That was the last thing on my mind. First thing was, "Let's buy a forty-eight inch screen color t.v." They had made a mistake, and I had convinced myself, "Hell, enjoy it; it's their mistake; they can't do nothing to you."

I bought me two V.C.R.s. I got nice clothes. I got a couple diamond rings.

Second check came, I bought a brand new Cadillac. I didn't have much credit in California, so when I got that check, I went up to the Cadillac dealer, and I said, "This is how much I get a month." They seen it was for $6000, and there was no credit check. I had the car the next day.

The next check came, I bought a house. I happened to be glancing through the paper. It had: 3-BEDROOM HOUSE; HANDICAP EQUIPPED. That was the thing that caught my eye.

The total payments were $136,000, $1200 a month. Which wasn't bad, with $6000 coming in. So I went after it. I got some good references from the Deans, the faculty, people who knew me through the student government. "He's a good person." "He'll take care of his business." So I was able to get the house. I would double up, paying $2000 a month, sometimes $2200, just to get ahead.

It was nice. It was in an exclusive neighborhood. People was in a high and mighty category there. The house had flowers and a big backyard. It had a swimming pool with an automatic lift. When I had a hard day and I wanted to unwind, I could roll up, press a button, and a little chair come out. I could jump in the chair and sit me in the water. I could roll straight into the shower. The guy who had lived there was paralyzed; he had it set up. It was a place a handicapped person would dream of. Everything was laid out perfectly for me.

I got expensive furniture. I furnished three bedrooms and only slept in one. I had six or eight color t.v.s. I had a t.v. in the living room, the den, the bathroom, the shower; all the bedrooms had color t.v.s. I paid $1500 for this dog, descended from a pit bull. I had rubber plants I paid $400 for.

Hell, I thought I was Harold Hughes, Jr. I was squandering the money. I looked at it this way. They might cut me off any time. It was their fault. Therefore, I ain't gonna save nothing. If I save something, they might take everything I saved. So each month, I spent all the money. I didn't save nothing nowhere. I was buying things that was valuable, where, if anything happened, I could resell it.

I wasn't thinking much about Vietnam. It would come back and haunt me now and then, but it wasn't as strong as before.

Fully Armed

The money helped me a whole lot. I was comfortable; I could take care of myself, and when you comfortable, things that bother you don't bother you no more.

I was getting to be known pretty good. I had friends visiting from different schools. San Jose State. Stanford. We'd party. We'd talk about the school issue. Things was going beautifully.

I did lots of traveling. I went to France. I went to Italy, Germany, Paris, Switzerland, Canada. I went all over the world, except for home. I really liked Paris. I met lots of beautiful people. I loved the way they talked. I was supposed to stay two weeks. I stayed six. I met this young lady named Alicia. Then I had to go because I had to be back in school, plus I wanted to make sure my check came in.

Life was awesome. I had all the necessities I needed. I wasn't having lots of accidents with my body. I was lots calmer. I learned how to break dance in the wheelchair. I met this woman, Monica, and moved her in. She had a hair place where she fix hair and stuff. I told her I was married. I told her about why I had left my family and hadn't seen them in years. I was totally honest with this woman.

That extra money gave me the freedom to experiment. Maybe I felt I was being paid for losing my legs, which you can't put a price on. My daughter would come in my mind; my wife would too, but it wouldn't make me sad. Every time, I switched channels, like you turn the t.v. to another subject. I didn't allow sadness to bother me. There was times I didn't have a good time with this money, but basically life was good. That lasted damn near three years.

It was January 3rd, 1987. I had reservations for a trip back to France. Everything was taken care of. I went to the bank to draw $3000 out. I had, maybe, $1300 in my account. People say, "Your check didn't come."

"What?"

"Your check didn't come."

I call Social Security. They say, "Have you received a letter in the mail?"

I say, "What kind of letter in the mail, ma'am?"

"Mr. Polk, there has been an overpayment of $60,000."

I dropped the phone. Ah, shit, what am I gonna do?

The lady say, "Mr. Polk, Mr. Polk, Mr. Polk..." The phone still swinging off the hook. "...Mr. Polk?"

I pick up the phone. I say, "I don't get *no* more checks?"

"Mr. Polk, something might be worked out, but we have a 'Void' on your computer card, not to send you more money until $60,000 is repaid."

"How the hell am I gonna pay $60,000? I'm in a wheelchair, lady, don't you know that?"

She said, "I'm sorry. I can't help you."

I went back to the house. I got worried. "Boy, you got this Cadillac. You got this house. You got this expensive dog and woman. Oh, hell!" The next day, I received that letter she was talking about.

I got an attorney. He set up a meeting with this agent from the V.A. and Social Security. I sat in the car because I didn't want to go through it. Three weeks done passed; I haven't got a check; I'm behind in my bills. When he came out with his head down, he didn't have to say nothing.

He said, "They not gonna reinstate you until the full $60,000 is paid."

I said, "Did you make it clear to them that I'm a Vietnam veteran? Don't that count for something?"

"We went through that. They felt that you were wrong because you knew they was overpaying you."

"Hell, they made the mistake. I just went along with it. Is that entrapment or something? Hey, I know a little bit about the law."

He kept saying there is nothing he could do.

My next plea for help was through the D.A.V. I went through the D.V.A, the P.V.A, the AmVet. They gave me another hot-shot lawyer. He went to the Social Security people and had a conversation. He couldn't do nothing.

Things started going bad then. I dropped out of school. I resigned from my position. I started selling off assets to try and pay for the house.

At this time, I had accumulated an '87 Cadillac, a 1960 Cadillac and a '66 Mustang. I sold that Mustang for $1000. I sold the 1960 Cadillac for $650. I had an antique desk I paid $2000 for. I sold it for $500. I sold my little t.v.s. I sold my big t.v. I started selling my jewelry, my clothes, piece-by-piece, trying to survive. But by now, I'm caught up in this high-profile life. I was still trying to travel. I was going places like Miami and New York, state traveling now; I wasn't going overseas. I felt better when I go away and come back. I needed money to be happy. I still had faith it gonna start back up. Even though you don't get that full $6000, $3750 is lots of money too.

Things got really-really bad. The Vietnam issue came back into my mind. I started pulling guns and knives. That had stopped completely when I was getting that money. Monica left. We had a great relationship, but people abandon ship when that ship start sinking.

We had lots of fights. One night I woke up, and I had this gun in her mouth. I was like in a trance. Sweat was popping off my body in big bubbles like I was boiling inside.

She had turned pure red. She was shaking. After about thirty cups of coffee and a blanket around her, holding her, she calmed down, but she kept moving back like she thought I was gonna kill her. She said, "It's starting again—the same thing you put your wife through. I love you a lot, but I'm leaving you."

And she left.

The next day my dog left.

Bob Levin

I went to the Liquor Barn to get a case of Olde English 800. I come back to drink my misery away and talk to my dog. The damn dog gone.

I got back in the car and got drunk-drunk-drunk. When I woke up the next afternoon, my neighbors were knocking on the windows. A friend of mine named Fred said, "Man, you look like shit. What happened? C'mon, man, let's get you some food. No! Let's get you a bath!"

We talked.

"What you gonna do, man?"

"I don't know." By now, I done sold the most valuable things. I'm down to the second-hand valuable things. "Hey, Fred, you need a plant? I paid $400 for it. Lemme get $100."

"Hell, yeah."

I went into a drinking frenzy. I became, not an alcoholic, but a beeraholic. I was drinking a case of beer a day, sometimes a case and a six-pack. When it got up to a case-and-a-half, I was totally out of control.

Mail stacked up. I had about 100 envelopes with bills, creditors after me, wanting to talk to me, letters. Might have been some money in one; I don't know. I was afraid to open any letters, so I didn't open none.

I was losing all these things.

Next time I look around, here come this person I had got the house from. When he came in, I was on my drinking spree, looking crazy, looking at the last beautiful thing I had, which was the color t.v. Only thing left was a waterbed, the t.v, me, and the beer cans on the floor.

He rolled through there and said, "Holy shit, what is happening to you?"

I said, "I can't stay. Your home was so beautiful. I haven't tore it up. I just can't afford the place no more."

"What happened?"

"The government overpaid me $60,000, and I didn't report it."

"You didn't save nothing, fool?"

"No. I bought things. I'm fixing to sell the rest I got."

"I understand the situation, but you have to understand my situation too. I give you another month, okay, free."

"Thank you."

I tried to find a damn job. No luck. No luck in Antioch for a person in a wheelchair looking for a job. Nope. Antioch? Nope. Pittsburg? Nope. Walnut Creek? Nope.

I tried to set up my own business, fixing lawn motors, rotor tillers, things like that. The first week, I made $300. I thought everything might be okay. After that, I didn't get no more business. I haven't touched a lawn motor since, I got so disgusted. The few things I did work on came from neighbors sympathizing with me because they liked me. I believe one guy broke his outboard motor just for me to fix it. Really.

I got to drinking hard. I started thinking about survival. "Where the best place in the world to be homeless?" "New York?" "No. Too many people there." "San Francisco?" "Shit, no. Too many schizophrenic people there. You kill somebody, because you damn near schizo you self." "Berkeley? Lots of good thing happen in the sixties there. Lots of crazy things happen. Everybody in Berkeley want to save something. Maybe somebody want to save you. Fuck it, let's go."

The next day, I had a garage sale. A couple walking-people friends of mine helped me move everything into the yard. I got about $800. What I don't sell, I give away.

STREET

I run across some people who look homeless. Used to be a time I wouldn't even talk to 'em. I might talk, but I never gave nobody no money for being homeless. I used to say, "Man, that's pitiful. Ain't no way I ever get in that position." Now I said, "Look at you, Jimmy. You homeless now."

I said, "Brother, where do a person in a wheelchair sleep if you're homeless?"

A white dude with long hippie clothes said, "Come with me, bro."

He started pushing me to People's Park.

People's Park is a bunch of grass and dirt, half the size of a football field, two blocks from the university, right by Telegraph Avenue. Trees at one end. Tents all over the place. Lots of hippies and lots of homeless people. A mess of drugged-out, burnt-out people that had given up on society. This was my first impression. I'm there five minutes, and thirty-five police running through. I said, "What is going on?"

"Man, this is Berserkeley." The dude fire up a joint. "And the police harass lots. They don't like homeless people."

"Oh, shit," I said.

By now, everybody coming up and sitting down. "Hey,

man, who are you?" "Hey, man, let's get high."

I'm thinking, "Damn, this is cool. Birds of a feather flock together." I'm buzzing now. People stroking guitars. Dogs catching frisbees. People hugging each other. It looked like a peaceful gathering among brothers and sisters, black and white. I felt very comfortable. It was like God got behind me and put his hand over my chest and said, "Son, I'm gonna be with you."

I was asking for information. "Do they have any resources here? Where can I eat?"

"Right here, man. They feed here every day."

"Who feed here?"

"Churches come on Saturday. You can eat with the Hare Krishnas every day, man, but they don't feed meat."

I'm thinking, "Maybe I be vegetarian. It's a matter of survival."

The Park consist of spread out patches of people that hang around together. You got your group that's involved in marijuana, your group that's involved in the peace movement, your group that's involved in keeping it People's Park, your group that desire nothing but wine, your group that desire nothing but girls.

It took me a week to plug into the system. I talked with everyone. I would sit around with whatever group I'm in and hope somebody get lucky and get some money and drink with 'em or smoke with 'em and try to find out where we get fed or where the shelter gonna be that night. I was fresh; I was new, and people cared for me. I got as much help from people that was homeless as from people that was not.

Being in a wheelchair gave me an edge. Everybody asked, "How in hell can a person in a wheelchair be out here?" "I'm a Vietnam veteran, and the government took my check." People who had bologna sandwiches two or three days old or an extra pair of pants or shoes or a clean shirt, said "Here. You need this more than me." And everybody shared the information they received. "Hey, man, they giving away free sleeping bags up here." "Hey, they giving away free food here." "You can get a five-dollar voucher for clothes."

I felt, "It's not gonna be so fucking bad. All these guys share their bread with you, share their drugs with you; everybody love everybody." I looked at it as a new way of living. It was thrilling. That turned out to be not true, but that was the frame I had to cycle myself into to deal with what was happening.

Street people are very happy, very content with their lives. They have freedom; they have no bills to pay, and they don't want to change that situation. One street person I met was telling me, "I have graduated from U.C. of Berkeley. I have had money. I have had cars. I have had women. But I never had peace until I become homeless. I love it thisaway."

Like society, the homeless got rules. Before the food trucks come, you might have fifty, sixty people in line. If you get out of line, take you a leak, get you a beer, whatever, you put a rock where you standing. If a person move that rock, he will lose respect in the homeless people eye. If they see him hungry, they won't give him food. They will call him "an asshole homeless person." When you in line for the shelter, you see backpacks and plastic bags and grocery carts. You can't put yourself ahead of them. You do, the others gonna make you have a worse night's sleep than you gonna have. They'll steal what little you got. And if a person got a corner that they hustle on, you do not hustle on that corner. Word get around, and if you in a bind, you need help, you need a drink, the others gonna tell you, "Kiss my ass."

Blankets was the one thing homeless people do not share. And if you don't have a blanket, you are messed up. Every night, on the streets of Berkeley, it's cold. You fuck with somebody's blanket, they will hurt you. Not your food or your clothes or your drugs. Your blanket. That is Number One. It come before your partner or your girlfriend. Three o'clock in the morning, you got no place to run for cover. People will rip blankets from their kids to keep warm. To hell with their children.

The Park have their assholes. But those assholes are not homeless. You got young kids that have nothing to do but come up to the Park to play Mr. Bad and start fights and try to make a name for they selves. You got assholes that come grab the good clothes out of the Free Boxes to sell to Wasteland or Buffalo Exchange. There's not much homeless people can do about it. We have this reputation as being useless, worthless. If anything go down, we get the blame.

Being on Telegraph was a trip. Walking around was like being in a bowl, mixed-up and made a part of. It was one giant carnival. It was different; it was fascinating; it was like, "I only seen this shit on t.v." You got people walking by with Mohawks. I ain't used to seeing that. You got people in all black, with gold earrings in their nose. I ain't never seen that. You got homeless people with 30,000 bags on. I'm living that. You got skinheads coming through. You got college students, young and fresh, enjoying their young life you wish you had. You got doctors and lawyers. You got "Har-Re Krish-Na. Ha-re Krish-Na. Ha-re Krish-na," and you freaking out on that. You got black po-lit-i-cal ac-ti-vists. And you got your junkies: "Man, you want to smoke a joint and escape this bullshit?" All these different people walking up and down the same street. Each block you make was like walking through a different level, upper and upper and upper, never the same.

I got by, running miles across north Berkeley, south Berkeley, east Berkeley, finding out where they gonna feed at, going to the Salvation Army to get vouchers for Safeway, waiting for the—"Hey-ah, ho-yo, hee-you"—Hare Krishnas, giving the Food Project a quarter for a plate of spaghetti, standing in lines with 100-some damn people, fighting, sometime, for three-day old macaroni and cheese, four-day old tuna fish.

I was sleeping in shelters. The first bad experience I had was the first night. They said, "We can't let you in. You are a high-risk category." It was the first time a person in a wheelchair seeked refuge in a homeless place. All of a sudden fifteen or twenty other people started raising hell, so they let me in. That was my first taste of unity with the homeless people. It made the bond stronger.

The shelters moved from place to place. You didn't always know where, and if you did, you couldn't always get in, and if you got in, other problems started there. Shelters got fifty, sixty one-inch thin mattresses on the floor. I can't sleep on no floor. Paraplegics need to sleep on something soft or vibrating to keep us turning or we get sores. I had to sleep in my wheelchair. Doing that eight, nine, ten days in a row took an effect on my body.

On the mattresses, you got fifty, sixty guys, most of them snoring, most of them unsanitary, most of them disrespectful towards each other. You got to hang onto your clothes, your shoes, any valuable thing you have, or it be gone in the morning. I would put my stuff in a backpack and sleep on it with my head and wake up, and it still be gone. That's how good the thiefs was.

The shelters got one bathroom for that entire group. The first time I went, my chair wouldn't fit inside. When I had to go, I crawled. I crawled back out and had to wake somebody to help me back in my chair.

I was the only one in the shelters in a wheelchair. I was always the oddball, the center of attention, the conversation topic. When you have fifty, sixty guys lying on the floor and one guy sitting in a wheelchair, you got 100, 120 eyes on you. I made lots of people feel better, because they think, "Damn, I could be you. We the same, but it's harder on you. You can't lay on the floor. You got to crawl to the bathroom."

Five o'clock every morning, they ring this loud noise. Time to be up. You got to be out by six. Some days you be so tired you can barely lift your eyebrows. You don't want to go out.

It be a hot day or a cold, wet, foggy day, and you got no place to go. The only place you got is the street. Only thing you can do is find some alley with some cover that will get you out of that sun or that cold wet. Some days I couldn't find no place or, if I did, I got run off because of the way I was living. A bad day like this, the thing most homeless people do is beg like hell for change, get a bottle of wine, drink it, and pass out on the street.

In the morning, the shelters serve us food: bread, two-week old raisins, coffee, if you give it to a dog, it was liable to pass out. I was the last one to get any. When people wake up, they form a line, and by the time I'm ready, I'm getting the crumbs from the coffee and the bread with the green shit on it. Maybe one day out of seven, somebody would say, "Stay there. I'll get you food," but when you waking up at five and got to be out by six, you don't think about your brother man. It's all about "I got to get *my* coffee, *my* raisins, *my* bread."

There was lots of fights in the shelters, and, every time, it seemed like I was in-between. One guy be on one side of my chair, the other guy be on the other, and I would always be knocked down. I went through that about three times and started sleeping outside.

I stayed in the Park. I stayed behind Berkeley High School. I stayed behind vacant buildings. I would shake cars and, if they open, crawl in. I would go down by the waterfront. A couple times I went down in BART, somewhere where I'm not seen, where I'm not bothering no one, trying to stay warm, and BART police would hit my chair so hard, sometimes miss the chair and hit me, to chase me out. One night, it was freezing cold, and I caught the elevator down there to sleep in this corner from where the trains come, and I pulled this blanket over my head, and I fell asleep, and I smelled smoke, and I pulled this blanket off, and this guy had set me on fire. I said, "Why'd you do that?" and he said, "Fuck you, bum."

I would stay in a location until the police would ask me to leave. My cover was boxes or newspapers. I would put a quarter in the machine, get five or six papers, and make my bed. I even opened peoples' garages and got out before they got up. Once, I snuck in this garage had an old couch. It was the first time I had laid on something soft in months. I woke up about eleven and seen a plate of food. A lady came out and said, "I hope that helped. But you can't do it again because my husband might not like it." Another time, I woke up and a guy had a shotgun on me. Then he saw my wheelchair. "Oh my God, you crippled? Can I get you some breakfast?" "Yes sir." "Can I get you a towel?" "Thank you, sir. Sir, do you have a pair of pants?"

After six or seven months, I started panhandling. I was so hungry I just started asking, "Spare change for food? Spare change for food?"

Panhandling broke my spirit. I thought, "Boy, you are pitiful. Your daddy and momma see you doing this, you will break their heart. Why don't you pick up the phone and call?" But another voice say, "No. All you'll hear is 'I told you so.' If you go back, you not have the freedom that you love."

The first bill I got was ten-dollars. I went to Nation Hamburger, off Telegraph, and that was the first meal I had that tasted good. Don't get me wrong; when you in the street, you appreciate everything, but in my condition, I have to eat hot, fresh food. Food that they give you, food that is old, give me diarrhea. The last thing you want in a wheelchair is diarrhea. And I was in a wheelchair; I was having diarrhea; I didn't have no facility to change clothes; I didn't have clothes. And I knew it was 'cause of the food.

So once that first ten-dollars hit my hand, I said, "Hey, push that pride aside, boy. Maybe there's a future in this."

One of my friends told me, "There's 100 panhandlers on Telegraph. Why don't you try Shattuck?"

I said, "Where's Shattuck?"

He said, "Go up Telegraph till you can't go nowhere, and

go straight down."

So I rolled around, and I seen Wells Fargo Bank. I parked there, and that first day I made forty-seven dollars. I was able to get a room and hot food, and, from that day on, I been at Wells Fargo. That's my office. I should have a plaque up there. In fact, the Bank President will tell you, I am part of the building. I give directions. I watch dogs. I watch bicycles. I tell 'em which way to push the door. Three or four times, people worked inside would tell me, "Jimmy, this person came in, was dressed like this, said he planted a bomb." And if they was from the street, I'd know who they was talking about, and I would say, "He's full of bullshit," or "Be sure you check this out! I'm moving!" I am just a handy man.

Everybody know me. The police who walk the beat all know my name. People hand me money, and they do not say anything. I had policemen tell me, "Jimmy, you can sleep in a cell tonight," not to arrest me, to get me out of the cold. Christmas time, the police ran every panhandler off Shattuck except me. The other panhandlers got pissed. "How come we got to move and he don't?" Police said "Because y'all don't make me smile." I still get slack from people on the street about that. One time this doctor who had just moved into the building started complaining that I was deterring his customers. The police told me, "Jimmy, he's an asshole. Move across the pavement from the door, instead of beside it. That way, he can't say shit."

Alcohol is a big problem with homeless people. We use it to get peace of mind. It's hard to sleep when it's cold and you're hungry and you got no place to go. You drink three or four cans of beer, you be so drunk, you don't care. You go to sleep, and you wake up: it's a new day. People call you an alcoholic. We call it medication. Emotion lotion.

I won't do heavy drugs, but I do drink. I don't drink to where I'm falling out of my chair; but if it gets cold out, I will roll ten blocks to get a bottle of wine, so I can be warm inside.

And I know once I get to sleep, I'm not gonna get in trouble. I'm gonna wake up, say, "Thank you, God," and start asking for change.

But in People's Park, I almost got trapped into that alcohol thing. I was hanging with these guys, anytime one person make a dollar, a dollar-fifty, he get a quart. I said, "I ain't never gonna get up if I keep doing this. Maybe if I put more time into asking for change, giving people a smile, giving them a compliment, I get something in return."

Sure enough, it works. I always try and make somebody feel good, not because I'm expecting change, but because it make me feel good. Night time, I can think how I made this person smile and how this person made me smile. Just that makes you warm.

I'm a spare happinesser and a spare changer. I'm a counselor too. I'm willing to listen to a person's problems with their husbands, their boyfriends, the jobs, the bosses, the bills. Used to be, I was rugged, I was tough, I did all the talking. Becoming homeless, I listen to everything.

I have a comment for everything too. If you was a computer expert, I would talk to you about computers. If you was a teacher, I would talk about school. If you was a baker, I was a chef. If you was a drug addict, I could talk about that. And if you talked about God, I could get spiritual and quote the Book of Revelations.

And I touch 'em. My eye contact, my one-on-one conversation make it work. Sometime, I'm listening and talking to four people at the same time, and nobody moves, because I give 'em my attention. It's not about, "Here, give me your money," and I'm running down the street. I sit there, and if you ain't got no money, I say, "Hey, I understand. God bless you anyway, because you took time to talk to me."

I meet hundreds of people every week, and I can tell when something's on a person mind. I think God gave me the gift to pick up on people's feelings. One person was complaining about work. I say, "My friend, least you have work." He smiled. "Thank you." One lady was crying. I said, "Do you need somebody to talk to?" She said, "I need a friend. Let's have coffee." That day, I needed a motel room. It was raining. But we spent a couple hours talking. After we got through, she got me a motel room without me asking.

One thing about people who give you money. You got those who lay it straight in your hand. You got those who drop it. You can tell who giving it from their heart, who giving it out of sorrow, who giving it 'cause of a guilty conscience. Besides money, I get hugs and kisses too. Sometimes I smell bad, and I'm dirty, but the people don't care. They say, "Jimmy, we love you. You listen to my problems. And here you are, rolling around in a raggedy chair, with raggedy clothes, and you always smiling."

So I love it. I mean, I don't love it-love it. I like being out there, and I don't. I like being out there for a moment, but I don't like being out there from six o'clock in the morning till ten o'clock at night.

The street's the Wild Wild West, man. Crazy shit can happen there. And one thing it's proved, being disabled has not made me weaker. It has made me stronger. I can go down further than any person and bounce back. There ain't too many disabled people reached the climax I have. Maybe two in a million. The odds are very high for a disabled person to last two years on the street, panhandling, begging, being spit on, pulling out his gun, when I had a gun, pulling out my knife.

Even pulled out a water pistol one time. These three guys was gonna take seventy-five dollars I had panhandled. I had a water gun I found in a trash can. It looked real. It fooled me. That's how come I picked it up. Evidently, some kid's mother didn't want him to have it and threw it away. So I pull out this plastic gun, and they start running. "The nigger's got a gun. The nigger's got a gun."

My wheelchair got stolen many times. I jump out of my

wheelchair to sleep on a bench, and, normally, I wake at the crack of a leaf, but, when you tired, your body shut down; you don't hear nothing. I woke up one night, and my chair was gone. I crawled across Martin Luther King Park looking for it. I'm crawling. I'm crawling. Then rain started. I'm sitting on the ground, soaking wet. I put my head down. I was hollering, "Oh, God, help me!" Nobody was walking up and down the street. Nobody was hearing me.

One time, by Kam's Restaurant, somebody grabbed me, took my wallet, threw me out, rolled my chair across the street, and left. Fifteen or twenty people looking, and nobody would help. Nobody. I couldn't get my chair because of all the cars. My nose bleeding like hell, my arm hurt, my leg bag busted, and people just looking.

Last Christmas, I lost two friends. One guy was twenty-three, but he looked forty-three. He come from a distinguished family that wanted him to be something that he didn't. He started living on the street. Christmas Eve, he said, "Jimmy, I can't take no more. I'm not gonna kiss my parents' ass. I have found a way out. Come with me." "Where?" "San Francisco." We went down on BART. I thought he was fixing to show me that he got a job or that something good done happened. The train coming. "Jimmy, I love you." Runs right in front. It squashed him like a tomato.

New Year's, I watched this boy drink hisself to death. He had 120 ten-milligram Valiums. He poured all 120 in his mouth, drinking wine behind 'em. I'm knocking on peoples' doors. When I finally got somebody to call 911, he was dead.

On the street, you have to observe everything. Like a psychiatrist in an interview, he's watching the way your eyes roll, your head turn. On the street, if you want to survive, it's the same. You watch every little thing about a person: how they twist their mouth, how they move their butt. If I think a person is weird, I won't hang with him. I have had friends say, "Man, John got killed last night," and I been with John two hours earlier and know he left with somebody I didn't feel right with. Or "Artist disappeared" and, the week before, he was with me and went off with some stranger.

Some of these so-called charities discriminate more against the homeless than anybody. If you don't have a quarter, the Food Project won't give you no food. What kind of shit is that? Some people don't have a quarter. They getting paid fifteen dollars an hour, and they treat homeless people like dogs.

One time, I went to a church. I couldn't eat because I couldn't get downstairs. Nobody would give me no food upstairs. Now my attitude is: I don't stand in line for no free food. I go out and ask. I go to the church house to sleep or pray, but I won't go there to eat. They have hurt me. They supposed to be the House of the Lord. They supposed to be helping. These experiences hard to shake off.

And the Center for Independent Living? Man, I hate those fuckers. People there all got some kind of disability, but they think they better than you. They think that, because they got jobs, you should kiss their tail. That go off in the disability world same as the straight-up world. I went there. I say, "I need a place to stay." "Do you get any money?" "Hell, no." "Well, all we can do is give you a bus pass." "What? I can't sleep on no bus."

My friend's chair was messed up; they bought him a new chair. I asked for new tires, they said, "We don't have that program no more. Next." I got a big old sign and started picketing, they made me so mad.

I asked them for shelter. They wouldn't write me no referral to no shelter, bad condition as I am. "You shouldn't of let yourself get like that." First time anger made me want to push somebody out of their wheelchair, and I'm in one too. I said, "Just because somebody gave you a job, doesn't mean for you to come down on me." "Get out before I call the police." "Kiss my ass." So the word is around C.I.L., "When Jimmy Polk come, trouble's coming."

But right is right and wrong is wrong. Somebody help you, spread that help. Just because you doing better than I am, even though you in the same condition, don't look down on me. One guy, couldn't even use his hands, told me, "You make us look bad." He run some photography agency next door to Wells Fargo. He give me thirty-five dollars to move from in front of his building, because this model was coming, and he was afraid she wouldn't. My friend, I'll take that thirty-five dollars, because that's a bed, but it made me feel bad. All he had to do was talk to me like a man, and I would have been glad to move.

Don't get me wrong. There is pleasure out there too. People care about me. People try to motivate me. People turn me onto resources what, due to my situation, I haven't followed up on yet. People take me to things I never experienced before.

A young lady from Boston met me in People's Park. She played the violin and flute in this orchestra. I said, "Spare change, my lady? You sure are jazzy." She said, "Something about you I like." She came every day to buy me breakfast. She said, "I dig you. I want you to try something new."

"What's that?"

"The concert."

I never been to a concert. But she was so pretty, I say, "Let's go."

The concert was at Trinity Church. One homeless buddy had found me some shoes. One found me a clean pair of slacks. One found me a sweater and an earring. I am looking sharp. And I roll into this place. I'm the onliest person in a wheelchair. I'm the only black person. I'm the only homeless person. And I don't understand Mozart. I couldn't understand how come, before they start playing, when they just ZZZZUNNNN, making all this noise, people start clapping. I felt completely out of place. I didn't understand what the hell was going on. But she was up there, so gentle and so

Fully Armed

smooth, it was a trip. And when I roll out, the homeless sleeping thirty inches across the gymnasium from where the concert was. And I walk into my other world, and I felt in place.

My world's so damned confused, sometimes I ask, "Is I living a fantasy? Is I fooling myself? Do I need psychological help?" From the time I wanted to hurt Erwin Barksdale but didn't want to kill him, it seemed like I been two different people. I live one life, and then I step into another one. I'm always going back and forth. Even though things happen good for me, I'm still more comfortable in the street than in the motel room with a t.v. I don't have to be out there, but I am. It scares me. I like that bed. I love that bed. But every time I get around a four-cornered room, I feel like I am trapped in that P.O.W. camp in that cage. I leave my room, sometimes two, three o'clock in the morning, just to roll around.

Every day you wake up in a wheelchair, you have to be prepared. Before I got on the street, I was used to having more than enough. Then I had nothing at all. But I didn't care. All I cared about was not going back to Texas, to my wife and people saying, "You should of stayed." I didn't want to face those elements.

I put it to myself: "How you gonna adjust?" "I don't know." Then, like in Nam, every day, automatic, you put on your helmet and your gun—CLICK—I put on this disguise. I'm back in the jungle, but it's not a battle war this time; it's a mind war. Vietnam kicked my ass. I sure wasn't gonna let the street take my soul.

Street life made Nam look like it ain't shit. Street life is hard; it is heavy. You got to be tough; you got to learn control; you got to learn to take shit. I told one guy I was a veteran and got spit on. Then I told him I was homeless, and he came back and spit on me again. Any other time, I would have shot the motherfucker twenty times. I said, "God bless you anyway." Before he made it to the corner, he turned around, came back, gave me thirty dollars, and made me drink a six-pack with him.

In the street, if you don't know how to take shit and you ain't strong, you gonna lose. When I say "lose," you're gone. These schizophrenics walking around? They lost, and they can't come back. No matter how much help you give 'em, they can't. Me, I ain't never gonna get that lost.

Even today, to protect myself from feeling bad, I don't plan things as far as definite plan-plan-plan. I don't look forward to things. I live each moment at a time, because things keep changing in my life. I got lots of complications there. Every year since I been shot, I've had one major surgery. Every year. I keep feeling my body can't keep going under that knife. Sometimes, seem just when everything is going great—BAM—I get knocked down again. But I'm gonna keep getting up. If you try to better yourself, good things happen. Bad things happen too, but if you give up, everything go downhill, and you can't get nowhere being down.

Now, I don't worry about the bad things. I don't have no lots of money. I ain't got no this and that and this and that. But I got peace. That's how come, every time you see me, I'm smiling. I'm not worrying about shit. I'm able to wake up and have a smile, instead of wake up and say, "Ah, shit, I got to live through today." Regardless of where I'm at or what I been through, first thing I do is thank God and put a smile on my face. Sometimes it's hard, but I have figured out a formula to make it easy. I think about what happened nice yesterday, and I feed off that. I roll down the street and not worry if this bag gonna bust. If it happen, I say, "The hell with it. Be happy." I thought about that a long time before the song was made.

I can do things like that. I can reach inside my heart and find a happy button. I may have been able to do 10,000 things before. I can do 9000 now. I don't think about the other 1000. Now, I want to live. Before, I was ready to take myself out.

PART II

ONE

I interviewed Jimmy for one or two hours, three or four times a week. I transcribed the tapes verbatim. When I rewrote, I edited slightly, trimming here or there, making shifts to strengthen the structure. But the result was ninety-nine percent Jimmy: his words, his phrasings, his rhythms.

I wanted to tell Jimmy's story in Jimmy's voice. It was a remarkable story. It was a story that had never been told. It was a voice that had never been heard. Writers did not live lives like this. If they learned about or fantasized them, their recountings, whether journalism or fiction, whether in their own voice or some stylized version, lost some essential truth. The people with these lives—shattered upon the rocks of war and paralysis, drug addiction and homelessness—deserved to be experienced whole. The rest of us needed to know the full dimensions of where the world could cast our brothers. And while Jimmy had crashed upon terrain that seemed to me to be unmatchably grotesque, his presence in my office—open, upbeat, risen—inspired awe.

Listening to Jimmy was overpowering. At times, he would rock back and forth in his chair. His voice would choke or quiver. One leg would jerk uncontrollably. He would press it into submission with both hands. On occasion, he would call for a break; he could not go on. Other times, he ached to see what memories would be revived. "I never told my story in such detail," he said. "Some—like the Twelfth Mission—I never told anyone. I closed that door. I didn't lock it, but it's a long time since I looked inside."

Once, Jimmy said, "I don't dream no more. When I go to sleep, it's night, and then it's morning. So much horrible things have happened to me, it's like a protective shield. Can we sue the government for that, Bob? They robbed me of my right to dream." *They robbed me of my right to dream.* The words tore at my throat. Now he was dreaming again, and while his rememberings could terrify him, one night he dreamed he died twelve times, it seemed his life was being reborn.

Adele was glad I was excited. "You're like having a brand new, bouncy puppy in the house," she said. My parents praised me for my good deed. They called regularly to check on Jimmy's progress. "Is he still coming to work?" "Is he taking care of his health?" And Max was certain I had a gold mine on my hands. "What do you foresee, professor," he said one afternoon, peeping at me through a crystal he had taken to wearing around his neck, "Eddie Murphy as Jimmy? Paul Newman as you?"

"Too short," I said.

"Magnum, P.I.?"

"Too Republican."

"Robert DeNiro?"

"Lacks my sensitive, intellectual side."

I was so proud. I was certain my book would be significant: socially progressive in its revelations about the war, humanly affirmative in its recounting of Jimmy's growth, artistically rich as I wrote at the top of my game. It would also be important for Jimmy. I imagined him, financially stable from his share of its earnings, returning to school, getting a degree, using his skills with people, his experiences, and his living example to become a successful counselor or political activist. And, I told myself, if I was not exactly who I was, this would not be happening. Without my being a lawyer, I would have had no job to offer Jimmy. Without my being a writer, I could have offered no book. Without my specific personality—without my very self—we could not have met, connected, had our relationship root.

As our collaboration moved forward, it spoke to me in subtler ways. Jimmy was black and I was white; he was a veteran and I had marched against the war; he was Southern to my Northern, Gentile to my Jew, disabled to my being "straight-up." Our working together supported beliefs about reconciliation and cooperation that I had been dissuaded from holding for years. The idea that this man, so different than me, felt close enough to confide in me and trusted me to work in his best interests filled me with a sense of responsibility and worth. I was totally committed to the telling of Jimmy's story. In his terms, I felt "blessed."

Of course, at times, I had my doubts.

I would walk down Shattuck Avenue, where the extraordinary was usually announced in terms of "Three T-shirts for $10" or "All-Leather Biker Jackets $79.99," having just learned of prison camp assassinations and doctors inoculating U.S. service men with heroin, and think, "This can't be true! I do not believe it." Then I would go home, Adele would serve spaghetti and clam sauce, and, relaxed, reflective, my doubts would erase. "I mean, what's Jimmy got to gain by making this stuff up?" I'd say, "I'm not raising his salary. I've even stopped giving him change on the street." Or I'd bounce out of my study, where I was supposed to be straightening out six months worth of Blue Cross notices. "Where the hell'd he get those details? The scarf? The jeeps waiting for his plane? That dialogue before the Bumblebees last job? I'm the goddamn writer, and I couldn't make up stuff that good." Or I'd keep it simple. "Shakespeare knew the evil kings and shit would pull. You think we're so civilized, it's not happening now? C'mon." The next day, Jimmy would tell me about paralytics walking, and I would think, "Okay! That's it! I will not believe another word." But that evening, I would reconvince myself again.

Minor inconsistencies stopped bothering me. If Jimmy's account of one mission seemed to contradict some part of another, I had encountered enough witnesses unable to accurately remember what happened to them last Tuesday to consider his credibility impeached. Like he said, "Basically, everything is ninety percent correct. I might have confused some dates or things. Twenty years is a hard time to be putting everything exact. Ninety percent I can remember damn near each by each, but I get some of 'em mixed up because, for twenty years, I been trying to erase 'em."

And having lived through My Lai and Allende, Watergate and Fred Hampton, Noriega and Cambodia, I could accept Jimmy's fundamental premises. So when he responded to my objections that "The Army doesn't take sixteen-year olds" or "Your unit sounds like 'The Dirty Dozen'" with "This government does lots of things the public does not know," and "All them movies—'Dirty Dozen,' 'Rambo,' 'Apocalisp Now'—got a piece of truth to them. Whoever wrote 'em, got his ideas from somewhere." I would nod.

If my doubts persisted, I shared them. A professor of Twentieth Century American History, who read portions of my manuscript, was convinced Jimmy's story was true. A Vietnam veteran I told about the Bumblebees said, "I never heard of them, but, by sixty-nine, we were so crazy over there we might of tried anything." Max said Jimmy's story fit none of the customary street-crazies' scenarios with which he was familiar. "He doesn't blame his whole trip on some monster conspiracy, and he doesn't blow himself up into Captain Superdude. Here's a guy scared shitless, killing women and children, strung out, dirty, and mean. What cat, makes up a story, plays himself like that?"

Adele had met Jimmy. She'd heard all the tapes. "What I see," she said, "is this kid, intellectually and emotionally undeveloped, like any sixteen-year-old, let alone one from a small

Texas town, whose life is ripped open by this rape-murder."
We were at an outdoor table in front of the cafe at the Wrench Hotel. It was Saturday afternoon. The light was gold in the trees. She was drinking a mint tea, and I had a double espresso. A man in lederhosen was dribbling a basketball across four lanes of traffic. "Before he can heal and establish an adult self, he is thrown, terrified, isolated, drugged silly, into this literal jungle—a world that continually grows more twisted and horrific—from which he emerges paralyzed, all hope for normality gone.

"Given that, his account makes perfect sense. He may have certain facts wrong. His interpretation of events or peoples' motives may be in error. But what you're getting is, at least, 'metaphoric reality.'" She paused and adjusted her black glasses. "After all, what's any army but a specially selected corps of trained killers. Most of what Jimmy says is true. The rest is his limited attempt to make sense out of the hell that happened to him."

A lawyer friend in Oakland had an interesting reaction. I had never mentioned Jimmy to him when I asked him to read my chapters about Waxahachie and Vietnam. He called a few days later. "That's a great story. Some of the language didn't seem right for the central character, but, except for a couple details, it hangs together well."

"That's him talking, Albert, every word."

"That's who talking?"

"The central character. It's all true."

"Bullshit!"

"Whattaya mean 'Bullshit?' You just told me you believed it, except for one or two details."

"I did not. I mean..." Albert had been voting Republican since 1972. His daughter went to cotillions, and he served on State Bar committees. I could hear him trying to have this all make sense. He was a man trying to jam one more bulky sweater into an already stuffed trunk. "I thought you were giving me a new novel. I believed it as a story. I didn't believe it as true."

Jimmy could understand Albert's confusion. "Each veteran's mind's been tampered with so much, sometimes we aren't sure what the hell is happening. The whole thing was unreal. You seen things that you can't believe. You seen things that you can't imagine. You seen things that you're saying, 'This is a fucking movie. This is not happening. There is no way this is real.' But it's happening. It's real. I still don't believe it. I cannot believe the unbelievable bullshit I been through. It seems like a science-fiction movie James Bond 007 would make. I swear to God, if I was writing this book, I wouldn't believe shit, but it's the truth. War, everything is possible."

Jimmy agreed to everything I asked by way of corroboration. He signed releases for his military records, his medical records, his file from Los Medanos J.C., and the court records of his prosecution. One morning, in August, I came into the office, and he was giving someone on the phone our address. When he hung up, he apologized for the charges, but he'd called Waxahachie, spoken with his father for the first time in four years, and asked him to send his Bumblebee scarf, his medals, and a scrapbook the family had kept on him since high school.

But my strongest reason for believing Jimmy was before me. Him, homeless, in his wheelchair. His story would have to unravel a long way before it ceased to be compelling. The more I heard and saw, the more I doubted it would unravel at all. Nor did I want it to. In its vicious bleakness, it offered a world view which justified my own pessimism and cynicism, but in his personal victory, it provided what I truly desired: good feelings and hope.

Often, leaving work after a taping, I would sit in my car and tremble. Other people, their cars, the blue blossoms on the trumpet vine that spilled down the wall of my parking garage seemed to be held within a universe that was physically separated from me by the weight of the experience in which I was involved.

Jimmy had endured war and disability and poverty. Yet each day, he could say, "Things will get better, my friend." His presence challenged me to re-examine my own bowed state. It called for me to capture him so others might be inspired by his example. Jimmy, in the achievements of his self, was a Picasso or Joyce. Like all great artists, through his work, he altered how one saw the world.

So I was disappointed when Jimmy disappeared.

TWO

I'm tired of running. I done ran from everything. I ran from my family. I ran to try and escape Nam. I done ran. I done ran. I done ran. I done ran so damn much right now I'm not running. I'm tired of running. My life was steady running. No more.
Jimmy Polk 8-26-89.

1.

August had been a busy month for Jimmy.

Ron Dellums, Berkeley's Congressman, has a local office staff that aggressively looks out for his constituents' welfare. I suggested to Jimmy that he call them about getting his disability check restored. Two days later, Jimmy said he had been granted reinstatement of $1000 a month until his debt was cleared.

Jimmy bought pizza and Coke for the entire office.

Jimmy's first priority was housing. Through Berkeley-Oakland Support Services (BOSS), using most of his first month's check and a $125 loan from me, he rented a two-room cottage in the backyard of a house on Sixth Street, near Hearst.

He bought a refrigerator and stove. A social worker, who was one of his regular panhandling contributors, promised him a television and bed. The V.A. promised to build a ramp, so he would not have to haul himself up the two steps to the front door. When he called his father to tell him he was getting settled, he learned his daughter, now fifteen, wanted to visit.

Until September 1st, when the cottage would be his, Jimmy rented a room in the Lake Merritt Lodge.

He was also having fainting spells.

A doctor at Ft. Miley Hospital told Jimmy he had a bladder infection. He recommended surgery. They would insert a tube up Jimmy's penis and trim away a fatty growth.

Jimmy was frightened. Every time they operated, the doctors told him he would be out in a few days, but he would be held for weeks. "I keep having dreams that I die," he said. "I'm having an operation and somebody screw up and I'm dead. Maybe I'll go on in the hospital. Maybe not. If I do, I am coming out after three days if I.V.s be hanging off me like a Christmas tree."

II.

Sept. 1. Yesterday, when I'd seen Jimmy panhandling, he'd told me he would drop off a tape at the office he'd filled on his own. He didn't, and he didn't come in today. He is to move into his cottage, and I assume he is too excited or too busy to work.

Sept. 5. Yesterday was Labor Day, and the office was closed. Today, Jimmy is off, but he is not panhandling. I ask two regulars at the outdoor tables in front of Frenzy if they've seen him. "Probably away for the weekend," says a skinny man, whose cane had been carved to look as if snake is entwined around it.

"I guess so," I say.

Sept. 6. Jimmy does not come in or call. In two months of work before this, he had only missed one day. Then, even though I knew he could have been busy or ill or hurt, I had worried he had quit because he did not want to go on with the book. Otherwise, I thought, he would have called. But, I had told myself, if he is quitting, why did he start? Where was the hustle, the advantage to be gained? What about the good feelings between us? The next morning, Jimmy had rushed in, explaining that he had been arrested in Oakland on an old panhandling warrant and not allowed to phone. When I told him what I had been thinking, he said he would never "abandon" me.

I am worried again.

Sept. 8. No word. Maybe Jimmy got his check and, with his cottage paid for and surgery closing in, went on a spree. I hope it is not for long.

Sept. 11. Amelia calls five V.A. hospitals. None have a record of a recent admission for a Jimmy Polk. One sounds evasive. I call and ask if they would tell me if someone was there on a psychiatric hold. "I'd tell you we had a patient registered by that name," the receptionist says.

Amelia calls every jail she can think of. She calls several social service agencies. BOSS says they would have no record of the address of any cottage they had found for someone. At C.I.L., a woman says she knows Jimmy. "He does things like this periodically. And even if I knew where he was, I wouldn't tell you."

Amelia cannot bring herself to call the Coroner.

Sept. 12. I call the Lake Merritt Lodge. The desk clerk says so many people go through there she cannot tell me when Jimmy had been there last or if he'd been there at all.

Adele and I drive to Sixth and Hearst. We cruise a wide street with wood-frame, single-family homes on both sides.

We see no likely-looking cottages in anyone's backyard. We stop in a Senior Citizens' Center. No one has seen any thirty-six-year-old black men in wheelchairs in the neighborhood lately. I post a notice on their bulletin board.

Sept. 13. I go to the Bank of America where Jimmy cashed my checks. I tell the manager that someone who works for me has disappeared. I give her Jimmy's account number and ask if there was a direct deposit of his disability check on the first and a large withdrawal immediately thereafter.

"I can't give you any information without Mr. Polk's consent."

"I can't get Mr. Polk's consent because he's the one who's disappeared."

"Then get the consent of the other person whose name appears on the account."

"What other person?" I feel like I have taken in a lot of water and an going down for the third time.

"I can't tell you."

"How the hell am I supposed to get their consent then?"

She smiles and shrugs.

Sept. 14. My telephone bill arrives. There are no calls to Texas on it.

It is dizzying. I remember walking into the office and Jimmy, excited, giving someone our address and apologizing for the charges. Were they on last month's bill? Did he call collect? Did he spontaneously make up a fake phone call? His father's excitement? The promised scrapbook and scarf?

Sept. 15. The Registrar from Los Medanos calls. They can't release Mr. Polk's records until he pays off a promissory note.

"How much does he owe you?"

"Just a minute."

Promissory note, I think. Sounds heavy.

"Twenty dollars," the Registrar says.

"The check is in the mail."

Sept. 16. I had asked a college friend, who had served in Intelligence in Vietnam, how I might verify Jimmy's experiences. He has sent me a monthly newspaper called VETERAN. In it are two pages of classified ads from people who are trying to locate others they served with.

Martin D'Giff is looking for Animal Gunn.

Screwdriver Scrivner is looking for Jonesie, Doc Creasy and Sgt. Sweat.

Dwight Fish wants to hear from his crew on The Black Widow.

The Indian wants to hear from any Black Berets who served with him at a firebase twenty-two klicks out of Quang Tri.

Stephen Smith is trying to locate an airborne ranger who last lived on Deer Island.

Joseph Moroney is looking for any Berets or Seals who participated in the special operation "Nam" from November 1962 to January 1963.

I will not abandon you, Jimmy had said.

Sept. 19. The Los Medanos records arrive.

Jimmy Don Polk was a student from the summer of 1984 through the fall of 1985. He completed 28.5 units with a grade point average of 2.53. He took courses in Arc Welding, Gas Welding, Small Engines, Marine Mechanics and Automotive Brakes. He received two A's and a B in Student Leadership and Governance. He failed Foreign Car Tune-up and Emission Control.

Sept. 22. Who had Michigan in the Jimmy pool?

My answering service took a message at 9:38 p.m. "Jimmy Polk is in hospital in Michigan. Will call in as long (sic) as he can. He had surgery twice. Is doing okay. Will call next week."

I focus on the positive. Jimmy is alive. He has recognized our connection. I do not know why he chose to go to Michigan, rather than Miami or Mexico or Paris, for his spree. I recognize that by calling at 9:30 p.m., which is not the best time to catch me in the office, and by not leaving his phone number or the name of his hospital, he has kept me from contacting him.

Adele tells me Jimmy is "retaining control."

Sept. 26. Jimmy's military personnel file arrives.

Jimmy Don Polk was born in Texas, January 23, 1957. He enlisted in the Army June 27, 1975, after high school in Ypsilanti, Michigan. He served until July 28, 1975, at Fort Ord, California, when he was given an Honorable Discharge for not meeting "medical standards for procurement" at the time he enlisted.

III.

It was all a lie.

He had made it up. The three jeeps in the desert and the camp with no colors and the hole drilled behind his back molar. The knife twisting in his shoulder and his fear of entering the camp to shoot the Colonel and the man he had kicked and beaten through the jungle who had saved his life. He had not only made up Jorge but Jorge's wonderful religion, which permitted killing with a knife because Jesus had been pierced by nails. He had even made up the three missions he could not tell me about.

He was black. He panhandled from a wheelchair. But what had disabled him and when? Had he made up the nurse's slap and hip-hopping like a rabbit and cursing his parents for not helping him die? Was all that agony a fiction? Having come to believe Jimmy's story, incredible as it was, it is, now, more difficult to believe that he had made it up than that it never happened.

Sept. 27. "Unless you get proof to the contrary," Adele says, "You have to accept the records as true."

I don't say anything. We are at home, lying on our bed, a king-size mattress on the floor of our living room, surrounded by a two-foot high alabaster bear, a grandfather clock, stopped at 6:50 since 1971, a photograph of Bob Dylan in the rain. On our stereo, John Coltrane is running "My Favorite Things" through the jungle, knotting it around trees, lacing it with vines. Overhead, our mobile shifts and shifts and shifts again, red and white and blue.

"In 1975, Jimmy joins the Army. Thirty days later he's discharged."

"Drug addiction," I say.

"Drug addiction's a good reason. The Army doesn't want a hassle. They say, 'If you don't fight us, we'll give you an honorable.'"

"Makes sense."

"So Jimmy's eighteen. He's out of the Army. Later, an auto accident, a gun shot wound, he's paralyzed. As an honorably discharged veteran, he is treated by the V.A. He's around a lot of men who've been paralyzed in Vietnam. He doesn't want to face who he really is and what really happened to him, so he takes their stories for his own."

"But the records say Jimmy's from Michigan. Jimmy doesn't talk like he's from Michigan. He talks like he's from Texas. If he's from Michigan, how'd he know Duane Thomas and Calvin Hill were the running backs for the Dallas Cowboys in 1969?"

"You don't want to believe the story's not true."

"Damn right. If his story's not true, I don't have a book."

"You have a book. It's just different."

Sept. 28. I like Adele's theory. But I reread the manuscript. Jimmy's paralysis seems real, and his reaction to it deeply involves his having been wounded in Vietnam. It is hard to believe he could have taken something that painful and personal and woven it around a lie. It is hard to believe he could, then, recount this lie so seamlessly, without stumbling or pause.

now, I am stuck. I don't know how to move forward, and I am too involved with this project to jump into anything else.

The solutions I think of seem outweighed by their problems. I could fictionalize what I have. "Depressed, cynical, yuppie lawyer meets a crippled, homeless person and..." still seems an attractive premise. But my present frame of mind is unlikely to come up with the redemptive ending the market likes. "...[L]earns he doesn't know shit about what cynical is" will not do. I would prefer not to present as "depressing" and "repellant" again. I was counting on becoming a new Bob, warming as many hearts as "Rocky."

I have considered the post-modern: a "Jimmy" character lives his life as a "wounded veteran," an "I" lives his as a "lawyer-writer;" one story dissolves into another; the nature of reality and fiction and self are questioned. Already in my "true" narrative, I have decided to change some names, create composite characters, alter time sequences, make-up dialogue. Why should this make me an "artist" and Jimmy "crazy," me a credit to society and him a sociopath? Interesting. Trendy. Some critic somewhere might like such a book. But I believe there is a reality to Jimmy and a reality to me that the most powerful book would investigate.

I have thought about journalism. But uncovering Jimmy's true story would mean traveling to Waxahachie and Michigan, interviewing doctors and neighbors, reviewing court records and newspaper files. I don't have the time, the money, or the inclination for that. Besides, what would I have when I was done? It would not be as if I had discovered who killed Kennedy or set the Reichstag fire. And I still feel obligated to Jimmy. I don't want to write something destructive to him. If he needs to be a wounded veteran, what right do I have to take this away?

Adele thinks my involvement with Jimmy makes as good a story as his story of his life. She has urged me to emphasize my role in the narrative. I have resisted because, to me, my life seems ordinary and my problems trivial compared to his. Now, with him gone, my character gains lines. But if that is my way out, until I hear from Jimmy, let him review the records and respond, I have neither an ending nor a point of view. The work remains unfocused, incomplete, without message or emotional release. I have to wait.

Oct. 11. I tell Max about the military records.

"Outrageous," he says.

Grease drips from the ducks hung in the front window of the Ming Mong Villa. Crabs scoot about in their murky tank. We have been having lunch together for forty years. Hot dogs and ice water before Saturday matinees. Hoagies and beer after playing ball in the park. Anything we could get our hands on when we were stoned. The best parts of our conversations still have to do with *Tales from the Crypt* and "In Paradise," high school basketball greats and minor sixties socio-political figures. Only he and I together can erect our particular verbal collage. Without him, the part of me built upon attendance at "The Party the Rolling Stones Didn't Come To" would vanish like the smoke from Ming Mong's wok.

Now he dips his Kung Pao shrimp in the hot mustard. "Maybe Jimmy forgot to mention he re-enlisted in seventy-five. Maybe it took the Army thirty days to find out he was crippled. 'Stand-up when you salute, soldier!' 'That's a little difficult, sir.'"

"Like 'Sergeant Bilko' when they inducted that chimp!"

"Private Harry Speak-up."

I grin at the magic we have worked again. The present is stricken from the record. "Presto-chango! Gentlemen, for your enjoyment. Eight o'clock, Tuesday night, 1956."

Oct. 5. Adele gives me a collection of writings by Phyllis Greenacre, a New York psychoanalyst. In her paper, "The Impostor," Greenacre writes of the "very special type of liar who *imposes* on others... (an) identity, either borrowed from some actual person or fabricated according to some imaginative conception of himself." Imposters, she has found, are often physically or sexually handicapped and present themselves as someone wealthier, more accomplished, or more powerful to overcome feelings of helplessness and failure.

Greenacre also addresses the importance of the audience for the imposter. Some require "emotional support from someone who especially believes in and nourishes [them]," in order to carry out their fraud. But the audience is often less a victim than an unconscious co-conspirator. It wants to believe, because its needs are being satisfied. Impostors seeking an important role within a society, she notes, are most successful in turbulent times, when people hope for saviors. So, it would seem, imposters like Jimmy, if he is one, who play to smaller crowds, would do best with people, like me, who are personally unsettled.

And Greenacre has written on "The Relation of the Imposter to the Artist," another subject of relevance. She points out that many impostors' performances are rich enough to be considered works of art. Like the imposter, the artist is two people: "the personally oriented" and "the creative self," and both artists and impostors "hunger...for completion" to achieve a "satisfying identity..."

Oct. 20. A quadriplegic in a motorized wheelchair goes from table to table across Frenzy's back room. People shake their heads. One...two...three... I am his fourth stop. I reach into my pocket for a quarter. Instead of change, he asks me to help him urinate.

The bathroom has one toilet and one sink. Crumpled paper towels litter the floor. A hole has been kicked into one wall. Among the graffiti:

RACISTS, SEXISTS, ANTI-GAY PEOPLE, FUCK YOU;
THOSE WHO HATE OTHER PEOPLE HATE THEMSELVES;
THERE IS ONLY ONE RACE, THE HUMAN RACE;

WE ARE NOT ONLY ACCOUNTABLE FOR WHAT WE DO BUT, ALSO, WHAT WE DO NOT.

I follow the man's instructions. I unzip his fly. I remove the plastic bottle from his backpack and unscrew its cap. I hold the bottle to his penis. The man asks my name, how long I have been in Berkeley. I have locked the door, but I keep between him and it, so he can not prevent my flight. I consider the depth of the man's courage and of his humiliation. I worry that I am grinding the bottle too hard into his belly. When the stream comes, I feel it strong and warm through the plastic. When it stops, I empty the bottle, rinse, and flush. In my nervousness and tension, I have spilled urine on the man. I dip a paper towel in warm water and cleanse him. I recognize that, if I had not known Jimmy, I would have shaken my head "No." I feel expanded as a human being. But when the man leaves, I wash and wash and wash my hands.

Oct. 22. I have been reading about impostors.

In Cleveland, a woman who won gold medals in the Olympics in the nineteen-thirties turned out, at her death, to have been male. On Los Angeles's Skid Row, a man passed away who had spent the last two years passing as the barely known ex-welterweight champion, Tony Demarco. In Walnut Creek, a fellow has successfully been borrowing money from and scoring with young women by claiming to be a member of the Grateful Dead. In the ninth century, Joan (or Joanna) served two years as Pope, before being discovered when she gave birth to a child. George Psalmanazer, who was probably French, was acclaimed by Dr. Samuel Johnson and eighteenth century London as a Japanese expert on Formosa, because of his mastery of its history, geography, alphabet, and language, all of which he had invented. Count Cagliostro, who was neither a "Count" nor a "Cagliostro" but an alchemist, forger, con man, astrologer, prophet, miracle-cure physician, and founder of the Egyptian Masonic Lodges, so fascinated Goethe that *he* assumed a false identity in an effort to learn more about him. Sir Henry Morton Stanley, the "discoverer" of Livingstone, was so ashamed of his illegitimacy that he invented an adoptive family for himself. Prince Michael Romanoff, the aristocratic White Russian owner of a popular Hollywood restaurant, was actually Brooklyn's Harry Gerguson. Andre Malraux, described in the biographical note to *Man's Fate* as a veteran of hand-to-hand combat in the Canton revolution and Commissioner of Propaganda for the insurgents, had, in fact, left Indochina long before its outbreak, having gone there originally to steal artifacts from Cambodian temples. William Faulkner, who posed as English in order to enlist in the Royal Canadian Air Force, did not let World War I's having ended before he saw combat prevent him from returning to Mississippi, limping, wearing his unearned pilot's wings and uniform, and letting it be known, in an affected British accent, that he had been shot down by the Boche. Ferdinand Waldo Demara, Jr., a tenth grade drop-out from Lawrence, Massachusetts, found successful employment as Martin Godagart, a high school teacher in Maine; Brother M. Jerome, a novitiate in a Trappist monastery; Robert Linton French, Ph.D., Dean of the School of Philosophy at Gannon College; Ben W. Jones, assistant warden at Huntsville State Prison in Texas (where Jimmy's judge would have sentenced him to had he not joined the military); and Joseph Cyr, M.D., a Canadian naval surgeon (as whom he operated on at least three wounded soldiers) and had his career memorialized by the movie "The Great Imposter," where he was portrayed by Tony Curtis (himself born Bernard Schwartz.)

    My favorite, though, was Stephen Jacob Weinberg (or, as he preferred, Stanley Clifford Weyman,) who, with no education beyond high school, successfully passed himself off as "a lieutenant in the French Navy, several doctors of medicine and two psychiatrists, a number of officers in the United States Navy—ranging in rank from lieutenant to admiral—four or five United States Army Officers, a couple of lawyers, the State

Department Naval Liaison Officer, an aviator, a sanitation expert, many consuls-general, and a United Nations expert on Balkan and Asian affairs." Weinberg was entertained by President Harding at the White House, served as Pola Negri's personal physician, organized Rudolph Valentino's funeral, acted as personal adviser (and interpreter) for Princess Fatima of Afghanistan, and lectured medical conferences on how to improve psychiatric treatment in penal institutions—recommendations, the author of his story points out, he may well have benefited from in his later years.

I found Weinberg in St. Clair McKelway's *The Big Little Man From Brooklyn,* a charming account: light, affectionate, bemused. I would love to write such a piece myself. But Weinberg never worked in McKelway's office; they never had coffee together. And McKelway knew from the outset who and what Weinberg was. No deceptions and reversals shook his authorial ground. McKelway could set himself at the start as a detached, though admiring, biographer and work to conclusion in that pose. And Jimmy is no Weinberg. He does not flit from colorful role to colorful role. He has no gold-braided, epauleted uniforms in his closet, no cutaway coats or rented Pierce-Arrows. He seeks no newsworthy events to cast himself in. He sits in his chair, on his corner, his performance internal, private. Unless you asked, you might not know it was going on. Another book I came across may help me more.

In 1942, Joseph Mitchell published "Professor Seagull," a profile of Joe Gould, in *The New Yorker.* Gould was, then, fifty-three. Descended from a prominent New England family, a graduate of Harvard College, he was a five-foot-four, 100-pound, toothless, wild-haired, bushy-bearded, homeless, alcoholic panhandler, the self-proclaimed "last of the bohemians," who had been bouncing around Greenwich Village for twenty-five years, while writing *An Oral History of Our Times,* the world's longest manuscript—9,000,000 words and growing—eleven times the length of *The Bible*—set down longhand in hundreds of copy books, usually stored in friends' apartments and studios across the Village, but deposited for the duration of the War, for protection against bombing, in the cellar of a chicken farm on Long Island.

Mitchell's piece made Gould a minor celebrity. His panhandling receipts picked up. Taverns let him hang around because he brought tourists in. An anonymous benefactress began sending him a stipend for room and board to allow him to complete his book. But in 1957, when Gould died, the *Oral History* could not be found. *Joe Gould's Secret*, published in 1965, is Mitchell's account of his relationship with Gould after the appearance of "Professor Seagull" and how he came to believe—but kept to himself—that Gould had no manuscript or, rather, had only three or four sections, which he wrote and rewrote over and over again.

Oct. 26. I had sent my agent the Vietnam portion of the manuscript. He replies that, unless I "believe to [my] bones" Jimmy's story is true, there is no book.

Oct. 29. N.P.R. reports the story of Robert Fife. Fife, a veteran of 130 combat missions in Vietnam, had been shot down in 1966, captured by the Viet Cong, and imprisoned for fifteen days, caged, beaten, urinated upon, until he escaped. He came back to Utah, married, had two children, became a successful businessman. But, at age forty-six, he committed suicide, leaving behind a 450 page manuscript he had been unable to publish, detailing his experiences, a victim, his psychiatrist said, of post-traumatic stress disorder, another casualty of the war.

A local newspaperman obtained permission from Fife's widow to revise his manuscript. Researching it, he learned that Robert Fife had served eight months in the Navy, but none in Vietnam, before being discharged as medically unfit due to a childhood injury.

The New York Times has reported that both the founder of the Vietnam War Museum in San Antonio, who'd claimed to have been a SEAL—the only commando unit Jimmy said compared to his Bumblebees—and his top assistant, independently and unknown to each other, had fabricated their war service histories. I am beginning to feel like one of those people who believe the moon landing took place in a television studio. Combat occurred in Southeast Asia, didn't it? They didn't make that up?

Nov. 8. Amelia has seen Jimmy. He was being pushed across Martin Luther King Way by a friend. He said he'd just got back. She said we'd been worried; he should stop by the office. "Definitely," he said.

I call Adele. "Great. Now you won't have to go to Waxahachie. And you'll have an ending for your book."
"If you have an ending you like, tell me what it is. I'll have Jimmy make it up."
"Oh, it has to be true."
"If it works, what difference does it make how 'true' it is?" I am being difficult. I am not looking forward to seeing Jimmy.

Jimmy does not come to the office.

Nov. 9. When I turn the corner, Jimmy is in his wheelchair in front of Wells Fargo. He waves when he sees me. "How's it going, buddy?"
"Good to see you," I say, "You're fired."
Jimmy says that, after the V.A. doctors treated his bladder infection, they flew him to Michigan, where bullet fragments were removed from his spine. While he was recovering, he had to lie on his stomach for thirty days. He feels badly it looks like he ran out on me, but they would not let him call. (He "snuck" the one I received.) When he was released, he made the government fly him to Texas to see his family. (He does not say who kept him from the phone in Texas.) Now he

Fully Armed

is back, living in a motel because his cottage was damaged by the earthquake. Tomorrow, he will bring me his military records, his medals, and eighteen tapes he made.

"Great," I say. I do not arrange a time to meet. I do not mention the records I have. This is fascinating, I think, Will I hear on the tapes how he and Robert Jordan blew up that bridge? How he and *The Pequod* hunted down that white whale?

Jimmy's sneakers have holes. I have the sudden thought that he can walk. I see him as a youthful thirty-two, not a war-ravaged thirty-six.

Nov. 10. Jimmy does not come to the office.

As I head to my garage, at the end of the day, I see Jimmy being wheeled up Center Street by a husky man with an Afro and sunglasses. Jimmy is slouched in his chair, lifeless, inert.

I am not angry. I do not feel cheated or abused. Jimmy has given me good times. Whatever the truth—whatever was so terrible about his life that he had to make up a substitute—he has enriched mine. I cross the street to his side.

Jimmy apologizes. He had to go to San Francisco to apply for a replacement wheelchair. He can come in Monday, or we can meet over the weekend. He has the money he owes me, and he wants to return a cassette recorder I'd lent him.

I say I'd like to get together. I show him *The Veteran* and suggest we advertise for men who knew of the Bumblebees. I say I have been learning about Vietnam by reading *A Bright and Shining Lie,* Neil Sheehan's Pulitzer Prize winning account of John Patrick Vann, an American military leader, who had falsified *his* past in order to impress correspondents reporting on the war. I mention I have Jimmy's military records.

He does not blink. He has records too. Also bullets they took out of his back. He compliments my new, black Western hat.

Nov. 14. Jimmy still has not come to the office. This morning,

I crossed Shattuck so I would not have to walk by him. When I leave, at five-thirty, he is still on his corner. "You're working late," I say.

"Things are bad, buddy. Someone broke into my room and stole my stuff. I'm homeless again."

Jimmy is glad I stopped. He'd seen me avoid him. ("I had errands," I say.) He thinks a lot of me. He appreciates my belief and faith. But things are weird. When we get back to the book, we will be getting into strange shit. Some cover-up is going on. Records are around saying he was in the military only thirty-two days. His real records are classified, but he has a print-out, plus his Medal of Valor and two Purple Hearts and his bullets and his scrapbook in a locker at the Ashby BART station. "My story's true, Bob. It's important you believe that." Jimmy is speaking rapidly. He is sweating. He does not look at me directly. "When I was in the hospital, people said I was crazy."

Okay, I think, this is it. I kneel beside the wheelchair and unzip my briefcase. On the plaza in front of B. Dalton's, purple-haired, black-jacketed punks strut like grackles. A steel drum reverberates under the eaves of the Great Western Building. I show Jimmy his birth date, his place of enlistment, his service resignation.

"That's my signature," he says, like he has never seen this document before, "But how'm I getting a service-connected disability without no service disability?"

Good point, I think. But I don't know you *are* getting a service-connected disability.

I stand up. I return the folder to my bag. I tell Jimmy about Robert Fife.

He shakes his head. "Sometimes I wonder if I'm dreaming all this shit. But if it wasn't true, I'd be too embarrassed to come back to Berkeley."

We plan to meet at Frenzy tomorrow at one o'clock. He will bring his records.

Fully Armed

That evening, my brother calls. He has been reading oral histories of Vietnam veterans. He has found no mention of the Bumblebees, but a former SEAL recounts missions, while supplied with morphine and Dexadrine, with a Provisional Reconnaissance Unit composed of murderers, rapists, and thieves, bailed out of prison by the C.I.A. (and paid according to how many ears they brought in.) And the author of a book on the Phoenix program, my brother tells me, became interested in its operation, in part, because his own father's military records had been altered, so as to conceal where he had served and what he had done.

Nov. 15. 12:30. I arrive early, sip my espresso, and review my notes. I am disturbed that Jimmy will not admit his story is untrue. If his story is true and his records have been falsified, do I have to worry about the C.I.A.? Thoughts of car bombs and poisoned chocolates and telescopic rifles in book depository windows (and how I will hold my hats up) occur. If his story isn't true, do I have to worry about him? Now I am a good guy, but if I don't support him, will he turn on me? There are frightening people on these streets. I had one client, Lonnie Goode, who believed a surgeon had filled his abdomen with toxic waste. His threats frightened the doctor so badly he fled the state. Then I learned Lonnie had consulted another lawyer because he believed I had altered his hospital records since they did not mention the implanting of these poisons. Every time I read about one of those men who goes into the school or bank with his AK-47, I wonder what Lonnie is doing.

1:15. Jimmy has not arrived. I worry that making him explore his past and questioning what he tells me may upset the balance by which he maintains his grip on the world. If so, what can I do? Jimmy seems too involved with me for me to simply walk away. If I wanted to call things off, I would not know how.

1:30. Jimmy hurries in. He is glad I waited. The Red Cross has been trying to prevent the pre-earthquake homeless from getting benefits that were intended only for its victims. He had taken in a rent receipt for his cottage to prove he qualified as one of the compensable dispossessed—even though he was 2000 miles away when the earthquake happened.

I give Jimmy my new position. "I can't tell what's true. It's you on one side, the government on the other, and me in the middle. But, damn it, there's a story here. You're homeless. You're in a fucking wheelchair. If you want to go on, bring me your documents and the cassettes. Till then, we'll talk, get reacquainted, and figure out what we're doing."

Jimmy pauses. "Okay, Bob. As long as you keep an open mind, you don't have to believe me. I will prove it to you."

"And if you made it up, it's so good, we'll do a series: westerns, war stories, sci-fi."

I am relieved. Jimmy is not as wired as yesterday. I tell him everything we did to find him. "We even called Waxahachie information and got your father's number."

"757-1660," he says.

I look at my notes. The number is correct. Not a bad guess for a guy from Ypsilanti.

Nov. 16. Jimmy and I have coffee again. He is eager to talk more about life on the street. I wonder if this eagerness is an admission his Vietnam stories are false. He has brought me nothing. He says his cottage has been locked because of earthquake damage. He does not mention his BART locker. He does not whip out his wallet and show me identification proving he was born in 1953. I do not ask him to.

While we are talking, an ex-client wanders in. Dr. Zing is sixty-five years old. He wears Brooks Brothers suits with elbow patches and has white ringlets to his shoulders. He is active in the Sanctuary movement and hosts a cable t.v. show on extraterrestrials. In his case, he had complained an exposure to electromagnetic waves as an office temp had caused him dizziness, fainting spells, and boils. All physical tests were negative; he refused all psychological tests as racist, sexist and ageist; he refused to speak to one physician but had his history related by his "spiritual advisor," who turned out to be a schizophrenic on a day-pass from Alta Bates Hospital. After I obtained an excellent settlement, Dr. Zing filed complaints about me with the judge, the Bar Association, and the Anti-Defamation League, accusing me of incompetence, fraud, and duress. He and Jimmy nod.

"You know that guy?" I say.

"Yeah. His elevator don't go all the way to the top floor."

So we go on.

So much Jimmy does is reasonable and so many of his responses appropriate, it is hard to believe he is crazy. He knew his disappearance hurt me. He picked up on my avoiding him. He brought up the money he owed without my asking. He spots Dr. Zing as a fruitcake when corporate sponsors give him air time. Jimmy is aware, perceptive, open. He thinks clearly, demonstrates insight, has a sense of humor. He has found a successful way of coping with the street. If he is crazy, what kind of craziness is this? There may be delusion, but is there harm?

But where is the book? One day in the life of a crippled street person? A novel from such a character's point-of-view? I don't feel I could write either, and, if there is no book, why am I talking to Jimmy? But if I would only talk to him in order to write a book, what kind of person am I?

Dec. 1. Jimmy has bought me a cassette recorder to replace mine, which was stolen. He has not repaid my loan, but when he talks about his debt, he adds the twenty dollars I paid Los Medanos for his transcript. While I'd like to think this acknowledgment demonstrates his honorable nature, I recognize it may stem from a conscience guilty for wasting my time. Or it may just be good PR, bonding me more deeply to him and setting up some juicier scam. I also note the fact (but do not dwell upon it) that he no longer mentions his records or medals or bullets or tapes.

Mainly, we seem to be in the process of becoming—it seems strange to say it—friends. He tells me how life in the shelter is getting him down. I tell him it's a phase; you have been through worse; hang in there. A few days later, I bitch about the frustrations of dealing with claims examiners who won't return phone calls and clients who renege on settlement agreements, and he repeats this advice to me.

I seem to have become an important focal point for Jimmy. I am this responsible, middle-class professional, who treats him like a human being. Well, I can do that. We'll see where the writing goes.

Dec. 6. Jimmy tells me his mother is coming to visit. Many months ago, he had mentioned a half-sister in Pittsburg. I ask if that is where his mother will stay. "Damn, Bob, you do remember."

"Am I going to meet her?"

"Sure."

"If I do, the first thing I'm going to ask is how old you are."

Jimmy laughs.

Dec. 9. The movie "Born on the 4th of July" has opened to tremendous publicity. If we do manage a book, I wonder, will truly disabled veterans be offended by this false one? Well, Jimmy is disabled. He is homeless. He's not a total fraud. *The Times*, in its article on the Vietnam War Museum, quoted a veteran: "First the American people drove us into the closet. Now they are letting us out and...lots more people coming out of the closet than went in. I don't get it."

Dec. 14. Adele suggests that everything Jimmy says is untrue.

From his mother's visiting, to his spending Thanksgiving at a friend's house in the Berkeley hills, to his thirty-dollar-a-night motel rooms, to his now living on East 80th Avenue.

I had been holding the line at only the "important" things being untrue. Vietnam. His marksmanship. Killing Erwin Barksdale. Maybe his wife and child. "He has to live somewhere," I say. "What difference does it make if it's East 80th or Sixth Street?

"I'm saying the truth may have no meaning for Jimmy. Words may just pop out of his head like breath or dreams."

Dec. 22. Christmas is doing well by Jimmy. Each day he displays for me more items his clientele has given him: thermal socks, an old black suit, a German chocolate cake he can barely lift (and which he offers me.) (I, the successful professional, have received a tin of nuts from an orthopedist I send $12,000 worth of business a year and a box of chocolates from my photocopying service.) He has enough money to treat himself to the Hyatt-Regency for the weekend. (He does not mention visiting his mother.) Two-thirds of the spokes on one of his wheels have snapped; he can't move forward or back; he is in danger of toppling over, but he doesn't want to pack it in and miss what else may be coming. A friend with a liftvan may pick him up later. He may call 911 and order a replacement chair. "Ain't no problem. Just another chapter for Jimmy."

While we talk, the husky man in the sunglasses leans against the wall. This, I have learned, is Mo, another vet, Jimmy's "road-dog," providing him protection and aid. Mo lives in a residential treatment center, but when Jimmy is doing well, Mo stays with him and shares his bounty. Every morning, Mo wheels Jimmy to his corner. Every night, he wheels him home.

Dec. 26. Jimmy is back on the corner in a "loaner" wheelchair with more gifts: a sweater, a 100% cashmere scarf, a used leather jacket, which he will sell because it is too small, a bottle of Valium from the V.A., and a foot-long, inch-thick candy cane he gives to a little girl. Samantha, a pretty woman with long, brown hair is chatting with him. He says he did visit his mother. (Now it is the Hyatt-Regency he does not mention.) Except for his father's absence, it was the first time the whole family had been together in ten or twelve years. (Huh? I think. Were *all* his sisters there?) His mother wants to give him a haircut, clean him up, and take him home.

Dec. 28. I hang out with Jimmy. In half an hour, three people hand him bills and several others change without his asking. A woman, her hair in beaded corn-rows, gives him a tin of homemade brownies. "Did you get all you want for Christmas, sister?" Jimmy asks. "Things I want for Christmas, they can't give," she says, "Peace in the world." A man with a headset on pulls two pairs of pants out of a gym bag. "I know you don't want no more than two dollars for that," Jimmy says. Jimmy gives the man a brownie, saying it has marijuana in it, and the man throws a t-shirt with Groucho Marx's picture into the deal. An A.C. Transit driver tells Jimmy a social service agency has found her brother a house for $170 a month. They share the hope he stays off "stuff." "If he's got a habit, I got a habit too," the driver says, "Because he's my brother, and I got to support him." Jimmy exchanges news about FEMA money with a woman with a plastic garbage bag slung over each shoulder. He tells a woman with pock-marked cheeks where Chief has gone. He instructs an Asian tourist how to get into Wells Fargo. A tall, bearded man brings Jimmy two bolts for his wheelchair. Jimmy identifies a blond man in army fatigues as a vet who has a white rat in each pocket. He calls them by name and they come. "He's got a good heart," Jimmy says. "Plus you got to find something to keep you going." A plump girl in a leather mini-skirt and her boyfriend with shoulder length hair and a Black Sabbath t-shirt arrive. "Be with you in a minute, Samantha," Jimmy says. "I'm conferring with my lawyer." They go off around the corner until I am gone.

Dec. 29. I feel good. I am writing regularly. Jimmy has been telling me about the street. My only frustration is, when I want a description or a characterization or a punchy, summative phrase, no matter how I ask, he cannot supply one. If this was fiction, I could make it up. But this *is* fiction, I think, part of it—maybe most—so why can't I?

The role of truth in this process is fascinating. Despite the military records and the contradictions and the various proofs that never materialize, part of me still believes Jimmy. "What a book you'll have!" this part keeps saying. The rewards, if Jimmy's story is true—financial and personal—keep this belief alive. Does this mean I am living a fiction too? But most of me assumes that I am witness to a masquerade and that I must write from this position.

I still don't know how. Joseph Mitchell did not know until after "Professor Seagull" appeared that *The Oral History* did not exist. If he had, would he have written about Joe Gould at all? How less kindly would he have treated him? How much would the truth have hurt Gould? There would have been no free drinks or stipend; instead of celebration, he would have received sly winks and whispers as he made his rounds. In effect, I am trying to write "Professor Seagull" and *Joe Gould's Secret* simultaneously. This is not something the same person can do. What Mitchell learned between the two pieces changed him. It altered his relationship with his subject and the point-of-view from which he reported. I have not thought out how believing Jimmy's story false will affect what or how I write. I will not lie, but I do not know how best to present the truth or what consequences that presentation will have.

Jimmy, meanwhile, is abuzz. He complains of dizziness. Once, he says, he almost fell from his chair, but he is excited to be working on the book again. He uses it to square accounts with people or institutions that mistreated him. He finds validation in it as a person of worth. When I tell him that to be most successful the book will need a happy ending, he speaks of returning to school and getting his degree. (Max says that, when he was a kid, he wanted to be a musician because that way he could stay up all night, hang out in dives, and get loaded. The last time we met, he spoke wistfully of owning a small business. "Dive burn-out," he called it. "Even street people have mid-life crises.")

But with Jimmy something always jars me. Yesterday, I heard him tell Samantha, "I don't want you going up there alone." "What if I take Mo?" she said. Two hours later, she was back, handing Jimmy twenty dollars. Is he dealing drugs? Is that where his Valium went? Is that what the Black Sabbath fan wanted? Or am I being a suspicious, racist pig?

Jan. 2. I have a new idea. Conceptual art.

I will write Jimmy's autobiography as he tells it. I will set Max up as Weinberg Press, with a post office box address and a telephone answering machine. Weinberg Press will publish *My Story* by Jimmy Don Polk. Jimmy will sell it on his corner from his chair. The media will receive promotional copies. Reporters and camera crews will flock to him. If my reaction is any indication, the public will respond with sympathy and admiration. Donations will pour in. Production companies will clamor for rights to make a Movie-of-the-Week. A desire to know more will develop. Investigations will be provoked. The truth will be revealed. The public and the media will turn. Anger and vilification will follow. Meanwhile, I am writing this down. This completes the story. This is the true book.

My idea comes from reading about Marcel Duchamp and his influence on our understanding of Art.[1] Before Duchamp displayed his bottle rack and his inverted urinal, Art had been something hanging on a wall. After Duchamp, Art became

---

[1] Interestingly, Duchamp, himself, was an impostor. Part of his mystique and authority came from his having renounced Art for Life and ceasing creative work for thirty years. After his death, however, it was revealed that, during this time, he had been secretly constructing an entire tableau in the apartment across from his—one whose execution and substance seemed to challenge everything he previously had said and done.

anything—even shadow, even light or thought—which heightened awareness or moved emotions or altered the way in which one viewed the world.

My Story would fulfill Duchamp's precepts. For one thing, it would examine the question of what makes a book. That it is sold in stores and not from wheelchairs? That it is published by Harper & Row and not by Max? That it is written by an Author and not a Disabled Street Person? (Or a Lawyer, satisfying his desire to be an Author by hiding behind a Disabled Street Person?) It would ask why Jimmy should be prevented from telling his life story just because he isn't a writer and can't afford self-publishing and it isn't true. Why should someone's life story have to be true, as long as it is the story they have selected as their own? If this story is true enough to be believed or true enough for fiction (as my lawyer-friend suggested) or true for other people (as Adele's analysis proposed), isn't that enough? What is a book but an arrangement of words on paper? What does it attempt but to provoke responses from its readers? What are its author's aims but the attraction of a few dollars and a shot at fame? Wouldn't *My Story* satisfy these criteria?

My book about *My Story* would, also, ask that the public see that Jimmy has done nothing *to* it. Jimmy has been himself. The public has manufactured its own adulatory froth and whipped itself into outrage for revenge. Their attacks might be painful for Jimmy, but if we proceed, it would be because he decided his gain would be worth his risk.

Or maybe besides being a paranoid, racist bastard, I am out of my head.

Jan. 3. Jimmy does not appear for a two o'clock appointment we had made earlier. I am not worried. I work on other material. He had said he had to see someone about fixing his chair, and Mo says he is expecting him too.

Jimmy's latest news has been that, because his cottage is not ready, "they" have put "them" in a place on 62nd Street.

And he was arrested for indecent exposure when a policeman spotted him changing his pants in an alley to get ready for a date. (But other policemen in the station knew him, so the charges were dropped.) And that his mother will be visiting Berkeley this week. ("Great!" I had said. "Let me take you both to lunch.")

Jan. 5. Jimmy has not been around. Chances for lunch with his mother look slim.

Jan. 10. I am out of the office all afternoon. When I get home, Amelia has left a message that Jimmy called. I dial the number he left.

Jimmy is in "a lockdown unit" in the V.A. Hospital in Palo Alto. "Nuts" are on his floor. He is full of "bugs." He is hooked to five different tubes. He talks of tumors, plastic surgery, an alcoholism that must be cured. "The doctors want to re-make my body and my mind. I guess it will be for the best." He sounds weak and tired but speaks clearly and directly. "I was not going to abandon you this time, Bob, no lie. Your calling makes my day."

"Do you need anything?"

"A carton of Benson-Hedges mentholateds and some gossip magazines."

Jan. 15. Adele and I visit Jimmy. He is lying on a gurney, stomach down. He wears blousy, burgundy pajamas. Blue plastic wraps protect his feet. A catheter connects him to a urine bag. "I'm messed up, buddy," he says.

Jimmy says that his dizziness and passing out had continued. He had woken up on a park bench, in the rain, in the middle of the night, broke, filthy, smelly, soaking wet, talking to God. He promised God that, if he made it through the night, he would go to the hospital. The next morning, he rolled up to Shattuck, ran into a friend who lent him twenty dollars, and took BART to the end of the line. The bus to Palo Alto wouldn't pick him up because he was too dirty. He couldn't get a cab. The hospital wouldn't send someone. "I almost said, 'Fuck it,' and went back to the street. Then I said, 'I won't quit now.'" He got back on BART. He rode it two stops in the opposite direction. He caught two more buses. When he arrived at the hospital, he was so weak and dizzy and looked so bad, they thought he was going to die. He had an infected bladder, an infected kidney, and an infected liver. He had bed sores from his chair. A couple were "that bad kind of green." Now his eyes are clear; his skin glows. He has committed to a three-month treatment program. When he did, the doctor, who had seen the number of "Left Hospital Against Medical Advice"s in his records, joked, "Are you sure you're the real Jimmy Polk?"

He is the same Jimmy, with his wit and sociability and canniness. He jokes with the two other patients in his room— a middle-aged man about to be discharged following a hernia repair and a seventy-year-old afflicted by alcoholic dementia— and their wives. When Adele needs the Ladies Room, Jimmy directs her. When we want lunch, he leads us to the vending machines. He has scouted out a phone he may be able to use for free.

Jimmy says he must stop living "on that danger edge." He loves the street, but it will kill him. He must find out why he's drawn there. He wants a career. He wants to help people. He recognizes he is good with them.

"Yeah!" Adele says. "It's time to put your energies to something positive."

"Sounds good," I say. I wonder if our book will manage a happy ending after all. If his right words and good qualities can overcome his handicaps.

Before we leave, a man with a damaged larynx bums a cigarette from Jimmy. Jimmy tells us—as the man nods in agreement—that his disability is the result of having been stabbed in the throat in Waxahachie by Wanda Mae Favors, who Jimmy had been to high school with. "My class voted her Most Likely to Go to Women's Prison," he says.

Driving home, I tell Adele I was glad I was there. "If Jimmy had come out and told me he'd been hospitalized with someone who'd been knifed by his next door neighbor, that would have been the final straw."

Jan. 17. So what kind of relationship do Jimmy and I have? What kind do we want? What is best for him? What is best for me?

I do not believe I am overinvolved. Jimmy can make me into his "friend," but my focus can remain the book. The two are not incompatible. With all our differences, the idea of being friends is peculiar, but a case can be made. I like Jimmy. I enjoy his company. I am concerned about his welfare. I spend more time with him than most people. I *think* about him more than anybody but Adele. I drove three hours to visit him, when I have not seen people in years whom I've worked or gone to school with because I will not take the time to go into San Francisco for lunch. If he can use our friendship as an impetus to get treated—as he seems to be doing—I would be delighted. But if he does enter a treatment program and introduces me to his doctor, as promised, I will talk to that doctor with a book in mind.

If there is a danger, it is that I don't know what forms "friendship" or "loyalty" or "betrayal" take for Jimmy. At any point, wires could connect, a spark could fly, and he could turn on me. I cannot forget Lonnie Goode. But I see no paranoia or rage in Jimmy. I see someone with whom I am uniquely involved. I see a catheter stuck in him.

Jan. 22. Put everything on hold.

Jimmy calls. He is returning to Long Beach for treatment. "It's a better facility, and they want me back. I'm their top draft choice."

He is upbeat. He seems to be behaving like a reasonable patient. I will miss meeting his doctors (not to mention his

Fully Armed

mother), but I will hope for the best.
The book can wait.

THREE

While Jimmy was hospitalized in Long Beach, we exchanged letters. I sent him news of the office ("Burglars kicked in the door over the weekend, dumped drawers, stole my stamps..."), Shattuck Avenue ("A new man in a wheelchair has your corner. Glasses, mustache, missing his right leg..."), the city ("Telegraph was so freaky last night I felt safer walking in the street, with traffic, than on the sidewalk"), and personal matters ("Someone has abandoned two kittens in our garage, the first in the back seat of my car, the second, a few weeks later, jammed into a box, with newspaper stuffed on top to keep it from jumping out.") I forwarded newspaper clippings on efforts to crack down on panhandlers or clear the homeless from People's Park.

Jimmy's letters were regular, friendly, and short on hard news. They said little specific about his treatment. They made no reference to whether his story was true.

Jan. 28

What's up Buddy.

Just a few lines to let you know that I am fine but it is "Hell" down here. I am pretty busy and sometime stress out. I am trying to adjust to these surroundings but it will take time. Basically I here to get my life on the Right Track and to deal with the Fear and Tears I have about my Past. I am going through a lot of emotional feelings but this is helping me. Soon as I am out of here we will get together. I will be here 1/2 of the year but I am not running away. Kiss Adele for me and tell everyone that I said 'Hi.' Got to go. I really miss you all.

Feb. 24
Hey my Best Friend
   Thanks a lots for keeping me updated on what's going on. Tell everyone that I miss them and said Hello. I am getting better every day but this program is a strange trip. Their objective is to start us thinking like Society. It is working but Time are hard around this camp but worth the pain. I cannot leave the hospital, so I get by from help from the friend I have run across. I got to go.

March 14
Well Hello my Best Friends
   Thanks a lot for the update. Tell everyone that I said Hello and with God Help I will see everyone sometime in June near the middle or end. When I get Back to Berklery we will make up for the time I been gone with the book. They say that I am doing Great but they also tell me to slowdown and to take everything one day at a time. My program is both Good and Bad but we are making the Best out of it. for the first time in my life I am letting people Try To Help Me. There is a lot of restrictions here so I am not able to leave the grounds. The stages that I am at now is that I am dealing with my Fear, Guilt, Rejection etc.... I do see a Hell of a lot of Change in and out of me.

   I tried to prod Jimmy about the book. "I see several ways to go," I wrote: "One is that your story is true. That way, you have to show me proof. The records or scrapbook or medals or something. You have to say, "Call my mother and father. I have told them about you, and it is okay to talk." This would be a fascinating book.

"Another way is that you tell me your story is not true. You tell me what is true and where the rest came from. We discuss why you made it up and how you used it. This would be fascinating too.

"Another way is you say the story is true but you have no proof. My agent says this will not work.

"Another way is you say the story is true, but I investigate and find out it isn't. This could be a successful book too, but I don't know if you would be happy with it."

Jimmy replied five days later.

April 20.
Hello my Good Friends.
Hey, Man it was a pleasure to hear from you. Tell everyone I said Hello and to keep on smiling for me. I hope that I will be out in the middle of June but it is up to these people. I am working my ass off taking personal inventory of my self and life. I been dealing with these Ghostses of my past and my fear. These people are beginning to know me better than myself. I been thinking about the book and I *promise* we will *Finish* it. Right now this Treatment is the most important and then the Book and then School or Work. There is still a lot that I want to tell you and when we get together we will decide which way to go. Man o man I really miss you and Berkley. This place has been driving me crazy with their ways and directions. But I Feel good and have a new insight about myself. This is the first time that I haven't run away. Tell everyone that I will surprise them and that I am thinking of you guys. Got to go.

I did not mention the book again.

On July 3rd, Jimmy called. He had been discharged from

the hospital and was an outpatient. While there, he had kept a journal, which he was sending me. It would answer all my questions.

The journal was accompanied by a letter that began: FORGIVE ME. BUT THIS IS THE SHOCKING TRUTH.

Hello Buddy. After you read this your feeling or opinion of me might change. This is a letter of confession and this is painful for me. But your friendship mean so much too me that I will tell you the truth and I hope you will try to understand the whys, and I hope that we can make somethings out of the life that I have lead and the life that I have to live. I hope that you can still write about it because I want to share my life with the whole world. OK. I am Very Sorry and I Mean that for lying to you and if I did hurt your feeling or trust I am truly sorry.
When you met me on the Street I was insane. But I myself wanted to be that way because I didn't want to live. I was also doing drug and drinking. I thought that doing these things was helping me to be the nice Guy that I was and still is and I was trying to escape being in the wheelchair.
After years and years of trying to understand why all this shit happening to me I gave up. I thought that God was trying to hurt me for a reason that I didn't know. I got tired of trying to found out why and I couldn't. I tried so many times to regain my faith in God and myself but after things didn't change I kept slipping backward until I finally slip all the way to the Street of Berkeley where you saw me.
I chose to live in a fantasy world which I created myself. This gave me a reason to live and to pretend to be happy because after I became paralyzed my whole world change. So to deal with this, I started to drink and to do drug to invent these lie inside my head to feel important and worth something. I was trying my damness to make everyone and myself happy. And I did one Hell of a job day to night every day. But

in the process I did lie a lot. I felt good helping people Smile but I felt Bad lying to them. I pray to God that you understand this.

Bob please forgive me and lets still try to write a damn good Book. It will help a lot of people in my condition and drug addict and Homeless people. Thank you for being One of the Best friend that I had had and let me know where you would like to go from here. I am ashamed to face you or to talk to you after writing this but I will continue to work on the Book and our friendship if you like for us to. I am a Better Jimmy now. I still the same except I am free from THOSE GHOSTSES of the past.

FOUR

Jimmy Polk never served in Vietnam.
Jimmy Polk never killed Erwin Barksdale.
Jimmy's mother never came back.

I was born in Waxahachie, Texas, first—twenty-third—fifty-seven.

My parents' names were Jasper and Geri Polk. My father was a carpenter; my mother was a secretary. I have two sisters, Joanna and Annette, one older and one younger. One's a guidance counselor and one's a drug addict.

My parents fought, what seemed like, every night. They fought with fists and feet and fingernails, and once my father hit my mother with an iron. One day, when I was six or seven, I came home from school, and I seen my mother jump in a car with her bags packed. By the time I holler out her name, the car was going down the street. The memory I had was she was never coming back. My father told me, "She don't want nothing to do with you."

When she left, my daddy was in a total shock. He had lots on him, trying to raise two girls and a boy. He was working; he be tired, and he was really hurting for my mother. My feelings were all disturbed. I remember looking at the pain in my father's face and tears in my sisters' eyes and feeling I was the cause of everything. Of course, I'm hurting too, but I didn't show many tears. This is something I held inside, trying to be the little man my father wanted me to be. There was times me and him would sit up, and he would talk, and I didn't understand anything he was saying, but I knew he was hurting, and all I could do was hold him. Between my dad being hurt and my mom leaving, I was totally screw up. I still had a normal childhood, hanging around with kids, shot marbles, had a slingshot, but, deep inside, I hurt.

It was not a relaxing atmosphere. My father believed very strongly in discipline. That was the rule, and we knew it. He wasn't physically violent with us kids, but, if we did something wrong, we got our butt whipped with belts or switches off of trees. And he was always angry. *Always* angry. When my father would smile, happy, the whole house was happy. Most of the time, he wasn't like that. There is still lots of love I have for my father, but, back then, there was just as much fear. It was like being around a firecracker about to explode.

Dad remarried when I was ten or eleven. My stepmother worked for Haggar Pants. They eventually had three more daughters and a son, but she accepted us and loved us like we were her own. I don't call my stepmother "Stepmother." I call her "Momma." And I love her just like a momma. I had one that brought me into the world, and I had one that raised me, and I love them both.

But yet and still, I always felt misfortune, because I felt I wasn't really wanted. I was a pretty bright kid, but I couldn't understand, being as little as I was, why would a mother, who said she loved you, do this. And I got teased by the kids. I be in school, and everybody be singing, "Jimmy's-momma-left-him," as I'm walking down the hall. That hurted me. Me and my sisters, then, all we had was each other. We was hurting from what Momma was doing, and we was in fear of Dad. I had to find out who my momma really was. I had to confirm or disconfirm that she wasn't the *per se* 'ho, slut, not-lovin' person that people, my father, mention that she was.

When I was fifteen, my mother came back. Evidently, the girls had wrote letters, telling lies, saying that Dad was beating on them. I don't know if her agenda was to take us. All I know is I came in one day, and they telling me they fixing to go with Mom. She had remarried somebody in the military stationed in Germany. She asked if I wanted to go. I was playing football. I had a couple girlfriends. I had a nice job. I had just got a Mustang. Everything was great. Even though I was still hurting for my mother, I was still mad at her for leaving. Plus, I felt some loyalty with Dad. I stood in the yard, looking at my Mustang, and I said, "No."

Then my mother and my sisters drove off in one direction, and I jumped in my Mustang and roared off in the opposite, just stomping the gas. The police stopped me after three blocks and brought me back to my father. I was crying, and I said, "I'm gonna tell you the truth, Daddy. She doesn't love me."

A year later, things started getting distressful. I lost my girlfriend. I quit football. I broke my collarbone playing basketball. I got out of the hospital to see another girl, and I got in a wreck and tore my car up. Kids were teasing me because I got hurt and I was supposed to be so tough. And my father put me on punishment for driving a stickshift, with one arm, in the snow and wouldn't help me get my car fixed.

I called my mother through the United States overseas operator. Cost me twelve dollars, and I said, "Daddy's mistreating me. I want to stay with you." She got in contact with my uncle, her brother, telling him to get me a picture on my passport and some kinda shots. This process was in the works, and my father didn't know about it.

Then something terrible happened. I had run away from home and was staying at my mother's mother's, two blocks from us. I was laying on the couch; she came in from work, sat down beside me, kissed me. She lay her head back. She said, "I love all my grandchildren. I'm gonna get some rest." Three seconds later, she died.

I remember not bothering her, not shaking her, just walking out. I ran back to my father's house. My stepmother was there and my father. I didn't tell them my grandmother had died, and my father was bitching at me. Then one of my cousins called and said, "Grandma dead." I knew she had died, but I didn't want to believe it. I jumped up while my father was running his mouth and ran completely through a new screen door back over there. My father came over in his car, and he bitching at me because I broke the screen door. He wasn't understanding I was upset because I had lost my grandmother. I remember thinking, "Fuck, that's it. I don't believe you have any compassion or anything." That put the nail in the coffin for me to get away.

And I left.
Germany was an exciting time. I was a country boy in a new world, living a better life than what I was living. You got to remember, I had never been as far as Dallas, and here I was in Germany.

It was a joy. People were friendly. Weren't no funky stares. You wasn't followed around stores. Talking to people was exciting. Drinking beer was exciting. Smoking hash was *real* exciting.

We was there three months, and then we moved to Michigan.

Ypsilanti was a fast town.
I was living in the projects with my mother and sisters. I was working at Kentucky Fried Chicken. I was hanging around with musicians and smoking lots of weed. I went to school a little, but I quit. I was too spoiled by then to play football. I was all footballed out. I was chasing girls instead. I said, "The hell with school. I'm gonna go in the army."

I enlisted in the military. I was there thirty days, and I

rehurt my shoulder. I got a medical discharge and came back to Michigan and begun to get plumb wild. I started becoming a person looking for the good times. I learned lots of slickness. I hung around with bad people. Guys who robbed and steal, who took the easy way out and didn't believe in hard work.

I got in a bunch of mess. I escaped death one time. I was going with this young lady, her boyfriend had just got out of jail. One night we come out of a party with some friends, and as we get into our car, there's four guys with shotguns behind us, shooting out the windows, putting a hit on us. There were eight of us inside this Camaro, and I remember kicking the door open and grabbing this woman's hand and running, dragging her up the street like a caveman. When I got home, four of the guys had their guns, and they wanted to get these guys. I had never been in a situation like that. In Texas, we did our little fist-fights. But here I was in big time Gangsterland, and it was like, "Show you got some courage."

Another time I was with a guy and he robbed a dope man. I started going to bed with a sawed-off shotgun after that. When my mother saw that, she said, "I'm sending your ass to your daddy," and I was back on the plane.

Texas was okay. My father had a brand new Cadillac I knew I would get to drive.

My father was glad I was back. You got to remember, I was Daddy's son. I went to stay with him, and I got a job with Owens Corning Fiberglass within a week. It was a good job. In fact, it was the best job in Waxahachie, Texas. I started off on the line, something like a rover. I would check the glue; I would tally; sometime I would cut board. I learned all the different jobs in the department. I was earning $200, $250 a week. Back in 1976, '77, '78 that was damn good money. Plus we got an extra $100, $200 the end of each month, depending on how much fiberglass we sold.

I met my future wife walking down Frankabetto Street at Frankabetto Park. Evelyn Corrinne Hodges. The first four or five times, she wouldn't talk to me. She was fourteen or fifteen; she was going with this guy. I kept trying, kept trying. When they broke up, that was all I needed to know. I got my cousin to introduce us. When that happened, she said, "Ask my mother if I can see you." I was scared to death, but I asked her. Her mother said, "You kinda old, but if you be nice to her, it'll be okay, 'cause you gonna do what you want to do behind my back anyway." Finally, we was going together, went together, went together, and we found out she was pregnant. I didn't want my child to come into the world as no bastard, and I planned on marrying Corrinne anyway, so I asked her, and she said, "Yeah."

We had a one-bedroom apartment in the South Oak Cliff section of Dallas in a place with a swimming pool. I was driving a 1975 Buick Regency and taking night classes at a junior college, trying to get the feel of what would be the best end for me. We were paying a fortune in diapers, but it wasn't bad. I was such a proud sucker that I wouldn't allow Corrinne to work. I was taking care of everything. Our people would help us if we needed it, but I didn't want help when they offered and wouldn't accept it either.

Things got bad when Marvetta started growing. We lost the apartment because the bills got too outrageous. We moved in with Corrinne's family. We was breaking up and going back together. We had lots of turbulent times. Her mother kept trying to convince her that I wasn't good enough for her; I was gonna hold her back. At times I felt like that I had, because she had to get out of school to have Marvetta, but my main objective was to give my wife and kid the best I could. Only thing that was on my mind was how could I make more money. How could I get a promotion. I liked being the head of a family. I liked going home and having a wife and child there. But it was shaky. We quit going out when we got married. We stayed home and talked about our dreams, and, Lord

Fully Armed

knows, we had dreams. Those dreams help us eat bologna sandwiches for two or three days because my daughter had to have Pampers and food.

Those dreams kept us going until I got shot.

September 3, 1978.
I had just made love to my wife.
She said, "Honey, we need something from the store."
"Okay, baby, I'll get it." Bread or milk. Something like that.

They had a phone outside the store. It had rung, and, like a fool, I picked it up. "Hello."

Somebody asked for somebody. I don't even know who this person is.

Three men had got out of a car. Two went into the store; one stayed outside. Other people were getting out of cars and going into the store. All of a sudden—Shots!—Explosions!—Blood! A robbery's going down! I dove on a woman and her daughter on their way into the store.

The man outside shot me in the spine.

I lay on the sidewalk. Blood was pumping out of me. I was praying like hell. Praying, just praying. I was too afraid to close my eyes. The ambulance came, and the guy said, "You ain't gonna make it. Any last thing you want to say?"

I said, "I'm a veteran. Get me to the V.A. hospital. It's three blocks away."

He said, "I got to take you to Parkland." That was twenty minutes.

They got me to the hospital. I could not talk loud enough for anyone to hear. The doctor said, "No use trying to save him. Blood pressure's down. Pulse is weak. Tag his toe."

But I know I'm alive. I'm on this table. My eyes are open. I'm seeing everything. I'm trying to say something somebody can hear. I made a loud grunt.

The doctor said, "Wait a minute. This man is not dead!" Everybody started rushing over, sticking needles in me. They telling me, "Swallow this tube through your nose." I'm doing what they say. I want to live, and I'm scared as Hell, and I know that, if I die, I will be seeing the Devil next. Bad things I have did that nobody know about but me and God passing through my mind like a double-feature movie. I'm repenting and repenting and repenting. I'm seeing darkness. I'm talking to myself in the darkness. "Oh my God, I'm dead. I haven't made twenty-one. I have a wife and child. Who gonna take care of them?" All of a sudden, this great light come in, and I'm floating toward the light. I'm scared, and I'm shaking, and I know that I'm dead, and when I got up on the brightest part of the light, it was a doctor's flashlight pointing in my eyes.

A doctor asked my wife and father to let them operate. "He's paralyzed, but he might be able to walk over time. If we go in and get this bullet now, his chances are better, but the chances are also better he will die."

I wanted to tell them to operate, but I couldn't talk. I'm laying there in all this pain, thinking, "Say, 'Yes.' Say, 'Yes.'"

And my wife and my father say, "No."

I had been in the hospital three weeks when it got back to me that my wife was having an affair.

That killed my will. I was fucked-up, shot; I didn't have no control over my bowels. These are things I have to live with the rest of my life! I don't want to. This was the woman that was supposed to love me. Be devoted. I told her, "Don't come again."

I tried withering away. For a month or two, I lay in bed and wanted to die. Then I got angry. I thought, "I'm stronger than this. She just wasn't no good. God trying to show you something. You going to walk. Keep trying." I got back to my rehabilitation. I wanted to prove something to myself, to rebound and get my sanity. I wanted to walk up to Corrinne and say, "Go to Hell."

But I couldn't do it.

The hospital gave up on me. After I had tried so hard, they was gonna put me out. They told my father, "Take him home. We can't help him. All he's doing is taking up room." My father said, "No, y'all haven't done enough." Then one doctor said, "Let's work out something with a place where he can get rehabilitation." He contacted Houston V.A., and Houston say, "Hell, yeah. He's a veteran. He's paralyzed. He needs a spinal cord unit."

Houston was "Welcome to the World of Paralyzation." I did not have no private room no more. I was on a ward with thirty men in wheelchairs and one woman. People who been paralyzed ten years. People with sores over their bodies. People that are bodywise deteriorated. I was looking at what is and I didn't like it. I did not want to see what would be in five years, ten years, fifteen years. I don't want this shit.

So when they took me down to P.T., T.T., and O.T., I tried ten times as hard as the next person. I'm a new injury, and people tell me all I'm gonna get back I'm gonna get in the first year. I tried everything. They had to restrain me, tie me up, sedate me to keep me in bed.

They taught me to use braces. I got so I could get out of the chair and hop for miles. Then this kid, couldn't be more than five or six, come to see his father. His father was at the stage I had been, and he said, "One day I'll be able to walk like him." The kid say, "Dad, he ain't walking. He hopping." I lost hope again, and I lay those crutches down.

After I was in Houston nine months, they said, "Jimmy, it's time to go back into society. You got to accept you gonna be like this."

I moved in with my father and stepmother. Basically, my life was on hold. There was no objective in it. I was trying to accept that Jimmy was alive, and this was the deal was gonna be. I could not have sex. I could not control my urine. It dripped from my penis, down a tube, into a bag. I had no control over my bowels. I had to clean himself out manually, or I would mess myself.

I had to accept that most of my life was going to be spent in and out of the hospital. Physically, I didn't take care of myself as I should. I got infections whole lots. Our bodies so delicate, if we hit a bump hard, it'll turn into a sore. I had sores the size of my fist they had to go in all the way to the bone to scrape. One time, they opened me up like a fish and drained out everything inside. I was in and out of the hospital every three months. Back and forth, back and forth. Every time I come out, it was harder and harder and harder. I was dying little bit by little bit.

Corrinne would bring Marvetta by to visit. She wanted to reconcile, but I was still angry. I still had this picture of her with someone else. But I did not believe any other woman would want me. I would be lonely the rest of my life. I would die lonely. So I tried to forgive her.

We could play the role of being man and woman, but there was no emotion. There was no dedication. We were just going through the motions. She was going through it out of guilt, and I was going through it out of fear of being lonely. We were kids trying to deal with this paralysis, this new body I had.

If we went out, it felt like hundreds and hundreds of people were looking at me. I was always treated like I was helpless. Like I was in the way. Like I was an "it." Whenever I step out of the car, whenever I sit on the curb, whenever I go down the street, I was treated like… "What's that?" People felt sorry for me, but their feeling sorry hurt me too. People said, "I hope I never be like that." They said, "I remember when you was a child. You used to run so fast." One time, we were out with another couple. I had what they call "an accident." To look at her go through this with people was terrifying. By her sitting up at two o'clock in the morning, crying and shaking because she didn't know what was gonna happen or how I was gonna respond, I was seeing a beautiful, young woman turn into an old maid.

It was Hell. My disability check was one-third of what I had been making. Banks would not loan me money. There was nothing that I owned. Everything I had was being paid on and would be taken away. Getting my check was like getting a five-dollar bill, cutting it into a thousand pieces, and paying everyone a piece at a time.

I was drinking and smoking marijuana to forget my accidents, the embarrassments, the feeling a dog had it better than me. Corrinne started drinking heavy. She became a certified alcoholic, *very* certified, hiding liquor in the cabinets, in closets. My baby, crawling under the couch one time, came out with a pint of gin.

We had fights... I mean, "War of the Roses" didn't have shit compared to "War of the Polks." I would try to make her feel guilt. I tried to make her feel every bit of my pain. I convinced myself, if she had been at my side when I got hurt, some miracle would have happened. And she embarrassed me in front of friends. She told 'em what I couldn't do.

Yet and still, we was staying together. We both had one thing we truly wanted. That was our little girl. We both suffered pain for her. We both took her feelings into heart. That's what drug it out that long.

Finally, I pushed her totally away. We might've killed each other. I'm actually talking about killing. I would've killed us both.

I got off into another world. I was hanging out with gangsters. Bad elements. Very criminal people. People I didn't have no business with. Women came on to me to find out if I could do certain things, to answer questions they had inside their minds. Evidently I couldn't, because they didn't stay long.

Every two months, I would bring a new girlfriend to meet my father, my stepmother, and them.

I would lie to women, "I can't have sex because I have an infection." I would tell every kind of lie to keep from going to bed alone. I slept with one eye open and one hand behind my butt, because I didn't know what would happen. One night, I was with this young lady. I had an accident. She jumped out of bed and ran. A week later, I was using heroin. That was the only comfort I could find.

My attitude was "The Hell with life. I'd rather live it stoned." I was smoking lots of weed, drinking lots. I became what they call "a trash can." If you would offer it, I would experiment with it. I would take a bottle of aspirin if you told me it would get me dizzy. I took so many drugs I felt like my body belonged in The Smithsonian Institute. Like I had the cure for all mankind's diseases in my blood.

My mission was to punish God. Hell, I was insane; I was confused; I was hurting. It was the beginning of how I became "Nightmare on Polk Street." In Waxahachie, everyone knew and respect the fact that I got hurt trying to help others. I didn't get hurt over no bullshit. People felt sorry for me; the churches felt sorry for me. That hurt me lots too, people feeling sorry for me. I didn't want it.

And I was still having resentments toward my mother. I needed her touch. She only came to see me once, and it was like she was a total stranger. My mind was thinking, "Get the Hell out. You don't care. What are you doing here?"

I wanted to die. I wanted somebody to kill me. I was doing outrageous things, like driving my buddies and watching them rip off the dope man. I can't walk, and I'm in the car driving. I was dealing drugs myself. The police come around; they all knew me. I would want them to shoot me. Here I am, got a gun in my lap, and they bust through the door; they wouldn't arrest me. No matter what I do. They shake their heads, "Jimmy..." 'Cause they knew this wasn't Jimmy Polk. This is what the injury did to Jimmy Polk. They arrested my friends. That made me feel like, "Damn, I can't do nothing right."

Coming to California was like trying to get a rebirth. I felt that, if I left Waxahachie, I would maybe get motivated and start living again. I wanted to escape the daily routine of dealing with people in that little country town. I wanted something new. I made myself believe, "Maybe, if I go where people won't know who I am, I can create the person that I want to be."

Soon as my check came, I filled up my old 1963 Chevrolet and left. As I left, it was coming through my mind, "Now I ain't got to deal with this person. I ain't got to deal with that person. I'm gonna wipe my slate clean. Something great's gonna happen."

That car was so raggedy it smoked all the way.

Soon as I got halfway, I called my mother. She was manager of a club, "The Lido," in Pittsburg. My mother's been married more times than Elizabeth Taylor. Her name's done changed from Faire to Polk to Becker to Brown. In fact, I got so many fathers I can't keep count. But she wasn't married then.

She said, "Come on."

When I pulled up, she ran out and hugged me. "Boy, what are you doing?"

"I'm trying to find a life."

She closed the club down and took me to her apartment. Pittsburg got a marina with a dock and sailboats and beach. I thought it was beautiful. Hey, this is California! I ain't used to seeing boats and Rolls Royces and palm trees. Everything was new.

Even though I still had this resentment, I didn't want my mother to know what I was going through and feeling bad. So I created this person that being paralyzed don't hurt. This person that liked to get out and do things. This person that would make people love him. This person that would make you feel, if you had a problem, you could go to him.

I got a kick out of having people come up, smiling, look me steady in the eye and not at my wheelchair. Creating this image, I was able to sleep some. It was like I figured out the purpose for me in life. It seemed weird because it was a lie, but it seemed like a beautiful lie because its purpose was good. When it made somebody happy that I touched his life, I figured, maybe that's why God allowed me to be in this wheelchair.

People asked me what happened. They beat around the bush, but you knew it was coming. By the time they came out with it—"What happen?"—I had already told 'em. I always came up with the Vietnam War. That way I manipulated their feelings. People looked at me like "Oh my God, my country did this. You did not deserve it." Instead of just seeing a crippled man in a wheelchair, they felt compassion.

I got more understanding and respect and sympathy with those lies than by telling the truth. And I wanted it so bad that I kept doing it. As time progressed, I got wrapped up into it. I became this person I would talk about. And I would add more to make this person more dramatic, to make a person listen to me a little bit more, to make a person smile at me, to make this person even hug me. Back home, I wasn't getting those feelings. I wasn't getting hugged. Everything was cold. When I came to California, I started feeling warmth inside, and I was liking that warm feeling because I missed it. When I lost my legs, everything became cold. There was no strong, warm, loving feeling inside of me. I didn't receive any. I didn't allow myself to feel any. I don't know which one is which. Maybe both.

I kept trying to make that feeling stronger and stronger. But at the same time, I tried to make a person feel good about themself. It wasn't all about me. It wasn't all about trying to escape. It was me trying to find a purpose. Even though I got these malfunctions, these defects, I had to look for a purpose. I was trying to give myself the feeling of being wanted or needed to give myself the will to keep living.

I had great conversations. I read everything I could get my hands on. The Greeks. *GQ, People.* I would follow things happening in the world. I would give my opinions on issues; my mother wouldn't know what I was talking about. My opinions sounded damn good, like I was educated. I was creating friends that respect and admire me and come to me for advice. People above just people in the street. People who had objectives like nice homes, nice cars. People who worked for Dow Chemical and P.G.&E. People who belonged to the Elks Club. People who, I figured, could help me in the long run.

I had met this beautiful lady, Monica, a manicurist, and broke that two-month record. She was a good person. She understood my body and the frustration I had. We got a one-bedroom duplex in West Pittsburg. It wasn't in a drug-infested neighborhood. Drugs was around the corner, but they wasn't being dealt in front of my face. I was smoking marijuana and sniffing speed occasionally, not to get high but to feel normal and get motivated.

My mother said, "You got a good mind, son. Why don't you go to school?"

I said, "Yeah."

I was being resurrected.

I got into Los Medanos. I majored in small engine repair. I became the first person in a wheelchair to complete a welding class. That made me proud. Then I became the first black president of the student government. That made me even prouder.

I was doing great things. Learning about bills and propositions and Robert's Rules of Order. Running meetings. Learning how the government worked. Traveling. I had new ideas for the school. Used books for students who couldn't afford them. Flowergrams and break dance contests to raise money. I felt important, being sent to different colleges and hobnobbing with Willie Brown and those people, having a voice in what was going on. Articles were written about me. My picture was in the school paper every week. Teachers knew my name. Students knew my name that I didn't even know. People came up to me with problems, and I'm rolling off like Ironsides to take care of them.

My mind was growing intellectualwise. I was experiencing things that I never would have. I was looking for higher ladders to get higher in the world. I had not erased my past, but it was not so much in front of me. I wasn't thinking about my accidents. I was thinking about my wife every now and then, but I never let sadness overcome me. I would shake it off and get back to what I was doing. I was not becoming; Jimmy had become.

But I was so busy at the schoolhouse, I was not attending to my private world. I had become big shit, and I lost the people who had helped me get on this roll. Monica didn't feel she was in my life. Time I should have been spending with her, I was being shipped to another town to represent the school.

I was going to San Diego. I didn't ask her to go. I didn't *want* her to go. I was having fun where I was going. She got tired of it. She said, "If you want this romance to work, you got to start concentrating on me. You got to bring me flowers. You got to take me out."

I been living with this woman for a year. I'm real bigheaded. I said, "Ah, I'm not gonna go through all that stuff. If you don't like it, you can leave."

And she left.

And she never came back.

I started feeling that loneliness.

I got back into drug use. I'm trying to maintain this heart from exploding; I'm trying to maintain that objective I had at school, but you can't do that with drugs. It takes a piece of you every time you do it. I started going downhill again, but, this time, I was going all the way down.

My drug use got heavier and heavier. School work got lesser and lesser. Every time my heart hurt, I got high, and my heart hurt damn near twenty-four hours a day. I was shooting speed; I was smoking weed; I was drinking. I'm thinking, "Damn, see how hard I work. I did this. I did that. But nobody appreciate me." By asking these questions, I'm giving myself a reason for doing what I was doing.

I started missing classes. I stopped going to meetings. I'm catching sores all over my body. Since I got shot, Los Medanos was the best period in his life. Now, it was like there was a knock at the door: "Surprise! I'm back! Mr. Hell! And guess what? This time I'm even badder. We can have a fucking party." And I said, "Take me, I'm yours."

My mother seen what was going on. She said, "C'mon, son. Stay with Mom till you regroup."

In a way, being with my mother helped. In a way, it hurt. Things were still going downhill, but they slowed considerable. I had a room. My bills were less. I was still using, but I was going to school. I was trying to find Monica to make amends. I was willing to do anything to get her back. I was afraid I would never have another good relationship. I thought, maybe, if I hurt myself, she'd come back and take care of me. But her resistance was like a brick wall. There was nothing I could do.

I stopped going to school. I didn't do nothing. I'd wake up, get high, look at t.v., hurt. It was like I was safe in that little room with my mother. I knew I would eat every day. I didn't worry if I messed up. I wasn't gonna be thrown out. I'd lost all desire and motivation. Respect for my mother wasn't there. She was working; she had a boyfriend, but I was paying for three-quarters of everything around the house on my Social Security. I was feeling I was buying her love. I would use in front of her. I didn't care if I hurt her, because I was hurting more. I tried to make her feel the pain that I felt coming up without her. Every time she reached out to me, I bit that much harder.

I had separated from the world. I didn't have the courage to tell my mother, "Hey, something's wrong." I didn't want to call my father and worry him. The only person I had to talk to was myself, and the advice I was giving wasn't good.

I had to get out of this deep water I was in before I drowned. I told my mother I was going into a rehabilitation program at the V.A. Hospital in Martinez. I was gonna stay a year. But when I got there, their beds was filled. I had already told my mother they had accepted me. No way I wanted to go back.

A Vietnam veteran I knew come over. Joey Sherlock. He was in Special Forces. He had got out of prison a year earlier for killing a couple black dudes. He said, "What you been up to, man?"

"Man, things are bad. I'm homeless."

"Us veterans got to stick together. You can stay with me." He got a truck and took me to Berkeley.

Joey was living in an apartment on University Avenue, next to Taco Bell. The guy was a certified Hell's Angel. His life was devoted to a Harley Davidson motorcycle. He always had on a leather jacket and tattoos. He always had a bandito in his long, blond hair. The guy tote guns in his boot. The guy had guns between his butt. He kept a loaded gun in each room of his house, including the bathroom and kitchen. He had two pit bulls and a beautiful wife. She was paying the bills.

I'm staying in this trailer in back. It had a bed, a table, and a lot of damn ants. It was so small, the door was twice as thin as my wheelchair. I had to fold it to bring it inside. I had to roll up between the motorcycle and the tree, jump into the trailer, and push myself backwards across the floor until I could pull myself onto the bed.

Now and then, Joey's wife would sneak me something to eat, but he didn't want her waiting on me. They had this flight of stairs, forty or fifty steps, straight up. If I wanted to eat or shower, I had to jump out of my wheelchair, jump up a step, pull my wheelchair up a step, jump up a step, pull my wheelchair up a step, jump up a step... Sometimes, halfway up, my chair'd slip all the way down. I had to psych myself up: "Okay, Jimmy, you have to do this."

Joey was a recovering alcoholic, so being with him gave me time to dry out. Plus, here was this roof over my head. The guy was prejudiced, but he wasn't prejudiced as to me. If you was black and a veteran, you was okay. If you was black and wasn't a veteran, you was what he called you. He liked me, and maybe I didn't like some of his ways and words, but I liked him. I gave him respect, but he didn't give me respect in the way he express himself about my people.

At night, he would lean out the window, shooting off his guns, hollering about "Niggers." I wanted a new life, and I blocked some of these things out, but brothers on the block kept coming down on me for betraying the race, so, after three weeks, I left for Telegraph.

Those first weeks were a night in Hell.

I was doing things I never thought I'd do. I would stick my tongue out in the window of a restaurant, till somebody'd say, "Give this man some food." I'd ask people with a doggie bag, "Can I have that? I'm hungry." I'd wash anyplace I saw a water hose. If I was bad, I'd go into some establishment and wipe myself in their bathroom, not really wash.

I didn't have no money for supplies. One time my leg-bag busted, and I had to find a plastic bag in a trash can to put over it to keep from getting wet on me. Many times my leg-bag busted, and I had to waste water or juice over me to pretend like it was that until I could do a quick fix job. Many, many times I had conversations smelling like urine. I never knew when my bowels was gonna move, and when I did, I never had nowhere to take care of them. I couldn't go to fucking MacDonald's. They'd throw you out soon as they look at you. I had to wait till it got dark and crawl somewhere with trees. The first time I did that, it felt like I threw my whole world of values, morals, and pride away.

I looked bad. I smelled bad. I felt bad. The days were long. Rainy, cold days were miserable. It didn't matter if I went 'round with four shirts and three pairs of pants. Every night was cold. There was not a day I didn't wake up cold and hungry. It wasn't like waking up in a warm bed. I'd wake up, and reality'd punch me in the face. I had to endure getting my blanket stole, my clothes stole, my shoes stole off my feet. I had to endure having accidents on myself and not having clothes to put on and asking homeless people I didn't even know, "Do you have an extra pair of pants?" "Do you have a clean shirt?" "Do you have shoes?"

Many nights, I'd be sitting with three or four plastic bags tied together in a knot, one end tied to a bench and one end tied around me, to keep my chair from being stole. I'd be shaking in a thin blanket, needing to change myself but having no place to and it too cold to jump on the ground. Even drinking, I couldn't sleep, and if I did crash out, I would only get fifteen minutes, because, if I heard a crack, my eyes'd open. Those nights, I cried a million tears.

I called myself a three-way minority: black, in a wheelchair, and homeless.

I was centered in the Park two months when I met Ajax. I was with these people when a police came up, Officer Stone, nine millimeter packing. He started kicking clothes, looking through bags. I said, "Ain't that illegal?"

He looked at me like Robocop. "What's your name?"

"Jimmy Don Polk."

"You got i.d.?"

"Yes, officer." I gave him my V.A. card. He starts talking to his shoulder computer-microphone-whatever.

"We don't have anything on you. Are you homeless?"

"Yes. That's how come I'm here."

"Why all the damn homeless people come to Berkeley?" That kinda offend me. I said, "What the fuck did you say?"

He said, "What the fuck you say?"

"I don't want no hassle. I plan on living here. And you got no right to harass people less fortunate than you." Then I come up with this line to impress the people and establish some identity. "Hey, I fought before you even thought about picking up a pistol."

He loosened up a little. "Try not to stay in this Park. Lots of drug dealers here and lots of fights. Glad to meet you."

The next day, Ajax called me over. "You a veteran?"

"Yes, bro, I am."

Ajax was anywhere from thirty-seven to forty-two. He was from Oklahoma, and he always had on a green fatigue jacket and cowboy boots. He had a manslaughter case against him, and they gave him the opportunity of going in the service or going to jail. When he went in the service, they said, "He's whack-o, but he has talent. Let's use him as a fucking killer."

The guy was fantastic. He could be lying in the grass, and I'd say, "Hit that tree," and he'd pick a knife out of his boot and hit any limb you point to. Ajax was very cool and very strong. He never bit his tongue, as far as any feeling he had, but he never disrespect nobody either. He didn't start no shit, but he didn't take none. I have seen him hurt people. He been on the street since he left Vietnam. He came back; he wasn't appreciated, and he freaked out. He hated society, and he was leery of people.

The guy wouldn't get tight with nobody 'cept veterans. We both had purple cards, so we got to know each other. We'd drink beer and start reminiscing. He would give me part of him, and I would give him part of me. I'd listen to how he'd been pimped by the government; he'd listen to what I went through with my body. When he would come up with his war stories, I came up with war stories I had from other veterans. You got to pay attention you want to live a homeless life, and I always been receptive to things I could use to convince people what I'm saying is true. I would come out with "Ooh Shu," "Ho Chi Minh," "Kee Yo," anything that sound familiar, anything that click, "Maybe this motherfucker was really there."

Even though my part was bullshit, his part was real. I believe his stories with all my heart. I seen his three Purple Hearts and his Medal of Valor. I seen pictures of him and his buddies over there. I seen the way he described everything, the way he felt, the tears he shed. Every time he told the stories of his missions, he cried like a three-week old baby, and I'm no sissy or nothing, but I would hug him, because I could feel his pain. He felt like he wasn't alone, and I felt like I wasn't alone too.

The guy watched over my back good. He jumped in lots of peoples' faces helping me. He didn't let people disrespect me. He made sure I et. When people brought food to the Park, he got me and him food. Every time we slept out, when I'd wake up, he'd got hot food or warm food and coffee beside me. If I'd say, "Thank you," he'd be angry.

Ajax schooled me how to survive. The guy was The Best. I could not touch him. Whenever he went out, he would come back with forty or fifty, sometimes sixty, eighty, ninety, a hundred dollars, and get a room for us both. He taught me how to approach people. "If you see a person with a frown, say something to make 'em smile. If you see a person with a smile, make 'em smile brighter. Make people feel good. Make them realize they could of been you. But make them realize that in a diplomatic way. Don't shove it in their face. If you be nice and gentle, a person may not be nice and gentle with you that day, but they will come back, and they will remember you."

The homeless got a saying: "The game is showed, not told."

Fully Armed

For a month, Ajax carried me and him both, walking me through, giving me knowledge, sheltering me like a big bird a little bird. Then one night, he turned me loose and made me prove I was for real. He said, "I taught you, but you won't do it. Us veterans got to do what we got to do." I didn't want him to think I was a bullshitter, which I wasn't, but I was, so I decided to make myself like him. I developed some of his come-on, his rap. On the street, the first question come to people's mind when they saw me was, "How you get put in that chair?" I used to say I got shot in Vietnam. Now, when people asked, "You get shot in the war?" "Yeah. Sure was. Lemme tell you about it." I was telling true stories. It's just that I wasn't in them.

Once I got this push, I was smart enough to go to people who had good techniques. I researched from the best panhandlers in Berkeley. And there are some damn good ones. There are guys pulling in five, six, $700 a week, no taxes, no overhead. But these guys don't give you their game. You have to dig in close, do them a favor, show them you cool. One guy, I took to dinner. "Hey, I had a good day. Lemme take you out." Even though I knew he had a pocketful of money, I paid his way. They started giving me information: spots to go, good restaurants, movie theaters, best times of the week.

I watched their movements, but my style was my own creation. Most people know what homeless people do with the money they give 'em, but if you can make 'em smile, make 'em grin, share their bad times, spot the things they're feeling, you gonna make money. I can look at a person and tell if he's happy, if he's down, if something's on his mind, if he need to hear something good, if he need to be picked up, if he need to be loved. If a beautiful lady walk by, I'll tell her, "You sure are jazzy." If an ugly woman walk by, I'll say, "You sure are pretty." I would make a person feel what I'm seeing. "Your shoes look good." "Your tie looks great."

Your mind gets very creative living on the street. If you can play on somebody's emotions or sympathy, you will. Being homeless, you got no pride or conscience to hold you back.

Homeless people will send their kids panhandling, because kids got a better chance getting money than they do. The kid will say, "My momma and daddy and I are hungry." People give the kid twenty dollars. The parents take that, buy the kid a hamburger, tell it, "Go play," and get high.

Homeless people will have cards printed: I AM DEAF. I AM DUMB. PLEASE HELP ME. The bottom line: GOD BLESS YOU. They pass them out. They don't have to say a word.

Homeless people will talk to themselves, read pages that do not exist, pet dogs you do not see, get down on all fours and bark, piss on your shoe. They'll do anything to get you to say, "Okay. Here. I'm sorry for you. Get the fuck out of my face."

Homeless people will run behind cars, tap the trunk, and play like, "Hey! You hit me!" They will bump you, fall, and make you feel like you to blame. "How come you don't watch out for me? Why you be like this?" They make a spectacle: a bunch of people stop, you got work to go to, people to take care of, you don't want police to come. So... "Here. I'm sorry."

You got people who will bust out crying, "I need help! My child's hurt!" And they lying. One lady got this big stomach. She will run up, "I'm pregnant! I need money to get to the hospital!" The woman was born with that stomach. She use that malfunction in her body to get over.

You got people holding "Free Clinic" or "Food Project" boxes. Some of them people, that's their own box. Some, the box is real, but they got a key. One guy got two houses in Berkeley off his box. Say he makes $300. He might take $200 and give $100 in, and they split that 50:50 with him. The guy'd pay me ten dollars an hour to work my corner, so you know he's doing good.

So many people in Berkeley willing to help people down

on their luck that the homeless have an edge. There are people out there who need and people who are only out for money. Each person, if they have a drug habit or they're hungry, have some game, and it's hard to separate who's for real.

Some homeless people have skills. We had guys that play music and people put money in their hat. Steel drums, guitars, one guy, about three-foot two, a real midget, play the violin. My friend Jose had two dogs. He'd set one on a window ledge and one on its back, with its four legs up, put cigarettes in their mouths, and those dogs would smoke. The college students loved that. They gave him lots of money. This artist, Robbie, would buy a ninety-nine cent pad, draw you in a minute, and charge a dollar. He made his hustle that way.
The musicians, the ones giving entertainment, are some of the true, genuine homeless. They also some of the true, genuine junkies.

Some homeless people work. Guys will pick cans and bottles all day. They'll buy a Squeegee and a bucket, jump in the road, and wash your car. They'll go early in the morning on University Avenue, where people ride up for cheap labor. "I need somebody to mow my yard." "I need somebody to cut my tree." And they will rush to that—for half the minimum wage.

People will look for regular jobs. They will wash their clothes in jugs and hang them at night on trees, so they'll have fresh clothes to put on when they look. But a simple thing on the application, like "Name of Place of Residence," destroys the chance they have. They can't put no address down. They can't put "People's Park."
If you get a job, you got to have a different set of clothes each day. Being homeless, how you gonna protect that set? You can't bring it to the job in a cart. Go to People's Park with a shovel. You find enough shit buried for a safari hunt.

In Berkeley, a homeless person liable to have stashed something on every block, in every building, behind every trash can, in every tree.

And when a homeless person get a position, they are the first ones fired if anything goes wrong. I had a friend who got a good job washing dishes. He broke one glass, and he was gone. Evidently, the manager was stressed out and had to lash that anger at somebody. Because the guy was homeless, he was the one that come to mind. It's hard to keep up hope when the next day that hope is destroyed. You say, "I'm tired of one day feeling good, the next day feeling lousy."

If you can get your game good, you don't need a job. I got so I didn't have to ask for change. All I had to do was show up. I would sit in one spot and, before the day's over, have enough for a motel room or whatever I need to get through the night. One guy told me, "What the fuck I'm gonna work for, Jimmy? I'm my own damn boss. I don't have to go no nine-to-five. I got a place to sleep every night. If I catch a bus, I can eat three meals a day. If I want to drink, I can ask people for money and they'll give it to me."

My comment was—I was researching then—"Hey, man, what about objectives? What about believing materialistically? Wouldn't it be nice, man, to come home, stick a movie in your V.C.R., and get you a Diet Pepsi or a beer or something?"

He said, "Fuck that. If I want a movie, I'll go to La Val's, pay two-fifty for a pitcher of beer, and watch big-screen t.v."

Lots of homeless people didn't have no choice. They lost their jobs and went through their savings and couldn't get no work. There is very educated people on the street, not dummies, people with degrees, people from blue collar workers to college professors. But society has broke 'em down so much that they feel like they never gonna get a chance. Society done kicked them in their butt, their front, their sides, and they blame society for keeping them down. So when they do get money, they either gonna drink it up, smoke it up, or give it up.

On the street, drugs and alcohol is like drinking water. There is no sober people in People's Park. If they is, they just glancing by to look at the scenery. Some do it to escape fear; some do it to get high; I did it to be normal.

When I woke up, I was already sick from the night before, so the first thing I would do is a can of Olde English 100 or a half-pint of wine to mellow out. Then I'd drink three of four cups of coffee to get busy. During the day, on the streets of Berkeley, you gonna run across different people that have different drugs, acid, cocaine, heroin, straight speed, Valiums, codeine, whoever came through with whatever. I had so much pain and fear and daily things I couldn't deal with straight, anything that was offered to me or that I had the money to buy I did.

Cocaine and speed was my favorite. Cocaine gave me the illusion that I wasn't afraid of anything. It made me feel I didn't have no problems and I didn't need no one. All I thought about was that moment. Of course, when that feeling is gone, it make you cry, it make you pray, it make you drink to get back on flat, normal ground. Speed made me know everything. It made me a doctor, a psychiatrist, a psychologist, a philosopher. It gave me the answer to any problem anyone possess, even my own. Speed made me think of things before they happen, as far as planning my next moves. It also made me stay up three, four, five days straight. Here I am on the street, and I ain't got enough energy to push my tires. That's the downside. Plus, you hungry; you frightened of asking people for money, even though you been asking a long time. Speed made me face the fact that I didn't like asking people for money but I had to. I was very vulnerable coming down off speed.

Basically, I couldn't get through the day without drugs and alcohol. When I went to sleep, I had to have it. When I woke up, I had to. I didn't see that as a problem. I seen that as a solution. After I got hurt, I started getting high to deal with being in this wheelchair. I felt I wasn't functioning right unless I was high. I felt sharper, like I communicated better, like I could deal with insults or whatever came my way. Like a normal person wake up, drink orange juice, give him that Vitamin C, drugs was my Vitamin C. It wouldn't make me steal and rob; it would make me hustle. Drugs and alcohol made me productive.

Street life is lived one piece at a time. When I went to bed, I would stick a dollar in the hole in my shoe or stash a soda or potato chips in my backpack, so I knew I could eat the next morning. If I knew I was going to do drugs or get drunk, I would bury ten dollars somewhere, so I knew I would have something left when I was done. That way, no matter what happened, I was ready for the day I needed to set myself up for the next night.

I was always looking for the easiest, most efficient way of taking care of myself. Being the onliest one out there in a wheelchair was my edge. And I was an actor. But after I completed a scene, it wasn't about me getting their money and booking. I would kick back, hold a conversation, and smile. It wasn't a fake smile. I had other objectives in mind, but I was giving back a little. Making people feel good was how I dealt with what I was doing. For me to get, I had to give. And the more people gave me, the more I gave them. Give me a penny, I'm gonna give you a penny's worth of happiness. Give me twenty dollars, I'm gonna give you whole lots of happiness.

I had my tricks too. Say my backpack was already stuffed with food and somebody gave me twenty dollars. I would buy a three-dollar sandwich, put the sandwich on my lap, the seventeen dollars in my pocket, and when the person came back, they'd say, "See you got something to eat, huh." "Yes, sir. Thank you very much."

If I had a good day, I would get twenty one-dollar bills and pass them out to my fellow homeless brothers. Then when I had a bad day, I had twenty people who'd let me have a couple dollars too.

After a while, at Wells Fargo, I didn't have no worries. Every day, I knew somebody would buy me breakfast, lunch or dinner. Every day, I was guaranteed fifty or $100. At night, no matter where I was sleeping, I couldn't wait to get back there. Anytime I made that hill, I was home. I felt safe. I felt protected. I felt love. I felt like I had nurturing. First thing I heard every morning, "How you doing, Jimmy? Would you like a cup of coffee?" If I had my head down five seconds, somebody'd pick it up.

This was the comfort I had been looking for. The emotions I felt during the days was good, but still, at night, when I was alone, it was bad.

After I got shot, I had fired God out of my life. I keep going back to this wheelchair because, before, my life was fantastic. The wheelchair was the flip side of the coin. To deal with reality, I had started painting a picture in my head. As the years went by and by and by, I made it greater and greater, changing pieces of the picture to get me the feelings I needed. Subconsciously, I knew it wasn't true, but talking about it, I was that person coming out of my mouth. We was one person, even though it was one lie.

I was living and feeling everything I was saying. When I was speaking of those things I said I did, I believed it. It was really real. No one could make me stop. My performance became stronger each time I did it. It was a way to get people's attention, break the ice, and get to know them. I needed money, okay, but I also needed somebody to like me, and I could see the people's faces, the awe, the concern coming out. The people came back with their problems and talked, and, if I had a problem, which I always did, they were there for me. They was more there for me, by me creating this person, than if I had told the truth.

It was an imaginary world that I found peace in. An imaginary world that put me secure, as somebody you could respect. A world where I couldn't be hurt anymore.

Being Mr.-Person-to-Talk-To-Everyday-on-Shattuck so long, I developed lots of friendships. It started as a game, but I ended up caring for these people. They helped me every day. They were giving me more compliments than I was giving them. It was like, "I'm gonna throw what you dish out back in your face." One kindergarten class would come gather 'round my chair and sing me songs. "Row, row, row your boat..." "Old MacDonald had a farm..." One little boy gave me a penny and a hug every day. His mother didn't say, "No! Get away! Don't touch him!" She picked him up and put him on my dirty lap. One lady, worked around the corner, told me, "Some guy left his wallet in our restaurant. We looked in it to return it, and he had a card: 'To Whoever It Concern: If anything happens to me, give everything I possess to Jimmy Polk, the young man sitting outside Wells Fargo Bank.'" It blew me away. I don't know who this is today.

Something started creeping back inside me, like pieces of my soul. I started feeling, "Hey, I am worth something." But guilt started too. Each time I received some compliment, that guilt hit me strong. "You know you living a fucking lie." Every hour on the hour, someone was telling me how I had affected their life, and when they did, that guilt would come. I started feeling bad when people gave me something. I started rejecting my clientele, no matter how bad I was hurting or how bad I needed a fix or how bad I needed a room. Those strangers had become friends, and my likeness for them had turned to love.

I was sick November, December, and the first of January. I had pneumonia. I had sores. The things I'd been doing had caught up with me. I was having flashbacks: how I used to have pride in how I looked or in working hard to earn a check or a relationship. I couldn't shake them. My body was telling me it was tired of me abusing it; my mind was telling me there was a part I wasn't using.

From a homeless person's point of view, I was doing good. I had established my corner. I could function with no problem. It should have been easy to stay in that position. But, spiritually, I was stripped. I believe in God; I never seen Him flash a lightning bolt, but nights, lying on a bench or in a motel room, things I had erased from my mind was coming back, like He was haunting me. I couldn't sleep. I couldn't rest. It was like, "No way is you going to sleep. You gonna look at this." I shed more tears the last weeks I was on the street than when I got there. I became a regular crybaby. I'd look in the mirror to wash my face and say, "Who is this person?" Cocaine couldn't help me. Liquor couldn't. Whatever was offered couldn't help. It made it worse. If I did get drunk, I had to pass out, because I couldn't stand the guilt and pain.

I was tired of getting high to be normal. I was sick and angry and disgusted at myself. I was educated. I had a good mind. My communication with other people was great. I was basically a damn good person. But the things I was doing was fucked-up. It was insane. This wheelchair had made me quit the life that I had, and I couldn't adjust the way that I had to. I had did some Jimmy Don Polk research, trying to stay in this thing and live from this thing, and it didn't work too good, ending up on the streets, a drug and alcoholic.

The last three weeks, I isolated myself. I didn't go to People's Park. I didn't go on Telegraph. My homeless friends could search me out; I wouldn't search for them. All I was searching for was who I was and who I wanted to be. I went off into a haven inside myself, struggling to get out of this hole I had dug. I would kick back and watch. I was seeing people I was and people I could be and people I was gonna be if I kept going. It was like "Show and Tell, Jimmy Polk."

I had to either get up from the ground, knock the dust off,

and get back into society or kill myself. That thought did cross my mind. "Why don't you run in front of a car or bus or steal a gun and shoot your head off?" But I didn't have the courage. So... "Let's go to Plan B. Let's get help." You know, we got "Off" and "On" switches like the light. Mine came back on. I didn't turn it on. Some force greater than me did that. It was His decision. Or Hers. Or Whoever.

That rainy Saturday night, somebody had gave me $100 and I had got messed up. I woke up on that bench, soaking wet, alcohol in one hand, drugs in the other, and I said, "God, I'd like to hire you back. Just help me get to Palo Alto Hospital."

FIVE

You played a major-major part in me deciding to get myself together. Other people I met on the street came at me out of the goodness of their heart, but they had pity or sympathy or guilt to get rid of or thought it was the rightful thing to do as a human in society. But the feeling I got from you was you wanted to help me, as me, and not as somebody feeling an obligation to help somebody. It was true friendship. It was like, "I don't care what position you in, I'm with you."

I had many offers to get off the street. Many people offered me a place to lay my head. But no one had suggested I work for them. That was a little respect there. It's like, "You not fucking disabled. You got some quality and stuff you can do." It wasn't about "Po' Jimmy." And I was willing to work for you and make one-third what I was making on the street. Anytime I leave a fifty, sixty, seventy dollar hustle to work for a person, I know it's real. I felt better being around you and the people in the office than on the street. I felt better. So I kept coming. I was taught: "You want good things, you sacrifice."

It helped. I'm not standing on the corner of Shattuck no more.

I planned to end this book with a chapter that began with Jimmy making these remarks. He had actually made them in August 1990, but I intended to set them in the context of a conversation he and Adele and I would be having in his apartment, during a visit to Long Beach she and I had scheduled over Thanksgiving weekend.

That visit never occurred.

During his hospitalization, Jimmy had completed a modified twelve-step program for substance abusers. He had joined Alcoholics Anonymous, Cocaine Anonymous and Narcotics Anonymous and, as an outpatient, continued to attend meetings of these groups. He was sharing an apartment by the beach with Marvin, a quadriplegic, and a woman who was Marvin's attendant. "I'm at a peaceful moment," Jimmy said. "I got serenity. I'm watching the breeze blow and the birds fly. It's tripping me out."

As part of his treatment, Jimmy had to take care of any "unfinished business" that remained with important people in his past: his father, his mother, his wife, his daughter, me. Marvetta, who was now twelve, and with whom Jimmy had not had contact since leaving Texas, wanted to see him. Jimmy arranged to spend a week with her at his mother's in Pittsburg. During this visit, he came to Berkeley for a day.

Jimmy rolled into my office wearing a Hawaiian shirt, sharply pressed dark slacks, highly polished shoes. His hair was oiled and curled. He had two gold chains and a gold bracelet. Adele and I spent the afternoon with him. We had won-ton soup at Kam's and sat outside Cafe Frenzy. Jimmy was excited and nervous and thoroughly upbeat. While we were together, thirty or forty people said "Hello" to Jimmy or hugged him or asked him where he'd been or told him how good he looked or that they'd missed him. Jimmy liked the attention. He liked it the most when the people did not recognize him at first, because that confirmed his transformation. He did not want us to leave him alone or take him to People's

Park, though. He still felt at risk out there.

After Adele and I dropped Jimmy off at the Rockridge BART station, she said this: "The key moment was when Jimmy said you didn't have to believe his story and let you exist for him apart from his lies. He had given up on reality himself, and he still wasn't ready to face it, but he could allow you to, and he could then begin the process of catching up to you.

"Before, people he told his fantasies to would come and go like they were fantasies too. You stuck around and continued to be real. Plus, you offered him this book, which he could see as giving his life purpose. You wanted a happy ending for the book, and he wanted one for his life, but he knew he couldn't have this if he kept putting forth lies. Your saying you would like him without his lies made him more willing to try to make reality work. But to do that, he had to go back and explore and work to catch up to your idea that it would be okay if his story wasn't true. It's taken him this seven-month journey to get there and put you in touch with his real self."

A few days later, Jimmy sent me a silver pin he had received from A.A. It said, SIX MONTHS SOBRIETY. ONE DAY AT A TIME. He said that it was the first time since he was twelve that he had been sober for so long. He wanted me to have the pin because I was his best friend. I put it on my key chain. I was touched.

In September, Jimmy enrolled in junior college. He was taking basic courses in mathematics and English. He was thinking of becoming a counselor or paralegal. Finances were a problem: his G.I. benefits had run out, and he was not yet eligible for a student loan. Transportation was a problem: the school was across town from his group meetings, bus service was erratic, and one driver refused to operate his lift for Jimmy's wheelchair. But Jimmy was determined. "Everything'll work out," he said.

Jimmy filed a complaint with the bus company about the

driver and had his shift changed. He arranged rides to and from campus with friends. He borrowed money to buy books. People in his groups chipped in and bought him a typewriter and cassette recorder for his lectures. He reported that his grades were good. A few weeks into the semester, the Dean allowed him the use of a room and equipment, and Jimmy started the school's first twelve-step program.

On October 21st, when I called, Jimmy told me the hospital wanted him to come in for a "tune-up." They thought he was pushing himself too hard. He was resisting the suggestion because it would mean dropping classes. "Everything'll be all right," he said.

On October 28th, the attendant answered. "Jimmy's not staying here any more. We don't know where he is. Maybe he'll call you."

In the creative writing class where Adele and I met, she once said, "In fiction, endings can be happy or sad, depending on where the author arbitrarily declares one." Later, in our life together, we would walk out of a movie if we were satisfied with where the director had us and did not trust his or her intentions for the remainder of the reel.

This was not fiction, but I was the author, and I declared this story done. I held nothing against Jimmy. I did not curse the slips or mourn the flaws which had cost me my projected resolution. I wished him luck. I sympathized. I hoped for the time I would pick up the phone and hear, "How's it going, buddy?" But when I next passed Wells Fargo, I had to force myself to look because I was afraid I'd see him.

I had desired uplift, but I could no longer wait. It was time to sink or swim, fish or cut bait, pull up stakes, move on. I could live with that, I told myself. In fact, I could embrace Jimmy's rise-and-fall struggle openly. My published novel ends with its protagonist, a minor-league basketball player, alone, at night, on an outdoor court, shooting baskets against the wind. The existential labor of moving rocks uphill was okay by me.

Jay Martin, a psychoanalyst and English professor, writes, in *Who Am I This Time,* that all people invent "a reality in which to live. We do not discover reality, we construct it." People who feel empty or weak, people whose self-confidence has been shattered or whose trust in others has been destroyed may seek strength from identification with powerful figures. They may fill their resultant vacuums with imaginary selves. When the real world seems "inauthentic, fragmentary or unavailable," only fiction may make it seem complete. But it is not only the damaged or the ill who use fantasies in their development, Martin tells us. All people will, to some degree, look at James Bond or Madonna or Ernest Hemingway or Albert Camus and say, "This is how I will be." Jimmy did it; I did it; we all do it. Sometimes you hit the ball out of the park; sometimes you whiff; sometimes you foul the sucker off your foot.

"It's the issue of the ideal," Adele said. We lay together on the bed, the mobile shifting, red and white and blue, in the unfelt currents, Bob Dylan—who once carved his self out of chunks of Woodie Guthrie—remaining in the rain. "You met this guy, wanting something to happen inside you, something to reaffirm life and make you whole. Law wasn't working for you. Writing wasn't. If you had been happy with law or with fiction, you wouldn't have been wandering the street so ready to meet people. And you met Jimmy, who had this life that was greater than any you could have imagined. It fascinated you. It seduced you. And the irony was that it had been made up by someone who couldn't stand his own life and had replaced it with his own fictions.

"You both had very different lives you were dissatisfied with. You both wanted to do something about them. He told you his stories, the product of his dissatisfaction. You listened, and your listening and your responses were the product of your dissatisfactions. You wanted to make a difference in this person's life and, in doing that, make a difference in your own. You wanted to make them both come out right. That's your reason for the book. Jimmy wanted the book to make a difference for him too. Then, through the telling and the listening, something big and real happened for Jimmy, and, as it happened for him, it happened for you because you were having this impact you wanted.

"Things were set in motion. They got better, but they didn't get perfect. Your impact did not produce the ideal. That's frustrating to you, and it's frustrating, somehow, for Jimmy. He had made up a fictional life, and it didn't work for him. Then he tried a 'real' life, and, while things got better there, they didn't become perfect either. His new life became intolerable, and he had to run again. But, in life, you can't have it as you want it. You must accept compromised improvement."

I wrote that down. I gave the PRINT command. It seemed that things were over.

PART III

1994

In February 1991, we had learned our house needed major structural repair. Shortly after that, my father died of liver cancer. Then I was flung into bed for a month by an undiagnosable, untreatable viral hepatitis. I would lie there, sweating my way through six t-shirts a night, thinking of my financial burden, the loss of my parental safety net, my suddenly too-real, personal fragility.

When I returned to work, it was with a new attitude. My commitment to my clients had been strengthened and my sensitivity to their needs heightened. (Which did not mean I did not slam the phone down on them now and then.) I had even begun to establish a gratifying, though offbeat—or, perhaps, gratifying *because* offbeat—writerly *persona*, regularly contributing essays and profiles to *The Comics Journal* ("The Magazine of Comics News & Criticism,") which occasionally put my name on the cover ("Bob Levin on *Yummy Fur*,") as though it meant something.

Jimmy re-established contact with me in late December of that year. He did not give me many details about what he had been doing; I did not ask for any. We kept in touch. He remained in Long Beach, recommitted to A.A., and seemed to do well. He achieved certification in computer literacy (WordPerfect, Lotus 1-2-3, Microsoft Word, Quattro Pro, dBase IV, and MS-DOS) through the V.A. He sought office work, while putting in ten to fifteen hours a week at the hospital for well under minimum wage. He spoke at local detoxification centers and rehabilitation units. He found a one-bedroom apartment through a program that partially subsidized housing for the elderly and disabled. He completed a semester at Long Beach Community College, receiving two As and a B.

My efforts to place our manuscript, with the muted climax I had appended at the time of Jimmy's second disappearance, had been unsuccessful.

If I were going to get anywhere, I decided, absolute honesty would be required. How, for instance, I would need to know, had Jimmy really been shot?

"Happen just like I told you," Jimmy said when I called. "I left out of the apartment to get some, I think, milk. The two men shot me."

"That," I said, with a somewhat sinking feeling, "Wasn't what you told me." I mentioned the woman-with-child that I—and some others—had our doubts about.

"I must of wanted to make it seem like I got shot for something, instead of I got shot for nothing," he said. "I left the apartment. I went in the phone booth. A car pull up with two guys in it. One of them mention something about, 'Can you tell me how to get to Waxahachie?' I said, 'Yeah, I can tell you.' All of a sudden, I see a gun, and they saying, 'Give me your wallet.' I say, 'Fuck you.' The guy kinda nod off, like you drop your head for a minute, and I seen an opportunity to get the hell out of there. I started running. Next thing I know—BAOW!—and I'm flying across the pavement. As I hit the ground, I felt a hole in me, but I wasn't hurt. I couldn't move, and I couldn't breath, and the guy backing back, trying to run the car over me backwards. That tire stopped two inches from my nose.

"I was crying and scared and trying to negotiate with God. 'Please let me live for my daughter. Don't let me die for my daughter.' I thought he would hear me better if I asked on her behalf than mine. I passed out and woke up surrounded by people. I lay on the ground questioning God, trying to make God feel guilty. 'I know people who rape and steal, and I didn't do those things. Why is this happening to me?'

"The ambulance came. I asked the guy, 'Will I live?' He told me, 'No.' I passed out and woke up, and I was on this table, and a bunch of people sticking tubes in my throat, in my nose, in my guts. A lady doctor asked me, 'Can you move your toes?' I said, 'No.' They looked sad, but I didn't care because I was waiting to die.

"Thirty days after I was in the hospital, my wife told me she was seeing another man. I was destroyed. I didn't have no function over my body; I didn't have no sex function; I was like a baby, diapers and all. I lost hope of walking or anything. She was what gave me the motivation that I had to walk again, that I had to do my best."

Something was bothering me. "What were you doing in the phone booth?"

"I had met this young lady," Jimmy said. "And I had plans to go see her. Damn, Bob, you do make me face some issues."

Okay, I thought.

The week after Christmas, Adele and I flew into the Orange County Airport. When we turned onto the Pacific Coast Highway, we were in a land of Jaguar dealerships and sailboat marinas. By the time we turned off, we were at Amigo's Mufflers and Nite Owl Liquors, the Quan Dang Convalescent Hospital and two young men in Raiders jacket being braced against a patrol car.

Jimmy's building was the largest—three stories high—and handsomest—a well-scrubbed gray with blue trim—in several blocks. It had a security gate and an interior courtyard with potted plants and a fountain in which two decoy mallards bobbed without attracting company.

"Glad to see you guys," Jimmy said. He wore a purple-and-red sweatshirt and bluejeans. He had two gold rings, a gold earring, and a quarter-inch gold-link necklace that spelled out COWBOYS and sported a Lone Star. His hair was clipped into a Carl Lewis crew-cut, with a short, thin, up-the-regiment pony-tail behind. He was heavy around the middle, but his shoulders, chest, and neck looked strong.

Jimmy's apartment was handsome and rich and immaculate and astounding.

We sat on a plump-cushioned sofa in front of a lemon-oiled redwood table. On the table were several pamphlets—"God is With You" by Swami Muktananda and "Self-Realization" by Paransa Yogananda were two—and the black, Bible-sized A.A. "Big Book." Amidst the foliage of a potted palm, a five-foot ficus, and hanging Swedish ivy, sat statues of the Buddha and Shiva. (A grid of *Playboy*s on the floor dispelled any notion that Jimmy's thoughts were solely of the spiritual.) Glass chessmen squared off on a hardwood board. A reclining ebony woman, nude, held a light globe aloft on one raised foot. A spear-clutching warrior flanked her on the shelf. "That guy's been dropped so many times," Jimmy said, "I'm surprised he's still standing straight."

On the walls were a twenty-five year old pastel portrait of Jimmy's mother, her stone-green eyes bright and strong, a more current photo of Jimmy and her embracing, and a color snapshot of a pig-tailed two-year old. ("Marvetta?" we asked. "Her daughter," Jimmy said.[2]) Incense burned. A computer screen, where "America On-Line" linked Jimmy to cyberspace, pulsed. (When, later, he demonstrated his mastery, codename

---

[2] Before we left, Jimmy would show us their Christmas card. "We couldn't buy you anything," Marvetta had written, "But we wanted to send you these words, 'We love you.'"

THEPOLK's first entry was "Any beautiful ladies out there?") The fruits of his three-year sobriety also included a seventeen-inch color Hitachi, a V.C.R., tape deck, and C.D. player. When he pushed his remote, we were engulfed by Chopin. "I wasn't the type of person who went around telling the home boys how much I loved classical music," he said. "I felt funny enough about who I am. But listening calms those beasts inside me that I once was and still am if I give up the journey."

We spent that afternoon and evening and the next afternoon and most of the afternoon after that with Jimmy. This is what he said.

I was living with Marvin in a complex with six or seven guys in wheelchairs. I was going to Long Beach C.C. and A.A., and I was about six months sober. I had flew my daughter from Texas to my mother's house. I was trying to make amends for abandoning her when she was little. When she came, she hugged everybody except me, and when she left, she hugged everybody except me. So, again, I felt like a piece of shit. I said, "Fuck it" and started using drugs again. One night I came home, and Marvin had changed the locks on the door.

Where we were living, guys who had gone off the program before weren't kicked out. It hurt me even more because we were the only two black persons. He should've given me a chance, but he had this big old note, saying, "Jimmy, I love you. But you need help, and you can't stay here no more."

I went up to Anaheim and Cherry. I seen those guys I had scored the dope from. I had $400, enough to get my feet started. All I had to do was spend $100 on someone, and he would tell me everything I needed to know. A guy showed me the alleys where the drug connections was at. He took me to an abandon garage where people slept at. It was a great location: Bank of America on the corner and a liquor store fifty-feet away.

I sat in front of the Bank of America from six o'clock in

the morning until ten, eleven o'clock at night. This time it was different. People in Long Beach react to panhandling different than Berkeley. They was very mean. But since I was the only one in a chair, people was more willing to give to me, even though they was mean, than they was to anyone else.

But it was like a bunch of dogs fighting over a bone. People got their own special gifts for getting money, and you in competition with them. You got your fast talkers, that talk so fast you give them money just to shut them the fuck up. You got your rough-handlers, that will bluff their way over, forcing you to give them money. You got ladies who take off their kid's clothes, put it in her purse, and beg for change to buy some. And you got people like me, who put sugar with it, who try to make a person feel good about giving something. You going against all them.

My daily meal was a bag of Lay's Potato Chips and, maybe, a taco from Jack-in-the-Box. The rest of my money was for crack cocaine and Thunderbird. Crack is pretty powerful stuff. Once you got money in your hand to get it, you in euphoria, imagining how wonderful you gonna feel. Your mind's excited; your stomach's growling; you're skipping down the alley on adrenalin.

Once you got the drug, you excited to get to a place to put it in your pipe. If you got no pipe, you use an empty soda can or break off a car antenna and stick some burnt-up Brillo pad on the end. I used to brake off an antenna a day and have ten pipes on me, so, when the stores closed, I can sell the pipes for five-dollars each or share a pipe with people got their own drug. I was a street person that was able to think ahead.

I got to be known as a cool guy. You know, "He share his dope. He cool." I got to be lots of people's buddy. I had it set up where I was sending people to score my dope for me. If they came back, they got a chance to get high with me again. I had a partner that I pay with dope to protect me from the elements who don't care if you're in a wheelchair or if you're blind; they will rob you. I had people all I had to say was, "I'll give you a hit if you get me a pair of pants," and I would have two or three pair of pants from the fences before the night's over. They might not of fit, but they was pants. And I convinced the liquor store owner that it would be nice to have my disability check signed over to him every month and set up credit, where I could get a short-dog every morning and a short-dog before closing.

I got into the drug scene real hard. I became a runner. On four flat tires, I was a runner. I had successful business people hand me $1200, and I would score them ounces I was buying for, maybe, ten and kick me out $200. In street terms, I had it going on. In my sick head, I'm doing business. I did a service. I didn't beat these guys as bad as other guys would. That made me better than them. You could trust me. Y'know I can't run from you no way.

So my life got pretty comfortable. It wasn't about digging through no trash cans for me. On days my clientele came, I didn't have to panhandle. But if days was bad, if no one came and I was out there, cold, trembling, smelling bad, my mind racing with what plots I gonna come up with or what lies I can tell or what hustle can I make to get my drugs, I did some awful things. If a person was brave enough to rob another person, I would play look-out. I would sit in front of the bank and watch the people getting money out of the teller machine and make a mark, like rub my nose, and let that person know, "That's the victim." I did some horrible things like that.

You have to understand, when you living that kind of life, you work real hard not to be human, not feel things, to do whatever it takes. On the streets of Long Beach, I had become one of the lowest, non-human persons there was. There was times I was full of piss and shit for thirty days. There was times when I didn't have fresh clothes. There was times I had so much dirt over my body I was blacker than what I really was. Water and soap was harmful to me. I had dreadlocks down my back; they was matted, and I'm pretty sure something was living in them. My eyes were so brown you couldn't see my pupils. There were days the garage was full—NO VACANCY—and I been banned from damn near every motel on P.C.H., I slept all night in the rain. The cars go by, and nobody would stop. Nobody would stop. There was terrible cold nights like that. Police have come fifteen times in a day and told me to get my funky ass away from the property. They wouldn't take me to jail, because I smelled so bad they wouldn't want me in their car. I left, and when they left, I came back.

Some mornings I would sit under a tree and watch the people go by in their beautiful cars, and I would get envy and jealousy and cuss God out. I couldn't understand God's logic of who he help and who he didn't. I seen bad people have it so much better than me. One guy, all he do was rob people, and he drive a Cadillac. Have gold all around his fingers. I never was a robber. I never harmed people as far as purely harm-harm people.

Of all the painful things that make me feel bad, the worst was when I was at the bus-stop, dodging cigarette butts people passing by was flicking at me. This mother and this little girl, boy, whatever came by, and the kid looked at me and stopped his momma and say, "What's that?" That hurt the shit out of me. Again, reality sit in. "Jimmy, look at where you at and what you doing and what you have become."

People thought I was strong and brave. They looked up to me, by me being in a wheelchair living on the street. But I cried lots. At night, when I was out of drugs and alcohol, the stores closed, nobody to ask money from, it was rough. I was tormented about my past. It was like hell right up inside my head. I thought about being shot. I thought about being abandon. I felt ashamed of being in my family. I felt ashamed that I did the same thing to my daughter what my mother did to me. I was angry at who had kicked me out of their house. Who had did me wrong because I was smoking a little dope. It made me feel good to imagine this dream. Here I am, dead. My mother and father crying. I'm in the coffin. "Yeah, motherfuckers, see what y'all caused me."

I played that scenario often. And you know what? It works. After I ran through all that shit, I was able to push it away and say, "Fuck it." And then it was daybreak again. It was time to try to survive another day.

Then a friend was killed. Slick Rick. He was a hustler; he was a robber, and he was a thief. But he treated me better than a lot of people. He had a sensitivity side to him that you normally don't show on the street. A few times he asked me how I was doing, and I said, "I'm doing fuck," and he say, "Let's get high." He would give me twenty-five dollars, say, "Get a room, man. Get off the street." And I would take the twenty-five dollars and go back to the dope man. Then, too, he was the type of person who would rob you in daylight.

We had been together. I had made a good hustle; he had made a good hustle. We was supposed to meet back up to get us a room at Howard Johnson. But he didn't show.

What happened was, I was rolling down this alley to find some little corner I could lean to the side for the night. It had to be between one and three. You got to understand, for me, the safest place in the world was a dark alley. I didn't feel good in the light. To get to those spots I was sleeping in, I had to go through dark alleys. To get to those spots I was smoking in, I had to go into a dark alley. So going through an alley at night was comfortable.

And I met up with Rick but not the way we wanted. I think he was dead. He was pretty dead to me. And I found myself going through his pockets. Here I am, thinking he's one of the best friends I got in Long Beach, and I'm trying to rip him off, you know, figuring he's dead, he ain't gonna need it.

I got his drug out of his pocket, and I rolled on down the alley. I stopped at this car port, and I took a hit, and it occurred to me how low I had become. I had got down to a level that I never figured I would get down to. I always managed to hold onto some feelings for some people. Something within myself that I thought was human. But it was gone. It wasn't there no more. It hurted me. It hurted me real bad. And maybe I got scared. I didn't get scared that anything was going to happen to me. I got scared of who the person that I really was had become. I took a hit off the crack, and I thought I had done bad dope. Then I got my dope out, and I *know* it was good dope, and I took a hit off it, and I couldn't get high. And I remember looking up, and I said, "If You real, if You can fucking hear me, help me. Send me a sign."

I cried myself to sleep, and I woke up: I was getting pissed on by a dog. If I could find that dog today, I'd buy him a steak.

I got a quarter, and I called the V.A.
Ms. Greta Gomez said, "Where are you?"
I said, "Anaheim and Cherry."
She said, "Where you living?"
I said, "Anaheim and Cherry."
She said, "Sound like you got a bunch of arrows in your ass. When do you want to come in?"
I was thinking, I got this covered. I got one more good shot. I say, "How about tomorrow?"
She said, "You got one hour. Do what you got to do."
In that hour, I do what I had to do. I rolled in, and they was happy. And they had tears in their eyes too. They had never seen me like that. My liver was hanging over my chair. I had these dreadlocks. I had four flat tires, and my front tire was hard rubber. I had pants that only closed this far. I had a t-shirt rolled up here. I smelled so bad that five minutes into the conversation they was on the other side of the room.

I can't tell you why I came back. I know I was tired. I was tired of being tired. I don't believe I was wanting to come into no program to get myself better. I just wanted something different than what I had.

I was laying on a gurney for thirty days because my butt

had rotted out from sleeping in the chair. My liver was shot. I don't know if I had a bladder or not. I was under enough antibiotics to sink a whale. I had burns where I had tweak out at night smoking in the alley and, thinking I heard police coming, stuck the hot pipe in my sock or pants or belly, knowing I can't feel. I was a human skeleton; I was a living corpse; physically, I was gone.

It was awful. I started experiencing things I had never experienced before. The head nurse would sit by my bed and hold my hand, and I would just see her hand. I was talking, and the voice would come out later. I was seeing snakes with polka-dot bow-ties singing "The Thrill is Gone" on the walls. It seemed like they was scrubbing me with wire bristles. People would look in the room, and I thought they was the F.B.I., the C.I.A. Not the police, the *F.B.I.*, the *C.I.A.*

They wouldn't let me off the ward. They put a sign on me said I was a health hazard. Then I made a deal. It took them four hours to cut my hair, and I went to my first A.A. meeting from there.

I was going to meetings telling people, "Fuck y'all. I want to get high." Sometimes I would lie and say, "It's so good to be sober," but I wanted to get high because they were telling me to do things that didn't make sense. "Surrender." Hell, I surrendered every time I got beat. "Find a power greater than yourself." How in the hell am I gonna find a power greater than myself? "Live in the moment." I'm not used to living in no moment. I'm used to thinking about tomorrow: where I'm gonna sleep at; where I'm gonna score my dope at; what's gonna affect whether I make it through the day.

I was in a bunch of fear of saying where I came from because I'm feeling they won't understand. I didn't hear nobody that was pissing on themselves, stealing clothes, begging for food, sleeping in the rain, getting spit on, getting cigarette burns, getting set on fire, being cussed out, being chased by the police the day the drug man wants his money. I'm not hearing none of that from these people. I told everybody, "Y'all full of shit. It will not work for a person like me." They said, "Keep coming back."

So I kept coming, and they kept welcoming me, offering their experience and strength and hope. See, my attitude was "The world is a shit sandwich, and each day I got to take another bite," and they was teaching me my way of thinking was wrong. These weren't just people from the hospital, they were people from outside, giving up their free time and holidays, visiting me, like they gave a damn about me. They taught me to commit to the fellowship and to take direction and to ask for help. They taught me to look and listen and hear. And I decided to give it my best shot. I said, "I'm gonna do what these people say. Then I can die in peace, because I can say to myself I did try."

One day one of my teachers took me to a Yogananda camp outside L.A. As I was passing through the garden, I started noticing the flowers. I started noticing the trees. I started noticing everything in a way I had never noticed before. I said, "What the hell is happening?" He said, "Relax." And I started thinking, "Did he slip me some drug somewhere down the line?"

So we go over by this pond. He say, "Call the ducks." I said, "How the hell am I gonna call some ducks? I know you got sobriety and all this, man, but you have fucking lost it." He said, "Call the ducks." And he have taught me so many other things that I trusted him. And like a fool, I was saying, "Quack, quack, quack, quack, quack," and from across the river, the ducks came straight at me. Chills came all over me, and I said, "Maybe this is something I can look into."

Even as a kid, I wanted to be you or someone else. I never wanted to be me. I wanted to be my friends, because their life was so better than mine. There was no sense of unity within myself; insecurity was always there. It was taught to me from seeing the infidelity with Mom and Dad, from seeing the fighting with Mom and Dad, from seeing other people having more than I had or getting things easier or being called "Big-Headed" or "Dumb." Watching my cousins get favoritism by Grandma and Grandad, watching my dad treat other kids better than me, I focused on all that shit.

I was fed...I was fed so much bad information coming up, it still make me angry. I was given bad information when my dad told me that all women were like my mother. They gonna fucking use you and use you up. That created that wall of "I better hurt her or leave her before she get that opportunity." That's bad information. I was given bad information by the preachers telling how God is this punishing, cruel God that is gonna put you straight to Hell for all these sins. Hell, at some point, I had created so many sins that I didn't think I had a shot at it, so why try. I see now that God is a loving God, and He's gonna forgive us, as long as we keep asking. I had bad information on that. I was given bad information when teachers told me, "Jimmy, you a fool for wanting to be a lawyer; you ain't never gonna get that far. You can't grasp this data. You slow here. You slow there." And I take a test, and I fail, and I say, "You're right." It killed the spirit for me trying again.

Lots of people gonna say, "You should've been stronger." I wish I was. But I wasn't. Until a person in a situation, you don't know how strong you going to be. I have never felt myself to be really dumb-dumb. I always felt, deep down inside, I could be any person or anything I wanted. But I didn't have enough motivation or self-esteem to keep trying. I listened to society tell me how I had to start off from the fucking eight-ball or how I wasn't going to be able to get to this point or that point, whether it be an education or a nice lady or a home or a nice car, and I believed that. Any time I got close—BAM—something would hit me, and it would prove society right. I got knocked back so many times, I said, "Fuck it, I'm gonna be just what society tell me I am."

If there was anything my kid or my grandkid ask me, I

would tell 'em, "Baby, no matter how many times you fail at something, keep trying. Keep fucking trying. Till the day you die. Don't be like fucking Daddy; he stopped."

I became homeless by choice. I didn't have to be homeless. I stayed homeless by choice. It was the easiest, safest way for me. The other life never worked for me. Several things happened that was overwhelming. The deal with Mom had something to do with it. The deal with Dad. Being shot was major, because now I got a body I don't want.

Not being able to have intimacy with a woman the rest of your life! That's a hell of a reality to a young man twenty years old. That was the most major concern to me. Not walking was second, okay. I mean, "Fuck not walking." It's the other deal I want. Having all this stripped from you at the tender age of twenty and not being a bad person, working hard and going to college to support a brand-new family, and all this is taken from you because of a worthless situation that I didn't contribute to and that should never happen. It was like, "That's it. I'm checking out."

I wanted to drop out of life, and I was too cowardly to do it with a gun. I'm afraid to live, but I am afraid to die. I'm afraid to kill myself, but it's okay if somebody else do it. It don't make sense, but if you do it for me, fine. I stopped fucking caring about anything or anybody. It was hard for me, because I'm a caring person. But I thought it was a weakness, because all it ever brought me was pain. Anybody I cared for, all they ever gave me was pain.

So what do a person do? Stay fuck-up not to deal with this. I ran away from everything. I pushed that misery to the furthest edge, living a scandalous life, becoming a drug addict, alcoholic, homeless person living in a chair, whether it was cold, whether it was raining, whether it was sunny, feeling shame and guilt and insecurity and pity and remorse, and all that shit was telling my mind, "It will always be this way." I was on a self-seeking suicide mission, running away from who I was, who I became, what reality is, because I never believed my life was going to get better.

It was very painful. And I'm not gonna say that pain has gone. But I handle it different. A.A. gave me tools I didn't have. It has put me on a highway of openness. If I practice meditation every day, consistent, my mind become very still. That's good, because I'm the kind of person, I start thinking, I'm way over here. And I'm way over here. I don't meditate to glow in the light or fly up in the cosmos or go on astro journeys, none of that shit. I do it because it give me peace of mind.

A.A. have give me another chance to love myself and to love others. I'm trying to be responsible and stay clean every day. I'm trying to maintain a nice home and gas in the car and get an education where, one day, I can tell Social Security, "Go kiss my ass." On a daily basis, I try to help someone else who is still suffering. I had no purpose before this. Yeah, to get loaded, but I had no purpose so far as helping someone. And I'm not as scared as I used to be. I'm waking up in the morning and jumping in the chair knowing no matter what happen I'm gonna be okay. No matter *what* happen. I'm *knowing* that. I'm not waking up thinking who can I fuck or who's gonna fuck me.

But I never know what life gonna throw at me. It's not no fun being in a chair. I'm susceptible to everything, especially bed sores. U.T.I. infections, they just come. If I eat wrong, I get sick for a week. If I eat a can of corn, I might have diarrhea for two weeks. Ain't a damn thing I can do about it. Kaopectate or anything ain't gonna stop it. If it do, it gonna impact me, which mean a trip to the hospital. If I take a job and I earn over $300 a month, Social Security cut me off. I could bump myself, be in the hospital three or four weeks, and lose everything. If anything big happen, like a flat tire, it can throw off my whole budget. And things always coming up at me from the past. Student loans they ain't even bothering the doctors about. Bills I created five or six years ago. I been paying everybody a little something out of my pocket for three years, and someone still gonna say, "Fuck you. We gonna sue. We gonna do what we can to take what you got." Responsibility's a bitch, but it's a must.

I had a terrible month in December. I was close to going through a full semester for the first time in my life. But the last two weeks I got sick. I had to go in the hospital, but I couldn't stop, because that was what I always did. Before, going in the hospital was like a gift from God, because I knew I could con all the drugs I want. The hospital was like, "Maybe God do like me." Now I do everything in my power not to go in.

I stuck it out, and when I did my last test, I went up to the hospital, and they put me on a table, and the doctor look in the scope, and he said, "Damn! You got stones blocking your whole bladder. We need to take them out."

I said, "Let's do it."

So they drag my legs open and strap 'em down in the chutes.

I said, "Y'all got to do all this?"

He stuck this rod up my penis—ZING—and I started hollering.

I had told 'em, "Don't give me no anesthetic." I was stupid. Recovering alcoholic had nothing to do with it. If a doctor administering drugs, you go for it. It's in the Big Book. It don't say, "Sit there like a fool and hurt." But I'm thinking, It's gonna be quick; it ain't gonna hurt; I'm bad; I'm tough; I'm Hercules. I had a nurse beside me, holding my hand. I hold her so hard she was on her knees trying to get away. For three hours, it went on. Pure pain.

I come out of the hospital, and my transmission went. Then I got robbed. It was like, "I'm on Social Security. I get these few hundred a month. Sure, I got this roof over my head, and I can pay this bill and that bill and that bill, but I'm fucking miserable in the process. I'm stuck in a certain level, and it's never gonna get no better. Why struggle to do good when I could struggle less doing bad?"

I called a friend. He made some soup and told me to come up.

I told him, "Fuck it, I feel like anytime I try to obtain something to feel comfortable with, it's gonna be vandalized or taken from me."

He said, "I know. But the bottom line is we don't drink or use over this. Go through the feeling. You'll be okay. That's what you gonna grow from."

And I'm bitching, "I don't want to feel."

He say, "You don't want to feel human."

Piss me off. But I had to laugh.

The past three years is like rewriting my life.

It's been difficult to get honest with myself and others. Some of the people I had to make amends to didn't accept my amends, and that hurt me. I thought everybody supposed to forgive. Contacting people and saying, "What can I do to make this right?" and they give you some outrageous quote it would take a lifetime or a river from God to do is scary. It's scary when someone offend me, and, instead of "Fuck you," I say, "Okay, I'll pray for you." Pffh. Pffh. Don't even feel right coming out of my mouth. Hearing of people who stay sober for fourteen or twenty years and go back is scary.

I know if I stop doing everything I've been taught, I'll be back on the street. I could live like that, but I could die. That's a choice I haven't made yet, but knowing I can survive out there is dangerous thinking to play with. I'm walking a fine wire, and if I stop, I'll fall. And we know what happen to Jimmy when Jimmy fall.

This whole thing is new to me. In the street, if I do this move or that move, I knew what to expect. Being sober, I don't. I go to Newcomers' Meeting, and they think I'm a guru. I go to Old Timers' Meeting, they tell me, "Shut-up. You still a baby." It's wonderful. I'm exploring the side of life which I used to call the square or not-cool. Damn, I wish I was square a long time ago.

The most important thing I've learned is not worrying. Take it easy, slow, enjoy yourself, and, whatever happen, take care of it. I lost hope before, then I regained it, then I lost it and I regained it, then I lost it, then I regained it. One thing different today, the hope that I have is realistic. I don't have the hope I'm gonna wake up one morning and do the jig. It'd be wonderful if it happen, but it probably won't. I'm not setting myself up by putting expectations on and, as soon as something damage that expectation, saying, "The hell with it. Time to move on."

My life is a long way from what I'd like it to be. I'm materialistic. I like having nice things. Maybe I won't get them, but looking at other people, who have been down similar to me, getting their new cars and new homes and having their ladies and purpose in life, impress me. Somewhere in my heart, I feel, since they did it, I could do it. And they tell me I can.

I dream like hell now. Since the accident, sleep was just a state of closing the eye and waking up. I didn't dream because I didn't believe in anything. Today, I have some of the strangest, wonderful dreams. Places that I'd like to see and like to be. Having a nice house and lady and dog.

I have a clear picture about what I don't want and a clear picture about what I'm trying to get. I would like to have comfortness and peace. Happy experiences would be enough for me.

Couple million dollars be fine too.

The streets are a big part of my life. I am grateful for all the deals I went through. I can pass down the street now and talk to that dope addict and that homeless person and understand where they at and not feel that I'm better. And I can share with another person that come in off the street. Let that person listen to me, it might give him some hope.

And it feel fucking good when someone say, "What you said stopped me from drinking." Or they tell you what you said three months ago to them. That is like being recharged. I don't want to be no guru, and I'm not trying to be a good boy scout, but I want to give back what's been given to me. If that's all I get, that's great. It's better than what I had.

When a person spend all his life running and seeking and that person don't find and give up, from that moment he start going backwards. If I'd put that effort into something I was trying to become, I'd probably be it by now. But I always put conditions on people and places and things. By doing that, I put up a wire to be hung. Whether I was a success always depend on a certain amount of time or money or energy or whatever. Any time I fell short, it was, "Fuck it. Let's move on." It wasn't about dusting myself off, taking a deep breath, and asking for help. It was about me believing I had to do that myself. And in life, you can't do that. You have to have help. If you don't, you gonna be a lonely motherfucker.

I still have the insecurity of wanting to do things perfectly. My head is like a bad neighborhood. If I go in alone, I'm messed up. I had so much bad information and got so many issues and fears I didn't want to deal with that, if I go in alone, I'm damned. Now there are people to show me that quality of life that I'm trying to attain and that quality of person I wants to become. I'm learning that, when we hurt or we got the feeling we ain't shit, we become that. And I'm learning we can calm that feeling down.

Christmas Day, I spent with my sponsor, his wife, and her sister's family. They love me like family too. We had dinner and exchanged gifts and drunk and eat and hung out. The dogs love me; they was all over me. We just had a good time. They hugged and kissed me and accepted me into their home.

Lots of areas in my life are being healed slowly. I'm learning lots of people do care about me. People accept me for my character defects and everything and still love me. And that's weird. That is weird.

Kinda nice though.

I don't know who I am yet. But I know I'm becoming a person that I kinda wanted to be.

Most days it's wonderful to be Jimmy.

AFTERWORD

The Orange County Airport is named for John Wayne. A thirty-foot tall statue celebrates this archetypal American fighting man, who, in actual life, had less shots fired at him in anger than Jimmy Polk.

"Before there had been only Jimmy and his chair," Adele says. "Now there is a real life in a real apartment with phones ringing and friends dropping by. He even has a dish with change for the washing machine, and it's his change. Do you realize what an achievement this is?"

Of course, I claim. How could I not? But, actually, a part of me is disappointed. Some retrograde portion remains hooked by his original recounting. Throughout our three days together—while this man, who once slept with dogs, took us to dinner and entertained a visitor who lectured about Krishnamurti and went off to his job and decided when it was appropriate to inform the building manager that the soda machine was not working and was considerate enough of us—and of *himself*—to know when our sessions had gone on too long— this shameful segment has worried at me constantly. Was what I was hearing *good* enough? Was it *moving*? Was I getting what I needed? It nibbled at me here; it nagged at me there; it woke me up and flipped me about like I was a chop for bread-ing. That part of me had sought a pot of gold, not quarters. It had clove to Jimmy out of a hunger for thrills and spills and blockbuster adventures. It had wanted something more dramatic than the banal randomness of drive-by evil. It had yearned for a tragedy calibrated upon forces more vast than a passing infidelity. It had hoped for more swaggering sagas and more mythic beasts than those roaming the crummy streets of Long Beach. It had craved the rhetoric of salvation, an apogee of consciousness, not the gingerbread homilies of A.A. while hop-skipping toward a white picket fence and a bungalow beyond. Recognizing the basic unworthiness of my position, I listen.

"When you have a childhood like Jimmy's—abandoned by your mother, abused by your father—it is crushing. He had no one to trust and no chance to build an authentic self to deal with an adult life. To be shot on top of this was catastrophic. He'd try to raise himself up, but some rejection or insult would become the reason to abuse himself again.

"Now, Jimmy's on his way to developing a substantial self. A *real* self. He is allowing himself to depend on other people. The metaphor that is the key," Adele says, "is the group of buddies with special skills that keep each other alive in desperate situations. That's what Jimmy imagines brilliantly in his Vietnam stories and seeks to recreate on the streets. Now, he's seeking it again, but with people who believe in the worth of functioning in the real world, sane and sober, who have struggled with the same sorts of things he has, with degrees of success, and won't be scared by what he does or goes through. He can become a 'baby' again, but this time he won't be crushed. He'll be allowed to do what he must do and learn what he must learn to locate and create the real, adult Jimmy Don Polk, who can love and be loved, trust and be trusted, who can take care of himself and find pleasures without having to beg them or steal them or make them up." She takes my hand. She is excited and happy for Jimmy. She rubs her cheek against the sleeve of my black leather jacket. I give her a squeeze.

We walk down the terminal's corridor. The walls are hung with the drawings of elementary school children. The topic is "Flight." Their planes and starships soar over battlefields and sweep into space. I am accompanied by thoughts of Max. The last time I had seen him, he believed himself infested by parasitic worms, which he was treating by dosing his abdomen with peroxide, roasting it under heat lamps, injecting methamphetamine into his thigh, knotting belts around his waist so they do not creep into his brain. That was four months ago, and because I was involved in his having been hospitalized, he has decided I am allied with the forces of evil and not spoken to me since.

Behind Max extends a line of friends, their steady, silent tred traipsing from here to oblivion. Dirty Dave Peters, who had the greatest E.C. comic book collection of any kid I ever knew. Ultimately an unfulfilled writer, himself, turning out for-hire pornographic originals, Davey shot an ex-girlfriend and overdosed on pills. And Pumps Pompey, who, in back-to-back games, once out-scored Richie Golloff and out-rebounded Dukey LaGuarde. Pumps ended up a glass artist in the Sierras, where, drunk, he fell off a cliff. And Travis Charge, whose water-pipe first turned me on. Already tuned-in sufficiently to have dropped out of Penn, Penn State, and Temple, Travis simply disappeared. And glorious, red-bearded Harvey Fessman, lead trial counsel for both the Mt. Airy Eight and the Ebony Coalition. Despondent over a third divorce and a practice that was crumbling like the Berlin Wall, the Fez locked himself into a room and carved both wrists.

It occurs to me how constricted have been the stories that allowed me to feel significance. Like the good burghers of Orange County, I have insisted upon honoring John Waynes. I have been unable to celebrate the everyday heroics and courage—and good fortune—required to live a stable, productive, consistent, enduring life. I have been induced to regard Jimmy's incredible effort as though it were skimmed milk. The lunacy it was not has obscured for me the miracle that it is. Jimmy's effort has been immense and his journey profound. He has honored me, perhaps more than I deserve, by allowing me to bear it witness.

NOTE

Fully Armed is a work of biographic fiction. "Jimmy Polk," "Bob Levin," and "Adele Levin" are the true names of true people. Their stories are true too (they are, in other words, "true" stories.) However, no other named character is real. They are composites or creations; names have been changed and material facts altered.